RAYYA DEEB

SENECA
REBEL

THE SENECA SOCIETY BOOK I

ATM Publishing
299 6th Avenue #4
Brooklyn, NY 11215

AcrossTheMargin.com

ISBN: 978-0-9972417-0-9

Library of Congress Control Number: 2016941031

First Print, First Edition 2016

Cover Design by Miss Anonymous

Explore Seneca

SenecaSociety.com

&
MEDIOLOGY
PRODUCTIONS

For my daughters.

1

MY BOTTOM LIP split straight down the middle from a combination of breathtaking G-force and peppery dry air. It stung like crazy. The skin on my cheeks pressed tight against the bone. I crinkled my nose at the motorized odor of BoomJet fumes, and blinked continuously to try and moisten my eyeballs.

I was a BoomJet virgin. I'd only flown on a regular jet once in my sixteen years, but one time was all it took to know this was far different. The low, monk-ish hum of the BoomJet wasn't like an engine's forceful whirr. It was hollow. Clean. Precise. Like the sound you hear when you press your ear to a conch shell, only amplified. There were no dings to say "buckle-up," no overhead fans or lights. Just a slick, amber ceiling. Dark gray automated belts strapped us into black rubber seats. The only familiar thing from the other, old-fashioned flight I'd taken before was how all the passengers were trying to meditate away their concern.

Nothing assured me that I'd made the right choice, but here I was, being hauled off to what was probably some kind of reform school, so I had to go with it. It was my own fault for thinking I could transfer that money unnoticed. My arms, piled high in retro friendship bracelets– red, purple, gray, black and blue– were plastered against my rib cage. My hands grasped the seat, and even though my palms were hot and clammy, they weren't going to slip. The force was too great. My ears popped. I swallowed, but that only made the throat scratchiness that was a normal part of my daily life in Southern California, worse. Hydration was impossible.

I sat, quiet, staring at a bulletproof mirror that separated us from the BoomJet cockpit, the faces of the other four passengers reflected in it. Just like me, each person moved only his or her eyes.

Mine shifted to look out into the acid-washed sky. The entire siding of the BoomJet was a window, one inch thick and clear as purified ice. Just one inch between me and a thirty thousand foot drop. Every minute, steam was released inside a paper-thin slit that ran through the outermost layer of the window, melting away any freeze before it had the chance to settle. I watched Los Angeles shrink to nothingness below. In an instant, as we rose above the cloak of smog, one of the most populated cities in the country vanished.

I was on my way to a place foreign to me in every way. I shifted my gaze forward again, and found myself staring back at my own reflection. Pale, because I spend less time in the sun than a baby's butt. Full lips chapped raw by thin air and insufficient time to find a Vitamin E melt. Suddenly an electric-blue digital read-out popped up and hovered in the mirror showing a countdown clock: 48:12. In under an hour I would be on the ground in Washington, D.C.

Just forty-eight hours ago I'd been twiddling my thumbs during a calculus exam I couldn't have cared less about. I closed my eyes, recalling those final moments of normalcy. My mind had been far away from that stupid math exam, thoughts bouncing all over the map, from Timbuktu to the shores of the Cayman Islands. Wanting to get home and see if my latest gambling bots were bringing down the house. Wishing I had some prickly pear cacao. Wondering if my dad was really dead. I always thought about my dad– every single day.

He used to take long walks when he wanted to think about things. We couldn't know how long a walk would last– an hour, two, sometimes even three. He never came home from his last one. After a day we got really worried because he had become super depressed about things at work. It had been a roller coaster the week before he vanished. Right before his depression kicked in, he'd been overcome with excitement. I've heard that's a sign of being manic, but I just don't think that's what was up with my dad. Either way, my mom and I never felt settled with it. I thought about it all the time. If he was dead, could he see me and was he proud? Or if he was alive, why didn't he ever come back? It didn't make sense that he might still be alive, because then he wouldn't have left us, or at least he'd have told us what was going on. I couldn't accept that he was dead.

My mom, on the other hand, was angry. One day she missed him and the next she cursed the fact that he'd ever existed. His pictures are still up in our house. They should be. He's only been gone three years– three excruciatingly long years. They say time flies, but for my mom and me the weight of it lingers, like the chocolaty aroma of roasted Guatemalan coffee that clings to my hair after five minutes at Café Firenze. It doesn't ever seem to go away.

I didn't miss a beat between each "C" I'd marked off on the math test because, quite honestly, it's absurd. The school administrators think I'm some kind of genius sheep. That my only purpose is to elevate the test scores of a public school on the brink of losing funding from the federal government. The rest of the class, deep in calculus hell, didn't want to hear about me, what a great student I was and how I'd save their advanced math program. All they wanted were tickets to Endless Horizon concerts and to get bent on Mojo Sticks.

Our school was probably the last one in America that still had LCD monitors. We were so far behind the current technology and everything else, too, and the gap grew by the second. In every movie or show I watched, the schools had holographic touch-screens, but not ours. In malls, hospitals and schools across the country, virus and bacteria were eradicated by UV sweeper bee-bots, but not at our school. We just accepted the pungent odor of industrial ammonia. It was there for our own good, according to the administration. My teacher, Mr. Malin, still used a phone. He had been fiddling with it as he always did during exams, but in that moment he'd had his eyes on me.

I had been so done with that exam. Judging by the look on Mr. Malin's face, he was so done with me, too.

"Finished already?"

"Yep." He was a good guy, but there was no way I'd give in to the system.

"A word."

Mr. Malin stepped up and headed out the classroom door. As I followed, I looked for any sign of approval from my peers across the room. I'd rather they see me as a misfit than some teacher's pet, but nobody seemed to notice my calculus test strike. The teachers did everything in their power to keep me on a tight leash. They all hated my anti-authority threads: *Nirvana Smells Like Teen Spirit* tank top, cut-off bleached jean shorts and black sneakers marked up with vintage Wite-Out pen art. Three dozen other high school juniors cranked out numbers as best they knew how, but it wasn't good enough for the administration. They expected me to bring up the test score average of the bunch, and I wasn't down with that.

It was just the two of us on the other side of the classroom door, in a drab hallway of empty concrete sockets, remnants of lockers from when kids still carried books to class. Nobody knew what would take their place. Not us, not the teachers, not the people who made the plans to get rid of the obsolete lockers. It didn't matter what the plans were anyhow. There was no money to complete them.

Mr. Malin eyed me with disappointment. The way he tipped his chin down and peered at me over his wire-framed eyeglasses will stick with me forever.

I figured things might go better if I spoke first.

"I know what you're going to say." My voice bounced off the cold, empty wall sockets.

"This isn't you, Campbell."

"If it isn't me, then who is it?"

"You tell me."

I couldn't look Mr. Malin in the eye because I knew that I wasn't being the best Doro Campbell I could be. But I was the Doro who could fight the tyrannical school system and deal with the judgment of all the kids at school. I wasn't a goody-goody. I was Doro Campbell, certifiable badass. At least that was my goal.

"You tell me why the most gifted mathematician I've ever had in my classroom wants to present herself like she's the worst. I just don't get it."

I blanked for an answer.

"The grades speak for themselves, Campbell. I wish I could do something more for you, but I just can't. You should really be in advanced calculus, but at this rate, you're going to end up repeating regular calculus your senior year and your gift will be flushed straight down the toilet into the bowels of the Los Angeles Unified sewer system. Do you know what it's like down there?"

"I don't really give a crap." I grinned, proud of my pun.

Mr. Malin dropped his head. He'd tried to get through to me so many times before. I heard him, but I'd already made up my mind. As much as I respected Mr. Malin and knew he respected me, it was all about the big picture. I wasn't giving in to the bureaucracy of this bunk education system.

Mr. Malin clenched his jaw. I felt bad for him. It was his life's work, seeing to it that his most promising students spread their wings and soared. His face muscles twitched a few times before he finally nodded in resignation and stepped back into class.

I remember thinking that couldn't be *it*. That it wasn't my destiny in life to be a mindless follower. I was more than ready to split from this place.

***

I was so deep into re-living what had happened two days back, that I missed the BoomJet's initial descent. There was no time to prepare. With uncanny speed we plummeted towards the earth at forty-five degrees, and then made a hard turn, parallel with the off-white concrete runway. A hollow thump and we landed, doing at least two hundred miles-per-hour. I was nearly suffocated by the restraint of the belts. My breath accelerated. We made a fast and abrupt, but considerably smooth, stop. I could breathe again.

Like I said, I was a BoomJet virgin. It kind of hurt, it went by super quick and before I had a chance to really enjoy it, it was over. We'd taken off from Los Angeles and landed on the outskirts of the nation's capital in forty-eight minutes flat. Before I left, my mom said that the last time she'd flown to the east coast, it had taken nearly ten times as long. As I tried to imagine her reaction to the crazy-fast trip I'd just taken, I realized how much I missed her already.

2

A MATTE BLACK SpaceFlex Passenger Flight Vehicle sat on the tarmac. What I wouldn't do for one of those. Ellen Malone stood up and smiled. "That's us."

"Awesome!" I thought, and followed Ellen off of the BoomJet without saying a word. I was dizzy and my legs buckled.

"Are you okay?"

"Amazing." I stood up straight. I didn't want her to see me weak, but that had been some intense G-Force. Ellen was fine, like she'd done this a million times. She straightened a crease in her blazer.

For the past three years the world had been crumbling all around me, but now it seemed someone was championing me. Ellen Malone. Although the jury was still out on her motivation, and the idea of reform school made me wince, I felt elevated here.

Next thing you know I was back in the air– this time, in a flighter amongst the affluent folk of metropolitan Washington, D.C. The airways just above the highways and roads had become transport paths for flighters after the federal government had approved the bill a few years back. Of course, it was made completely unaffordable to ninety-nine percent of the population, and since I didn't have a license and my mom had no idea I was a millionaire, the only time I had experienced flighting was when I'd hot-hacked a flighter with my best friend, Julie.

That had been one seriously ill-fated joyride on a sweltering day back in May. We'd cruised over the 10 Freeway, and I veered off to pull some tricks between a stretch of decrepit, old Mediterranean-style stucco buildings in overpopulated, underprivileged hoods, where no other flighters ever went. We were doing about fifty, level with the roofs. People saw us and were cheering out their windows. Julie was egging me on like crazy. We always instigated each other to push the limits. I dropped us towards the road, just above the first story of the buildings, and then gunned it straight towards one of them. "Waaahoo!" I shouted. No fear. Julie screamed, braced herself in her seat, and just as we almost smashed into the first floor, I pulled back and we jetted straight up the side and into the sky, where we were met by the flighter cops. Busted in a stolen flighter just two weeks before my sixteenth birthday. I did two weeks in juvie, three months of community service and my license was revoked until I turn twenty.

The upside was that while my classmates were inside being lectured on flighter technology, I was outside experiencing it firsthand. I still don't get what's so wrong with that. In any case, my mom did. She was pissed beyond belief. It was just another event in a long series of me getting in trouble. It was so worth it. My school counselor and administrators were convinced I was acting up because I had lost my dad. I maintain that it was because everyone around me was so boring, that I needed to be proactive and inventive in order to have any fun.

But this unpredictable excursion with Ellen Malone, *this* I would classify as fun. From the moment we touched down in Virginia, I had the feeling that life would never be the same. I'd never been east of The Rockies, let alone to the other side of the country. This was a whole new horizon. For starters, the landscape was a stark contrast to what I was used to. Los Angeles' glory days were long gone. My parents would tell me stories of a top-notch tourist destination that had slipped into an abyss of overpopulation and filth. Broken roads overridden with traffic around the clock. Baywatch waves covered in dudes and babes would be considered folklore if there weren't countless images to prove their existence. From Malibu to Hermosa, the ocean water was just too polluted to swim in now.

Unlike every single metropolis across the globe, the air was clean here in Virginia, the roads paved to perfection. Smooth and black. And as we cruised above the endless river of traffic that carved its way through the tall sea of deep green trees, I saw something we most definitely did not have in LA. An elevated, four-lane roadway built in translucent concrete. Ellen saw that I was fixated on it. "The Smart Road. It runs above Route 66 into downtown Washington, D.C., as well as down Highway 81 to Blacksburg, Virginia, where the technology was first researched, blueprinted and constructed for many years before stretching thousands of miles across the country," she explained. "Some of the session leaders you'll be meeting were recruited out of the institutions that developed this sustainable transportation system. If we get a little closer, you'll see the law enforcement vehicles, traffic and weather collection devices, medical units and commercial freight trucks traveling on it in automated, unmanned vehicles."

"I've seen footage of it. In LA we'd be lucky to drive one block without hitting a pothole. It makes no sense. I mean, people in LA pay taxes too. Or at least, they did."

"Taxes have nothing to do with this. It's privatized. We have Flexer Technology Corporation to thank for this."

"Hmm." I pulled my little blue flexer from my ear and twirled it between my fingers, suddenly getting that its role was way more complex than simply providing me with personal computing functions. The Smart Road was fascinating. Optical fibers the size of pins composed the entire roadway, and let us see straight down through it to the road below.

I looked around at the areas beyond the road itself. It was the end of September in Virginia and fall was creeping in. I'd always heard of "seasons" and now I was starting to feel it. Even though I hadn't experienced the infamous hot and humid east coast summer that had just rolled out, I could taste autumn rolling in. A cool, thick dankness lingered in the air, penetrating straight to my bones. Made me want some warm apple cider. I wasn't in Los Angeles anymore.

The flighter exited into a wooded area and landed us in the driveway of an imposing colonial-style mansion. White pillars. Red brick. I was so excited I don't think I blinked. This was a highly secured girls' ambassador house, where tucked away behind a thick grove of leafy trees, I would be staying for my pre-orientation. Ellen and I got out of the flighter.

"Welcome to Great Falls." Ellen was genuinely pleased to see that I was in awe. How could I not be? This place was unbelievable. Pristine, manicured lawns surrounded the estate, engulfing it in unending wooded serenity. Tufts of puffy, water-colored clouds traveled slowly in the pale blue-gray sky. The noise of the 405 was replaced with what I guessed were the soothing tones of crickets and bullfrogs, though I'd never heard those sounds in real life. I'd only seen places like this in pictures and movies. We were less than fifteen miles from the nation's capital but it felt like I was in a dream, floating in a kind of peace I'd only imagined until now.

"Let's go inside and get you settled."

Ellen had a nice voice. Melodic and warm like she could have been a blues singer in another life. My heart raced as I followed her through a terra-cotta red front door that was hit smack in the center of this perfectly symmetrical home. But my guard was up. I thought I'd been sent here because of all the acting out I'd been doing, and yet I was getting the red carpet treatment. It didn't add up. But until I had a reason not to make the most of what looked like a pretty sweet situation, I would.

Thirty-foot ceilings. Cotton ball-colored walls. Crisp light. Dark cherry wood floors so pristinely polished it looked like they'd never been walked on. A brass chandelier hung from the ceiling. Lights twinkled through its crystals, and just beyond it, a girl appeared at the top of the stairs.

"Jennifer, come down and meet our new guest."

I stared as a super sophisticated looking teenage girl descended from a grand staircase that wound down into the foyer. Textbook posture. Hair pulled back in a perfect French braid, impeccably fitted preppy clothes from head to toe and a striped silver silk scarf draped from her long neck. Not your typical reform school girl, I thought to myself. She slid her hand delicately down a solid wood railing that was as thick as a Boa constrictor.

"Hi. Jennifer Wallingsford. It's a pleasure to meet you." She extended her hand and waited a beat for my name. It hit me that this was the daughter of Congressman Frank Wallingsford.

"Hi." I was intimidated for the first time in longer than I could remember. "Dorothy." No idea why I said my whole first name. I never do that. Her dad was one of the most powerful men in the country, so that made her one of the most powerful daughters in the country. Actually– the entire world. I wondered what kind of trouble she'd gotten herself into to end up here.

"Doro is here from LA for a pre-orientation. We hope to have her join us this fall."

"Nice. Well, make yourself at home. I'm headed to my parents' house for dinner, but let me give you my contact info in case you need anything. Please, don't hesitate to flex me."

"Cool– great, that's cool. Thanks." I whipped my flexer out and pressed it against hers to swap contacts. Was this really happening? Her flexer was a flat, palm-sized red reflective mirror. Mine was currently set as a blue tune-plug since I'd been mellowing out to Bob Marley while waiting for the BoomJet to lift off, and hadn't morphed it since then.

Ellen was cool, calm and collected. I tried to emulate her vibe. She spoke to Jennifer with the ease of an old family friend.

"Thanks, Jennifer. Please tell your dad I'll see him first thing tomorrow to debrief him on my LA trip."

Was she using the word "debrief" in reference to me? She must have been.

Jennifer's eyes seemed sincere as they gently locked on mine before she headed out. "There are some spritzers and peaches I just put in the fridge, cacao in the pantry. Help yourself." She spoke with a confidence that was completely devoid of the notorious Capitol Hill arrogance. It completely blew me away.

I was feeling pretty darn important at this point and couldn't wait to get my hands on that cacao, though I've never heard someone my age use the term "spritzer." Just go with it, I told myself, not sure just how much cooler things could get. Man, was I in for something else.

3

THE CRICKETS AND frogs sounded like they were amplified onto loud speakers that faced my room. It helped soothe my nerves, as I lay awake in bed all that night. I couldn't get a second of shuteye, anticipating the next day's itinerary. This was all happening BoomJet fast.

One of the rules of coming on this pre-orientation trip was that I was not allowed to call anyone from back home, including my mom. I missed her and Killer so much. We had not been apart like this ever before. Julie just wasn't going to believe any of this, but I had to wait until I went back home for a visit before I could tell them all about it.

Despite only one good hour of sleep, I was considerably wired first thing in the morning. I could hear stirring in the house, but compared to the noise of the rat race I was used to, it all sounded peaceful. Hair dryers, showers, forks clinking on plates... usual sounds in an unusual place. Still, I didn't see a soul as I peeked my head out the bedroom door. I made my way to the bathroom Ellen had shown me the night before.

An hour later I was downstairs with twelve other teenage girls. They were all dressed in blue uniforms and were totally in the groove of getting up and out the door. Jennifer was there with another girl. My gaze lingered on her for a moment. I still couldn't believe I was living in the dorm where Jennifer Wallingsford stayed. She looked just as put together as she had the night before. She turned her head in my direction and as our eyes met, I quickly looked away.

"Dorothy."

Holy crap, she remembered my name.

"How was your first night?"

"Great. Slept like a baby." I don't know why I lied. I wanted her to think I was comfortable here. I mean, I was, but people generally equate lack of sleep to anxiety and all the things that come with that. Just like my dad though, I didn't need much sleep. My mind was naturally caffeinated and it just carried my body along for the ride. Especially here in absurdly gorgeous Great Falls.

Ellen had instructed me to take the flighter bus with the rest of the girls, where I would be met by a student representative whom I would shadow for the day. I found myself moving through the front doors of the mansion with the pack of girls in blue. I was in my Nirvana tank. It was a bit chillier than tank top weather but I just had to rock it. No doubt I stood out. I hadn't had time to wash it before I'd come on this trip, but it was sort of like my security blanket. It still smelled like coffee, too, which was both a comfort and a major tease because I needed one bad.

"Wasn't Kurt Cobain that singer who shot himself in the head?" Jennifer's friend inquired with a scowl hidden beneath a sour smirk.

I looked down at my shirt, "He was."

Jennifer's sour friend gave me a look as if it was *me*, not Kurt, who'd shot myself in the head– right in front of them.

"McKayla, this is Dorothy Campbell. She just got here from LA."

I didn't want to know McKayla, but if she was a friend of Jennifer Wallingsford, I wasn't going to oppose.

"LA. So, like, why don't you have a tan?"

Jennifer smiled at me as if to say, "Ignore her," without saying anything at all. So I did. It wasn't even two seconds before McKayla's attention was elsewhere, admiring another girl's motion graphic nail art. It was a deep blue lizard that flipped its red tongue out and flashed into a rose.

I got on the flighter bus with the rest of the girls and took the first empty seat I saw. The door shut and I heard the pressurizer filling. I turned to look out the window. Just as I began to admire the absurdly fresh scenery that nobody else seemed to notice, the windows glazed over in a mirrored blue hue and I was staring back at myself. I turned my focus to the flighter pilot at the front. He was wearing specialized goggles which I assumed let him see through the windshield, which now was mirrored too.

The flight was oddly disorienting. We must have made a

dozen or more turns, a few U's and some circles. What was the big secret? When we landed twenty minutes later, the blue mirrors dissolved, and once again, green took center stage through the windows.

The setting was similar to that at the girls' ambassador house, only this time against a river's edge. I figured it must be the Potomac. As I stepped off the flighter bus, mesmerizing, unapologetic white water rapids grabbed my attention. Turbulent waters slammed up against the earth, spreading stones in jagged, abstract patterns. As the morning dew disappeared, the smell of thick, grassy air filled my nose and its green taste settled down through the back of my throat. My previously chapped lips suddenly felt moist and revived. This was simultaneously unreal and as real as real gets.

Once again, I followed the pack. Having prided myself in non-conformity since as far back as I could remember, I took each stride by envisioning myself as the black sheep among all the girls in blue. No clue where we were headed. There were no buildings or signs of life other than a few birds and a squirrel or two. I swear to god I looked up and saw an eagle, and unless my eyes were cheating me, it was bald. Another legend I'd only seen in pictures. Was this a pit stop? I'd thought we were going to a school.

The blue herd of girls stopped in a patch of fairytale grass that was encircled in a shiny, metallic gold ring that lay flush to the field. It was probably about twenty yards in diameter. I looked around, perplexed and intrigued. Jennifer Wallingsford stood with McKayla and a few others, mingling in just the way mingling happened back at my school. She caught me looking at her and waved me over.

"This doesn't look like a school," I said.

"Don't worry, soon it will all make sense."

"If you say so." Jennifer was cool, but I wasn't going to buy into everything she said unless it made sense to me.

"Believe me, I know exactly how you feel. Even though I grew up in this area, nothing could have prepared me for this."

I heard a low hum and within seconds we were under a dome of gold aerogel that emerged from the ground and cupped us against the earth. A hydraulic system began to lower the circle of grass that we stood on. I braced myself, unsure of what was happening. Everyone else just relaxed and carried on with their conversations. This was completely normal to all of them, but it was so not-normal to me. In thirty seconds, we were grounded.

The dome disappeared and I found myself standing inside a structure filled with bustling human life. The architecture around me was phenomenal, a modern rendering of the best elements of American colonial style– just as I'd seen so far in the land above. Lots of teenagers and a few adults in form-fitting ultramarine blue uniforms filled these below-ground halls. I just stood there, taking it in. This place didn't seem like any kind of school, especially not a reform school. There was a galactic grandeur in the air that no school could generate.

"Dorothy Campbell." I turned to see a kid my age, smiling and extending his hand. I scanned him without moving my eyes– thin, shaggy head of dark brown hair, big brown puppy dog eyes, half-tucked shirt, braces, friendship bracelets. *Friendship bracelets.* I breathed a sigh of relief in finding a shred of something– *someone* I could relate to. I smiled back.

"Welcome to Seneca. I'm Timmy Reba, your *personal* student escort for pre-orientation."

And so, there it was– they called it Seneca.

"They told me I'm your shadow for the day."

"Please. Friends call me Reba. It's my last name. Mi padre es Puertorriqueno."

Reba rolled his R's with gusto. Electricity surged out of this kid's pores as if kinetic energy was harvested and redistributed through his braces. Considering where I was, maybe it was.

"I'm sure you're a little disoriented."

A little? How was this normal to all these people?

"Don't worry, you'll be up to speed in no time. Campbella. Is it okay if I call you that? It really works for you."

"Sure."

Reba waved his hand for me to follow him. "First things first, let's get you your blues."

4

Now I, too, was wearing blue. Although borderline
conservative, there was a sexiness in this getup. I imagined that
an air of slick sophistication blew through me. I pinched the
sharp collar, ran my fingers down six smooth pyrite buttons to
my waistline, which, after loose-fitting cotton t-shirts, had never
felt so exposed as it did right now. I decided to own it. I could be
a new person here. I could absolutely flex this outfit. And before
I looked up, I glanced down at my beloved sneakers with a grin.
This blue uniform thing wasn't so bad after all. I didn't feel like a
sheep or member of some Floridian mega-cult, I felt like an
astronaut, exploring the unknown. Except these unknowns were
not in outer space, they were right here below the surface of the
Earth. I wondered how far down we were.

This kid Reba was on fire, I'd never met someone with so
much energy. He'd get along well with Killer, I thought, as he
lead me down the hall with a pep in his step. He was so excited
when he spoke that his words all blended together and he barely
took a breath. "I remember my first day here– all tingly with

excitement and wide-eyed as I took it all in. Amendment. I'm *still* wide-eyed and taking it all in and it's been two years."

Now I wanted to hear everything, see everything and do everything I could at Seneca. It was the future. I was in the future. Talk about a self-fulfilling prophecy.

"Welcome to the future." He smiled.

What the heck? Was this kid reading my mind? He winked, then turned back to watch where he was going, almost knocking over a kid who had built-on robotic arms.

"My mistake, Yoshi."

Yoshi's left arm slammed into the glistening golden wall, sending a smooth ripple all the way down. The wall morphed right back to normal, not unlike the materials our flexers were made of– a sort of programmable metallic polymer. I wondered if these walls could be commanded into functions other than just dividing spaces, like I could command my flexer to form a cup, harvest rain and purify it to drink, or illuminate an entire room with any color.

Yoshi grunted at Reba, who stepped aside in awe. This Yoshi kid was so small he'd pass for a child ineligible for rides at the amusement park, but he clearly had larger-than-life capabilities that Reba was majorly impressed by. Yoshi continued on, glaring back at Reba, who just offered up a smile.

"Yoshi Higashi. What I'd do to be him for a day."

My interest was piqued. I mean seriously– kids with robotic arms?

"Come on, first session starts in three minutes, and they've got you booked in mathematic applications. Sick session. Wish I could qualify, but they got me searching out mock cadavers in the Aboves."

I had no clue what that meant, and judging by Reba's reaction, he could tell.

"Don't ask."

I didn't. I just followed, ready to devour this landscape. The halls were completely golden, some brick and some smooth, but all golden. I noticed several of the walls morphing into objects. First I saw a guy approach a wall and it morphed into a water fountain. The water moved with him to meet his mouth. At the water fountain back in my school in LA, we had to press a button and bend to the water. The thing had been around since the 1980's. I wanted to see more and more. What else could these walls do, and what was behind them?

And then, my world about stood still, for the first time in my life, in the most unlikely of places and times for stillness to occur. A doorway appeared on one of the walls, and from it, emerged a guy about six foot tall, my age, buzz cut, pale skin tone just like me and rocking dark blue combat boots. Our eyes met like magnets– he had one blue and one hazel. I swear to god, if love at first sight existed, this was it. I was rendered a believer in one single instant. In that moment I felt like I knew him. Or at least I wanted to know him. Those lines were happily blurred.

"Campbella? You coming?" Reba was ten steps ahead of me,

looking back. He saw who I was scoping out and I could tell it made him a little bummed, but he tried to hide it.

"Yes, sorry, this is all just so..."

"I know. It's new, exciting, different, etcetera, etcetera... but don't lose focus. It's easy to lose focus here."

No kidding. "No way. I'm totally focused."

As I followed Reba down the hall, I looked back over my shoulder. Blue combat boots was gone. The farther away I got from him, the closer I wanted to be. I had to find out who he was, where he was from, why he was here.

5

QUANTUM PHYSICS APPLICATIONS, mathematics in epidemiology, quantum computing freestyle, Seneca civics and ethics, and last, but not least, mathematics in religion. Yes indeed, my schedule was a mind rush. I learned that there was no such thing as paper in Seneca. They only used a stone paper that was made from a calcium carbonate quarried in Virginia and other places in the world too. Absolutely everything is either sustainable, compostable or can be safely reduced to components that create energy. Human waste for example. When we use the toilet it flushes into a "poo-renew" system, as the S.E.R.C. Scholars joke, that breaks it down in skyscraper-sized drums alongside each Seneca City center. The ecosystem within this subterranean city is a dream come true to every hippie in the history of the world.

How could I ever go back to Los Angeles Public School? I couldn't. My dad would have been all over this situation. Man, did I wish I could share this with him. This was exactly where I needed to be. One second I think I'm headed to reform school to pay for my crimes, the next I'm in Disneyland for tech junkies. I mean, let's get real for a second, though. It had definitely entered that "too good to be true" zone. Something was up. I just didn't know what. Yet. Yeah, I wanted to know, but part of me didn't. I felt like a kid in a candy shop. I couldn't resist the sugar, wasn't so concerned about what came next. This place didn't even have grades. It was all performance and incentive based: do well and you were rewarded with awesome mini-adventures. Do bad, repeat the session via tablet until you get it right. If you don't get it right, you don't leave the session. Everyone got everything right, eventually. I quickly learned that that's just the pedigree of the Seneca population. I was flattered that I was considered to be on that level.

Reba picked me up after my last session. "And how would you rate your visit to the future thus far, Lady Campbella?"

He didn't just have pep in his step; it was in his vocab too. And his shaggy hair had an air of happiness too, as it sashayed back and forth. Reba was growing on me, and I had a feeling that we were going to be good friends. Then I started to think about Julie. I'd be so far away from her. We wouldn't get to hang out every single day like we had for so many years. Maybe I would get the hook up so she could come visit via BoomJet on the weekends. Could dogs stay in the ambassadors' house or would I have to leave Killer behind with my mom? There were a lot of unanswered questions, but no matter what, I knew that nothing would ever be the same. It couldn't be.

"This place is insane."

"Chica, you ain't seen nothin' yet."

"Well then, show me more, Rrreba." I rolled my "R" just like he did.

"Easy, tiger– all in due time. Your last stop of the day is at a location in the Aboves. Ellen Malone is taking you."

"Okay." The way he said it sounded so mysterious. Like it wasn't a part of my day that he was excited to share. But I wasn't worried, because so far everything Ellen Malone had shown me was ridiculously slick. And most of all, I was ready to get past today to start tomorrow and see Blue Combat Boots.

6

BACK IN A blacked-out flighter with Ellen Malone, I was riding high at twilight in Great Falls. The cabin was soundproofed against the dwindling traffic outside. Taillights and headlights flowed towards infinity in both directions. I knew those lights were like the ones that passed by my mom, and we were somehow connected this way.

"You seem happy here. Different than when I first met you just a couple days ago."

She was right. When I'd first met Ellen, I'd been ready to go down swinging.

I'd just had that unfortunate hallway conversation with Mr. Malin and had headed home to the small two-bedroom apartment I share with my mom in Culver City. I figured she'd already heard from Mr. Malin about that pointless calculus test and I was ready for round two of, "What are we going to do with you?" I pulled my flexer from my ear and held it to the sensor to unlock the front door.

My dog, Killer, a sweet black Pomeranian, greeted me every

day with hops and licks. That day was no different. Despite everyone else's disapproval of my academic fall, Killer showered me with unconditional praise. Apartment 14W was Killer's kingdom, and I was his queen. This pup of mine was an expert in extracting the warm fuzzy side of me that, believe it or not, does exist. I scooped him up to my face where he unleashed a barrage of ticklish licks.

"Killer, I missed you so much, my sweet, sweet baby boy." I remember suddenly feeling that something was off. Drenched in dog breath, I looked down the hallway and noticed that my bedroom door was wide-fricken-open.

"What in the...?"

I always left it locked. *Always.*

I quickly, but gently, put Killer down and tiptoed down the hall while he jumped at my heels, squealing for attention. As I inched along, I heard the murmur of voices. My heartbeat flat-lined and jump-started into a race.

I closed my eyes, took a deep breath, then turned and looked through the doorway– there was my mom, sitting with her head in her hands. I was floored.

"Mom?"

"Dorothy!"

"What are you doing in my room!?"

"Doro–"

"This is so messed up–"

My eyes darted to the ground where I saw the three heavy-duty flexer entry locks from my bedroom door that had been removed and scattered. My mom had let me secure my room after my dad went missing. She knew I needed a sense of security as well as the privacy to deal with grief in my own way, on my own time. And she much preferred that I was in our home behind locked doors than out getting into trouble.

"You broke my locks?!"

Storming in, with Killer yapping away at my side, I instantly realized that my mom and I were not alone–

"What the–"

"Hello, Dorothy."

There were four men all in black, and a striking woman in a power suit. Ellen Malone. She wore a double-breasted metallic blazer and pants perfectly contoured to her body, an electric-blue blouse and three-inch shiny black heels with a silver stone at the base of each heel. Culver City fed Los Angeles with its blue-collared heartbeat. White tees and jeans were more common here than floral dresses at a Southern Baptist church service. Women in high-end power suits were never local.

So the people in my room clearly were not from around our neighborhood. One of the men took a step towards me. Just as fast, I took a step back, scooping Killer up from the ground in the same move.

The approaching man in black pulled out a badge. "Federal Bureau of Investigation."

Damn. I felt my mom's eyes burn a hole in me. Not just a little hole. This was a full-on fire blown in by the Santa Ana winds.

"Take a seat."

I sat on the edge of my bed, literally and figuratively. With all these people in my room there was barely room to breathe.

"Expensive equipment for a teenage girl."

"It was my dad's."

"That's nice," the agent sneered.

I'd claimed my dad's gear after it sat dormant in his office for almost a year. Floor to ceiling flat flex glass monitors leaving not an inch of wall visible to the naked eye. Thick, midnight purple velvet drapes pulled closed, their fibers shimmering in a blue hue that emanated from the monitors. The blue hue I lived for. The purr of electronics being cranked full of energy from a stand-alone generator drowned out the sounds of traffic from one of the country's most congested freeway systems, below us. The 405 delivered a polluted yet calming sound that could be heard in every other nook and cranny of our apartment.

"Your mother is going to prison."

"What?!" No way. They had to have been there for me, not her. I looked away from the FBI agents to my mom, who sat distraught and broken down. Mascara streaked down her cheeks like charcoal art. Killer panted maniacally, feeding off my anxious energy. I could smell his hot beefy breath. Gross. The whole scene was stamping itself into the impression center of my brain for many a replay at later dates.

"Fifty thousand dollars shows up in her bank account, and she knows it doesn't belong to her, but she doesn't tell anyone about it."

"I told you, I don't even have a bank account at InfiniCal Bank!" My mom snapped.

Oh my god. The whole situation was absolutely my fault. When all the money had started coming in I had set up a false identity at a bank in the Caribbean, created an account in my mom's name and transferred that money in to it. Obviously that false identity wasn't as foolproof as I had hoped it would be.

"*You* don't know anything about that do you?"

I remember searching my mom's face. And she searched mine. I could tell she instantly knew that I must have had something to do with this mystery account the FBI found that was in her name. She always had the answers, but at that moment she was completely incapable of counseling her misfit teenage daughter. I could tell by the way she looked at me that she was thinking of my dad, and that I was indeed my father's daughter. She always said that. I know I reminded her of him, and it both broke her heart and kept it beating all at once.

"Let me try that again..." The presence of the men in black in my bedroom shook me to my core and they knew it. It wasn't their first dance, that was clear from the mix of nonchalance and confidence in the agent's voice. "We're investigating your mom for wire fraud. If you know something about this and you don't tell the truth about it, you don't want to know how both your lives will change. And not in a good way." I figured that they must have had legit evidence, but all I knew to do was deny, deny, deny. I had to get my mom out of that situation. It wasn't her fault. My mind raced to find solutions. What should I do? What should I say?

An 8x10 black and white photo of my family tacked up above my motherboard caught my eye. It was the last photo of us all together. I looked at it every morning and every night and wished every single time that our life was still like that. My mom was a geriatric nurse at the hospital and my dad had a "job with security," as he always liked to say. For an instant, as her happiness in the photo conjured a barrage of memories of our happy past I nearly forgot her current despair. Normally I could get lost in that photo, but not then, in that salty, lingering moment that was all my fault.

"Doro, don't say anything. We're getting a lawyer. We'll fix this." My mom's body language didn't exactly match her words. I kept quiet, but on the inside I was bursting with worry.

Up to that time, Ellen Malone had simply been the woman in the metallic power suit who sat calmly in my peripheral vision. But when we locked eyes, she interjected, "If you all would give us a moment, I'd like to have a word with Dorothy alone."

The men in black obliged and they took my mom with them. "Thank god," I thought. That menacing pack of human wolves had my mom in tears and something had to give. Before she left she stared at me with a firm, 'Don't say a thing,' look. I wasn't going to.

Ellen offered a kind smile, obviously making an effort to quell my panic. "I've been looking forward to meeting you for a long time."

That was weird. I tried to calculate her motive. I wouldn't let her smooth talk me, no matter what. I'd thought I was invisible but what an idiot I'd turned out to be. I'd made one bad move because I'd wanted to help my mom out. We were drowning in debt. She did the best she could for us both, but now that my dad was gone our cost of living far surpassed her income, and we were in a deep, deep hole that was only becoming blacker by the second. I knew she was having panic attacks and trying to hide them from me. She'd say she had allergies and would go to the bathroom and cry. We couldn't even afford two flexers anymore. She gave hers up so I could keep mine. I'd felt guilty and helpless for so long. I had always wanted to help and finally I could. I knew creating that account for her was the only way to get her the cash. I believed that would allow the transfer to fly under the radar, but it didn't.

Ellen stood up. "I know what you're thinking–"

"You people always do."

"And I understand why you'd be guarded with me. But I'm not part of the FBI. I'm here to offer you help."

I don't know what it was with adults always thinking I needed help... but this wasn't about me anymore. I had reeled my mom in to this mess as a result of my criminal activity. I had no choice but to listen.

"Let's be honest. You and I both know where that money came from..."

I put on my best poker face. Wasn't talking, no matter what.

"But I don't care about that, Dorothy. What's done is done. Let me tell you what I do care about. Your mom is going to prison, unless we do something about it."

I crossed my arms and tilted my chin up to offer her my skeptical ears.

"The mandatory sentence for wire fraud is six years. I know you don't want your mom to rot away in prison. I don't want that either. Wouldn't wish that on anyone. I can make all of this go away, Dorothy. Are you interested in hearing me out?"

Although everything inside me said, "trust no one," I slowly started to feel in my gut that maybe she had come for good reasons. Maybe. I might listen, but by no means was I ready to offer compliance. "Not really."

"Alright then."

Ellen turned in towards my system of monitors, looking intently at it. There was no way she knew what it all meant. I noticed that the view through her glasses was blurry until she turned a tiny knob on the side of the frame and her lenses adjusted to the focal point: A numerical reading that was multiplying at what might as well have been the speed of light.

"Impressive."

She took her glasses off. Puffy, dark skin framed her kind blue eyes. A loose bun held up with no kinks in her hair. I could not get my hair up like that to save my life. My ponytail always had kinks. "She must be pushing forty," I thought, and wondered why in the world she thought my monitors were, as she put it, "impressive." She couldn't possibly have known what she was looking at. Not a chance.

"Did you know that you're the only person to have broken the algorithm for every major gambling site in the world?"

I was stunned. Who was Ellen Malone? Until I knew that, and what she was doing in my room, I was going to play dumb. "I don't know what you mean."

She gave me a smile as if to say, "How cute." No matter which way I played it, Ellen Malone was reading me like a book.

"Dorothy, I appreciate your sense of humor. We're both smart women here. Well, you might be smarter, and that's fine."

"It's Doro."

It was weird. I didn't know her. She was enigmatic. Yet against my better judgment, she was someone I wanted to trust. Wanted to, but wouldn't. She'd called me a woman, when everyone else considered me a kid. She already knew so much about me, and now I wanted to know about her.

"My name's Ellen. Ellen Malone. When I heard about what was going on here, I knew I had to step in. It would be a shame to let your genius go to waste. Those guys out there, they don't understand that. All they care about is the law, and that you've broken it. I can look past that because I see your potential."

"Thanks." It was a compliment after all, and so far I liked the direction of this conversation, considering where it was headed just a few minutes back.

"I took a BoomJet in from Virginia this afternoon to personally invite you to be a part of something. Something very special."

"Great. A cult. I should have known."

"Not even close."

"Sure."

She took a controlled breath and stared me down. As a matter of fact, she gave me the stare-off of all stare-offs. "Do I really look like I'm in a cult?"

I looked away.

"Cults don't recruit geniuses, they recruit the weak-minded."

She was right. Being facetious wasn't working for me. I needed to get my mom out of trouble, find out who Ellen Malone really was, and what she really wanted from me.

"I can go. I'll just let the men waiting in your living room know that I'm done here."

Ellen stood to go and didn't hesitate. She walked towards my door and didn't look back. My immediate future flashed before me. My mom being torn out of our apartment, hauled off to prison. Me on my own. I'd probably end up in juvie or even worse, some orphanage.

"Wait!"

Ellen stopped in my doorway when she heard my voice, but she didn't turn to look at me.

"I want to know what you came here for. What do you want from me?"

"Honestly, Doro, what I have to offer you is a privilege. It's something I wanted to do, not something I needed to do."

"Alright. I'm sorry. Please understand, coming home to... this... completely shocked me."

"Listen, I can't say I sympathize with you on this current situation. The law was broken and this is the consequence. I'm here with a solution, because I don't want you to flush your talents down the drain. I want you to bring them to a place where they can be refined and used for good."

First Mr. Malin and then Ellen Malone with the flush metaphor. Was something out there in the universe trying to tell me to get my head out of the toilet or what? As weird as it felt, the probability was super slim that a higher power was speaking to me through toilet metaphors. But still...

"Like how?"

"Oh, you'll see for yourself. I'm not asking you to simply accept anything as the ultimate truth. Just open your eyes, Doro."

"Okay. Eyes open. Mind open, too."

I felt our dueling presences arrive at some sort of odd alignment. Despite the friction, something clicked.

"Most of the people in this world don't get second chances, Doro. This is yours. It has everything to do with the future. With your future."

Over the next several hours, Ellen gave me one seriously

strong sales pitch. Probably the most convincing part of it was that she made it perfectly clear that she knew everything. She knew I had my hand in every major online gambling site in the world. Everything from poker and beyond, if there was algorithm-based security on their sites, I had pretty much had their number. Processes that entire departments in the government had been researching for decades had taken me just a couple of weeks to crack. If quantum cryptography couldn't stop the Chinese, it couldn't stop me. I'd written the algorithms to break the quantum repeaters that the sites had in place. This wasn't a learned skill. According to my dad, it was a gift. Ellen Malone saw it as that, too. Most people that were on the same wavelength as one another finished each other's sentences. But my dad and I, we finished each other's equations.

The systems in my room were set to work around the clock. My method was to create new identities, setting them to win and lose at a 75/25 ratio, and then shutting them down once they'd won more than about $500,000. I had been funneling millions of dollars from all of these wins into an offshore bank account in the Cayman Islands, where they don't ask a lot of questions when they see big sums of money come and go. In less than one month I'd racked up nearly a billion dollars. Getting to that point had been a walk in the park for me. I felt confident in the invisibility my secret identities provided, and thought I'd been careful not to raise any red flags. Unfortunately one red flag had been flapping in the wind. Some secret division of the United

States Government had its all-knowing eye on me.

During that conversation with Ellen I'd responded with equal parts resistance and curiosity, but no matter what I conjured up as Ellen's possible motives, I knew that going with Ellen to some reform school in Virginia was the only way for me to protect my mom. So the next thing I knew, I was here. Seneca City. Totally not reform school and nothing like LA. Ellen was right, I did feel completely different here.

"I can't believe this is all happening, I mean, I've dreamt that places like this existed ever since I was a little kid. My dad talked about this sort of existence all the time. Instead of bedtime stories, he would light up my room with flexer moonlight and tell me all about Earth's great potentials and how I would be a part of it all one day. Now it's starting to come true. I just wish he could see it."

"I bet he can." She was so optimistic. Definitely not the typical authority figure I'd dealt with in my life so far, always trying to suppress my spirit. She was trying to align with me and that was pretty darn cool. I wanted to feel her optimism, but I was still worried that all this goodness just couldn't be real. I wanted to be careful not to be blinded by the allure of a secret city which fulfilled all of my technological fantasies.

"So, what's the catch?"

"Catch?"

"Yeah, why me? Why this? Why now?"

Ellen looked out the window. The amber light filled her face with a glow and illuminated her pride for Seneca. She didn't have to search for an answer to my question. It came naturally to her.

"That's something you need to answer for yourself."

Wow, she was good. I pondered her statement for the remainder of the ride.

We suddenly emerged from the greenery into the city. The sky behind us was fading from the moody gray-blue I was so taken by, into a gradient of plum and orange. I could see that we were descending on the nation's capital.

The flighter crossed over a much more serene part of the Potomac than the raging river I had glimpsed that morning. White buildings reflected like glassy replicas in the stillness of the water. The Kennedy Center, the White House, the Washington Monument... one after the other. In a matter of three minutes I took them all in. We landed on the roof of a building. I could see the top of the Capitol. I was literally inside my last U.S. history class. Experience was replacing being lectured about stuff and it was fine with me.

"Ellen!"

A man in a mustard-colored tweed suit with a chocolate shirt and plaid tie greeted us with open arms as we emerged from the flighter. He gave Ellen Malone a huge hug and then turned to me, like I was his long-lost favorite niece. "There she is!"

He gave me a firm handshake.

"Gregory, sorry we're late, I wanted to bring Doro via the scenic route. It's her first time in D.C."

"And hopefully not her last!"

"Hopefully."

Ellen Malone and Gregory had similar smiles.

I flashed one right back, "Definitely not."

"Well, come on in, there are some people who've been looking forward to meeting you." And, with that, Gregory ushered us in through the door, past a security guard that looked like he might be Secret Service.

Gregory Zaffron had a great gait. I've always been super into people's walking styles. A walk says a lot about a person. My walk has always been smooth like butter. I try to blend into my environment, not bring too much attention to myself when I move. Gregory was the opposite. His steps were long and wide. His mustard jacket moved like a cape.

"Great day, ain't it?"

Ellen Malone and I looked at one another and smiled. Gregory hadn't said anything funny– he just *was* funny by being himself. There were an awful lot of characters here in this world of Seneca. I liked everyone I had met so far except for Jennifer Wallingsford's friend, McKayla. To top it all off, I already had heart palpitations over some guy I'd seen from a distance, and that's not even my style.

We approached a gargantuan, medieval-looking door. Gregory gave the guards in front of it a nod and they stepped aside as we walked in.

"Dorothy Campbell. You're finally here."

Holy crap. It was Congressman Wallingsford. And Jennifer was here, too.

"Congressman Wallingsford, sir, it's an honor to meet you."

"The honor is all mine."

Congressman Wallingsford, Jennifer and a power-packed, exquisitely groomed group of six men and one woman sat around a grand mahogany table in a windowless room. I tried to take in the tufted leather seats, intricate Persian rug, elaborate crown molding and the lemony scent of wood polish that I love. All eyes were on me. *Me.*

"Please, have a seat." Congressman Wallingsford pulled out a giant black leather chair for me right next to his daughter. Ellen Malone took a seat next to me.

"We hope you've enjoyed yourself so far."

"This is all so incredible, and everyone is so nice. I don't even know how to thank you for having me here."

Congressman Wallingsford had a certain look of determination– the aura of a man who knows what he wants and will stop at nothing to get it, a man whose path you wouldn't want to be stupid enough to cross. He took a casual seat at the end of the mahogany tabletop across from everyone else.

"Oh, you don't have to thank us. We should be thanking *you* for coming out to visit us here at Seneca." The people in the room all nodded in agreement. "So, thank you, Dorothy."

"You're welcome?" I didn't feel like I should be the one saying that.

Ellen put her hand on my shoulder. "I've got feedback that Doro here is perfect for the program. She fit in so well today. All of the session leaders had nothing but good things to say about her."

"So I hear."

I smiled. Congressman Wallingsford hadn't stopped smiling since I'd entered the room. His teeth were whiter than freshly cut coconut, with one solid gold cap peeking out from a bottom tooth. Seneca must be Land of the Smiles, I thought. Not a large man physically, at just about five foot eight and maybe a buck sixty in weight, Congressman Wallingsford still had a presence so vast it filled the whole room. You couldn't avoid his powerful gaze. A five o'clock shadow of peppery hair was just beginning to show through his once clean shave.

As cool as this was, things felt bizarre. Why were they all being so extraordinarily nice to me?

Congressman Wallingsford got up from his perch at the end of the table. "We'd love for you to stay."

I knew everyone kept saying things like that, but coming from one of the most powerful men in our government, I was awestruck. "Really? That would be... I mean, that's beyond amazing."

The vibe in the room was not normal, just like the rest of this abnormal Seneca situation. It was so many things all at once–exciting, scary, fun, confusing, exhilarating... addictive... I was swirling in a whirlwind.

Ellen turned and looked at me in earnest. "There is one caveat, Doro. In order for you to stay with us, you will never be able to turn back."

That took a moment to register. What did *never* mean? "Turn back," like I'd be out of the school system for good, or "turn back" meaning to LA? I didn't want to go back to my old school. I most definitely wanted to stay here and have this experience, but did she mean that I could never go home?

Jennifer spoke up. "Dorothy, this place *is* incredible. We all know it. This is an opportunity for you to be a part something huge that pretty much every other person our age will never even know exists."

"I hear you."

Congressman Wallingsford motioned for everyone to leave the room except for Ellen, Jennifer and me. I didn't even know who they were and now they were all gone. The focus on me was getting even tighter. I started to feel like I was being cornered and had to let them know where I stood before things got stickier.

"I have to be able to go home and see my mom, my friends, my dog, my apartment."

Congressman Wallingsford lost his smile. Uh oh. Things were going to get intense. I wished that we could just rewind to the cool stuff, like being in the golden hallway with Blue Combat Boots. I closed my eyes tight, and hoped this part would be over when I opened them, but it wasn't.

"The truth is, Dorothy, this is the one and only opportunity you will ever truly have in your life to change things. To make the world a better place for your mom, and everyone else."

"I don't understand."

"Billions of people– over half of the world's population– live in poverty. They don't have access to education, medicine, food, you name it. The things most of us take for granted. The climate has been undergoing a drastic change since before our time, and in the Aboves we no longer have the means to stop that momentum. You don't want to imagine the planet your children and their children will see if things continue in this direction."

"I get that."

"I hope you do. You see, things haven't changed because people haven't taken responsibility for altering this path. Until now. You've had a chance to experience the Senecan lifestyle. You're beginning to understand how forward-thinking it is. Trust me, you've just seen the tip of the iceberg. Imagine the possibilities if what we are capable of here in Seneca were to extend to everyone in the world."

I couldn't imagine it. It seemed too good to be true. But it also seemed that if anyone had the power to make that happen it would be someone like Congressman Wallingsford and his powerful government pals.

"That's the goal, Dorothy. But there is a plan and there is a price."

It was just too much to comprehend that the only way I could participate in this revolutionary plan for humanity was by walking away from everything I've ever known and loved. I had a feeling that what he was saying was one hundred percent authentic, but I still didn't understand why he was discussing this with *me*.

"So you're telling me I just have to accept the end of my life?"

"No, just the the end of life as you know it." Congressman Wallingsford finally sat down in the biggest chair in the room. "But for us, it's the beginning of a new life. A better life for all of humanity. But great change requires hard work, compromise and tremendous dedication. It doesn't happen overnight."

Ellen put her hand on my shoulder again. "Congressman Wallingsford is right, Doro. You have to think of it as a new beginning. You're someone whom we want and need to have as a part of the Seneca Society."

"Ellen was sent to bring you here because your unique talents would contribute greatly to the creation of this international society we're building. That's what Seneca is, Dorothy. A better tomorrow— for everyone on earth, not just Senecans."

This whole pitch was beginning to sound like a corny commercial, but at the same time I couldn't help being compelled by his argument.

"I don't get it. How is it possible to change the whole world?"

"Over the past ten years, we have developed a circuit of metropolitan hubs beneath the surface of the Earth in which human life can thrive. Each hub is equipped with its own contingency of the world's most gifted, intelligent, and healthy, citizens on the planet. The recruiting process started three years ago. We're dedicated to forming a society capable of overcoming the damage of the past before it's too late."

I looked away. How could I change things? I couldn't face the picture of urgency he was painting.

"Because of your qualifications, you, Dorothy, are one of the chosen to help do that."

I felt I had to respond in some way but I still couldn't commit to something that seemed like an insanely irrevocable decision.

"Of course I don't want to just sit back and ride the decline of civilization, but I can't just leave my mom."

"We understand the weight of the decision you need to make. It's never easy."

My senses warped. The room got smaller. All I could hear was the sound of my own breath. "But I just don't understand. What about my mom, why can't she come with me?"

Congressman Wallingsford turned to Ellen Malone. She was looking at me with compassion, as though she wanted to protect me, but still had to give me a crucial piece of information. "Unfortunately, there is extremely limited space in Seneca, and only the chosen can join us on this journey."

"So you're telling me you want me to leave my mom behind? Like we can't be a part of each others' lives anymore, at all?" Panic was setting in. I couldn't leave my mom. As much as I alienated her, and she me, she was all I had. I loved her to death.

She was my mom.

"Doro, you will be a part of her life in a different way. In shaping the life she can live in the future. Just think about it. This is going to take some time to accept. It did for all of us. But in our mission to ensure the preservation and quality of life on this planet, we are dealing with infinitely valuable information. You must understand that Seneca is beyond top secret in nature and must be protected as such."

I sat forward and dropped my head into my hands. I rarely ever broke down, but this was it for me. My breaking point. Leave, and be with my mom in a place where I'd never truly be able to make a difference, or stay, leaving behind the only person who loves me, who has done everything for me, but putting my gifts to good use for the betterment my mom's life and the world.

Jennifer looked to her dad for approval to speak. This was clearly something the three of them had been through before. "I lost my mom when I was twelve. At first it was horrible. I couldn't get through one second of the day without missing her. I cried more often than not. And this is no different. It's not easy to imagine life without your mom in it, Dorothy, but it is the only way to make a better life for you and her... I will be there for you, to support you in any way I can."

I felt trapped. "No way. I'm not leaving her."

"If you turn back, you will never be given this opportunity again," Ellen said.

"Oh well." Even though I said that, I felt deep inside that I couldn't walk away from this. I couldn't. But I couldn't leave my mom either! This had been in the cards all along and Ellen had built me up to give me this information and let me crash.

Congressman Wallingsford fingered his flexer sitting on the table in front of him. "We're ready for you, Gregory."

Gregory came in with another dude, probably about seventy years old, Indian, kind old eyes. He smiled. Go figure.

Congressman Wallingsford leaned over the table towards me. "It's time for you to choose, Dorothy Campbell. Will you join the society of the future? Now that you know what can be, can you really go back to the life you were living? Of indefinitely riding that stale status quo?"

"I– I have to talk to my mom," I stuttered.

"I'm sorry, you can't."

"This can't be okay, I'm a minor, I..."

Ellen took my shoulder again, this time more firmly. "Doro, I know this is extremely difficult, but it's the way things have to..."

"Difficult?! It's beyond messed up. I want to talk to my mom. You have to let me call her."

Gregory chimed in. "Once you make your decision, you'll have the chance to speak with her, but it will be monitored and you will be given a specific set of guidelines for what you can and cannot say."

"Don't you have freedom of speech in Seneca?"

"Of course we do!" Ellen said, "But you understand that we must be extraordinarily careful about how and when we bring this information to the Aboves."

Ellen was trying to comfort me with reason, but this time it wasn't going to work. Pleasantries and charisma couldn't calm me now. "And what if I say no?"

Gregory stepped forward and put his arm around the Indian man. "Dorothy, this is Dr. Ashvind Kulkarni. He's one of Seneca's top M.D.s. If you choose to leave this room without committing to join Seneca, he will administer a Cogniz-X dosage that will erase all memory of what you've seen and heard here in the past forty-eight hours. The drug will take effect in less than an hour, in which time we will transport you via PFV to Washington Dulles Airport, and from there you'll fly back to Los Angeles. You'll be back home with your mother by sunrise tomorrow, completely unaffected by what's happened here. You'll go on with your normal life, without knowing anything at all about the Seneca Society."

7

MY EYES WERE closed to help me think. When they were open, the sensory extravaganza around me swallowed my thoughts. How was I going to tell her? I thought of my dad. Would he understand why I made this choice? That this was ultimately the best choice for everyone in my life? I thought of my mom, alone and wondering why I'd never come home after my stint at a government-backed reform school. I thought of Killer, Julie, my visits to Café Firenze before I went to school. Joining my mom on house-calls to her patients that had become like family to me.

My mom, Layla Campbell, is a no-nonsense, hardworking woman. Her paternal grandparents emigrated from Lebanon to Glendale, California. My grandfather hadn't gone to college. He'd gotten into the food import business just like his father before him, and had become fairly successful off of selling yogurt drinks. He had married a Greek-American woman from the Greek Orthodox Church and my mom was their only child. She was an overachiever from the get-go. Spent summers hiding out, reading and listening to vintage LPs in the dark while other kids played video games and caused a ruckus all over the city. She was only nineteen when she met the love of her life– my dad– Johnny Campbell.

My dad was a small-town Wisconsin boy who'd come to Los Angeles to attend UCLA on a full-ride mathematics scholarship. My mom was in the nursing program and worked part-time in the student union, where my dad would come to see her every second of every day he wasn't in class. Like me, the guy didn't need to study and he didn't need to sleep. All he knew was math and my mom.

I hadn't chosen this path for my life; it was just the way things unfolded. And I desperately needed to rescue my mom from the terrible mess I had put her in. To her, this whole "reform school" plan could be the thing to get me away from the memories at home she thought were causing me to act out. She didn't have a clue about the big picture or the work being done below ground in Seneca. But if she did, I was sure she'd understand that they were legitimately trying to save the world. And she'd be proud that I could be a part of that.

I knew my job was to figure out a way to bring my mom to Seneca too. I just knew it. I would have to. My staying in Seneca or not wasn't really even a decision. It was the gamble I had to make. Ultimately, while the pain that rippled through my heart was beyond anything I'd ever felt, I was compelled from deep within to make the hardest choice I'd ever had to make.

I was numb. My fingers could barely move across my flexer

screen. It felt like my hands were frostbitten while my body was actually burning up. Even though they had debriefed me on what I could and couldn't say to my mom regarding my new 'school' and my decision to stay here, how I was going to keep the real information from her? If I strayed from the script, I would be putting my mom in danger.

The only thing to do was jump in and call. It was go time.

"Doro!" Her voice warmed my soul but singed it with agony, too. Would I ever see her face again, I wondered.

At hearing her voice I squeezed my eyes tight and fought a sob with everything I had. My chest seemed filled with sandbags, my palms sweaty.

I was alone in a dignified guest room, but I felt like I was being monitored. I didn't trust that it was safe to stray from the parameters they had provided for this conversation. A newbie in their world, I wasn't ready to test their boundaries yet.

"Hi, honey! How's your trip going? I want to hear everything!"

I was choked up but dug deep down to muster up the strength to say what I needed to say. To make my mom feel at ease no matter how far from reality my own comfort was.

"I love you." It came out without even thinking about it.

"Well, I love *you*. Killer is right here and he misses you, too. He hasn't left your bed since you've been gone. Only when I lured him out with a marrow bone from Romeo's Meat Market."

I laughed, and was glad she couldn't see the tears streaming down my face.

"I miss you guys so much. This is a great place for me, though. They're doing such cool things, and I've decided that... I'd like to stay."

"That's great, hon. I think something like this is just what you need. And they'll be lucky to have you."

"Yeah."

"Will you be coming home to pack? When should I plan on coming to visit?"

Nothing about this felt right to me, but I knew it had to be done— for now.

"That's the thing. They don't allow visitors... in the first few months... while we go through this big mental and physical cleansing process. But I think there is a parents' weekend after that."

"Really? Well... okay... I guess we'll plan for later, then. You let me know when, and I'll come right away, okay?"

"I miss you mom. So much. But I can't come home to pack if I want to stay here. They send government appointed messengers to retrieve the things I'll need."

"Wow, this is really serious."

"I know. I'm sorry we didn't get to say goodbye properly— or, not *goodbye*. You know what I mean."

"Doro, it's okay. We'll be together again sooner than you think. Until then, I'll have Killer to keep me company. You just do what you need to do, and know that I'm proud of you."

This was it. I was leaving my life behind. I truly believed that, despite what I had been told, my mom and I would be reunited one day. Hearing her voice confirmed that. I would never let her go that easily. Never.

8

THE SKIN UNDER my eyes was puffy and raw from crying all night. I know I'm like my dad and used to getting no sleep, but this was crazy. I was really feeling it now. I was dressed in blue from head to toe, descending on the gold-domed grass patch deep into Seneca, my new home.

"Campbella!" I was too tired to turn around. I didn't have to because Reba was by my side in a flash. His hair was more disheveled than the last time I'd seen him, his shirt half tucked in. He had been waiting at the entry point. "I am so crazy happy to see you today. You have no idea. It's always a crapshoot; will the newbies be back or not? You know? And you are, and that is incredible!"

"For who?" Even though I had made the choice, I was plagued with guilt.

"Two years ago, I went through exactly what you're going through, and trust me, it gets better. Even though we're a part of something so unbelievably phenomenal, that doesn't mean the other side of the sword doesn't affect us. We're still human. But you'll see. It'll get better."

"Thanks, Reba." I really did appreciate this bubbly guy. Yet part of me wanted to resist his friendship, out of loyalty to Julie. I felt like I'd be replacing her. My inner circle was being dismantled and rebuilt.

"I have to tell you, though, what you go through next isn't for the faint of heart. So hang on tight, and if you need a friend..." Reba held up his wrist. His flexer was in the form of a retro stopwatch. I took mine from my back pocket and we pressed them together.

"I gotta bounce now, chica, but how about lunch? I think we have it at the same time."

"Yeah, we can do lunch."

"Sweet!" And Reba was gone in the blink of an eye. I pulled up my locations map on my flexer. I pinpointed my first official session of my first real day as a citizen of Seneca: Mathematics in epidemiology. If I had to pick a least favorite session, this would be the one. I always hated discussing diseases but, hey, I get it, everyone hated it just the same and that's why they were so set on finding ways to eradicate it in this new society.

I looked up from my entry point to determine which of four golden hallways I needed to take. In my direct line of vision, about forty-five yards down, there was a perfectly shaped head with a buzz cut. My eyes darted to the floor. There they were: blue combat boots. I looked up. His face. Two mysterious, different-colored eyes with a depth to them I so badly wanted to explore. I wanted for him to see me. He didn't. I looked down the hall I needed to take, but he was headed in the opposite direction. By the time I looked back to where he'd been, he was gone.

The urge to follow him was magnetic. I moved without even thinking. I made it to where I'd last seen him standing. There were no doors in sight. Maybe one had opened up for him in the wall, like I had seen happen the day before. He could be anywhere. I needed to get to session, set to begin in two minutes. I definitely didn't want to start things off on the wrong foot by being late.

As I headed back in the other direction, McKayla Gordon, Jennifer Wallingsford's sour friend, appeared.

"Hi, McKayla." I figured if I was here to stay, it was probably best to play nice. No need to have enemies right off the bat in a brand new place. Neutrality was my goal.

"Not feeling suicidal today are you, Nirvana?" She smirked and eyed me as a doorway opened up in the golden wall for her.

"Not today, but thanks for your concern."

I watched her saunter past me, through the instant door and into her session. I glimpsed inside the room and was about to walk away when something caught my eye. McKayla sat in front of *him*. Blue Combat Boots was in her session. He looked up and saw me staring at him from outside the room. And just like that, the door glazed over in the mirrored gold and I was staring back at myself. Or a version of myself that was acting like a silly little girl with a silly little crush. A girl I didn't know. I snapped out of it. With one minute to get to session, I booked it back down the hall and made it to my seat with seconds to spare.

9

RATHER THAN JOINING the other girls of the dorm for our morning ride into Seneca, Ellen picked me up in a flighter with a driver and a special guard. These two were always with her. They were in the front. She was in the back. I wasn't sure where we were headed. But I was getting used to that.

She handed me a coffee. "Do you like mochas?" It was my first real whiff of coffee since the last time I'd been inside Café Firenze four mornings before. (Had it really only been four days ago that all this had begun?) I swiped the cup from Ellen's hand, took the lid off and slurped up the still unmelted whipped cream atop the silky, chocolate-infused espresso milk. One whiff of the rich aroma made my heart ache, made me miss my mom more than I ever knew I could. It was even more painful than missing my dad, I think, because I had chosen to do it.

"You made the right choice, Doro."

I took a sip– it hurt so good. "That's what I hear... I hope so."

"I made the same choice three years ago, when I accepted Congressman Wallingsford's invitation to join Seneca's Youth

Initiation Division."

Ellen was touching her necklace, her eyes chock full of sorrow. I felt an energy emanating from her that resonated with me. An understanding between us. She removed her necklace. It was a Yin Yang in silver and gold, with two diamonds as the dots, each encircled in the metal of the opposite side. Her hand started to shake. She opened it. It was a locket, and inside was a tiny picture of her and a little boy. He must have been around eight or nine. "It was the hardest thing I'd ever done. The hardest thing I'll ever do. Not a day goes by that I don't think about him, or a night when he isn't present in my dreams."

It was her son. I didn't have to ask. "What's his name?"

"Connor. I call him Con Con. He'll never understand why I never came home."

We sat in silence for the rest of the ride. I wasn't the only one who'd made a big sacrifice.

The flighter traveled deeper and deeper into lush greenery, away from civilization. It was quite possibly the most scenic trip I'd taken in my entire life. I saw virtually no signs of human life other than train tracks and a dozen or more freight trucks as we flighted down 81 South. The Smart Road was populated with automated vehicles. That was where the majority of the traffic was, if you'd even call it traffic, which you wouldn't. Besides the highway, the Smart Road and a flighter here and there, we were just like a brush sweeping across nature's paint palette, collecting all its richness in our bristles. My lungs opened up to the thick, moist air, my eyes as wide as an owl's in the dark of night. Except it was twilight, and the sky was still a deep sea blue, only just beginning its slow fade to black.

We reached a mountainous area of Southern Virginia and the flighter landed in a secluded nook, next to a lake. The water was still and inviting. As the seasons changed, the robust green that filled the branches here was speckled ever so lightly with maroon and orange.

"This is Claytor Lake."

"It's beautiful."

"Isn't it? All this is the result of a dam built on the oldest river in North America. It's an ancient gift that, fortunately, man has not yet destroyed. The dam once provided this region with much of its hydroelectric power. Southern Gate Electric, a utilities company owned by Congressman Wallingsford's brother, Billy, bought the dam five years ago and Seneca had it converted to power a large portion of the Northwestern Seneca hemisphere. This small area provides us with a substantial source of power that allows us to do the things we do. It's also used to cool our super computers. Right now, we're standing directly above the greatest computing center in the world as well as one of Seneca's premier medical hubs."

I looked around, trying to pinpoint any sign of this. Nothing. In fact, everything I saw was natural and gorgeous— the antithesis of the artificial world of computers. "You would never know."

"And for the most part, no one does."

The mysterious men in blue shadowed us. About a hundred yards down, near the forest's edge, I saw a circle of grass with a gold ring. The entrance.

"Come on, let me show you."

Our little posse met two more men in blue at the entrance, trading places with our original escorts who turned back to the flighter. We stepped onto the encircled grass patch. The gold dome appeared and then, quickly, we descended. I was kind of surprised that taking this advanced elevator down inside the earth was beginning to feel normal.

"Doro, this is where you'll be spending a lot of time once you go through your pre-requisite session work at S.E.R.C."

When the gold dissolved, the forest's sweet serenity was replaced by walls of computer monitors, all pumping out droves of data. This place was like my bedroom on insane mega steroids. An open workspace. People everywhere, young and old, of every ethnicity, working together or apart on intricate spreadsheets of equations and data. The buzz of machinery and voices blended symphonically. The smell of technology, what an aphrodisiac! Everyone looked enthusiastic about the work they were focussed on. This was an absolute wonderland to a tech junkie like me.

I started along a five-foot-wide gold path that ran through the middle of the open space. One group in blue caught my eye. They were all my age and were working with people of various ages, from a three-year-old girl to a man of about sixty. I skidded to a stop. One of those people was Blue Combat Boots. Everything around me faded to a blur, then pulled focus on him. Blue Combat Boots was working with the sixty-something man, taking stats from sensors on the man's body as he walked on a treadmill.

"Doro? You coming?"

"Yes... what's going on over there?"

"That's a regenerative medicine residency for advanced S.E.R.C. scholars."

"So what, like physical therapy?"

"Like growing limbs for patients that were either born without them, or lost them in situations like land mine explosions or car accidents. Even people who had their lungs removed from cancer can have brand new lungs that work better than the ones they were born with."

This was absolutely amazing. These patients were moving their arms and legs as if they'd always had healthy ones. Scientists had been trying to perfect this advancement in the Aboves for decades. Here in Seneca, it was so normal that not only doctors were analyzing patients' progress, but people my age were, too. And one of those people was Blue Combat Boots. This guy wasn't anything like the ones I went to school with back in LA. Oh no, he most certainly was not. I stood there watching him as he and the older man shared a joke.

"There will be plenty of time for you to explore all of this, but today we have a different agenda."

I looked at Ellen Malone with the wonder of a kid on Christmas morning. If only I could stay in this spot for just a few moments more. But she didn't return my "this is going to be fun" look, and so I followed her, looking back until I was beyond where I could see him anymore.

"There's an awful disease endemic to Seneca that comes from an abundant fauna in the Southeastern Hemisphere. Necrolla Carne. It's an organism that slowly eats away at the human body, causing a long, drawn-out death. It's something you never, ever want to witness."

"Um, *that* is repulsive. Makes my skin crawl just thinking about it." Ellen was amused as I scratched furiously at my arms. Talk of disease always made me feel the symptoms. Just like my dad. He was always washing his hands thoroughly, all the way up to his elbows.

"Fortunately, our medical research and development team has developed a vaccine that immunizes us from it."

"A shot? I'm getting a shot today?"

"It's not too bad."

"It's the worst. I hate shots. I hate needles. I might pass out."

Ellen laughed. I did, too, but out of nervousness, not amusement. Soon we entered a medical wing that made every doctor's office I'd ever visited back home look like an exhibit in a history museum. Ellen explained that I wouldn't see a doctor unless a problem arose, and that was only three to five percent of the time. Instead, a lot of my experience would be automated or handled by technicians.

I followed the footpath map to the med-unit, which had been transmitted to my flexer upon entry. I marveled at the white touch screen with blue typeface that covered the entire length of the wall. It was an automated system that managed the devices within each med-unit and was overseen by a few med-techs in powder blue lab coats. My flexer notified me that I had reached my med-unit, so I stopped and went inside as the golden door opened.

My instructions were relayed to me by an automated narration in a calming female voice: "Take a seat." "Roll up your sleeve." "Open your mouth."

Even though I was a little nervous, I laid back in a robotic chair that did all the work a nurse or doctor always had done in the past, and surprised myself by thinking that I trusted this machine more than I would an actual doctor. My physical statistical data was transmitted from the chair back to the computer for analysis and report, and the machine said, "You are healthy, Dorothy."

If this technology already existed, why couldn't it happen up in the Aboves? No sooner had I begun to ponder that than a voice instructed me to expose my left shoulder for that dreadful shot.

10

I WOKE UP in a haze and a cold sweat. I was literally drenched, back in my bed back at the ambassadors' house. Ellen Malone must have brought me back while I was out cold. Things were a little blurry, but after a moment, I regained focus and grabbed for the glass of water at my bedside. I downed it. That vaccine was no joke. Luckily it was preparing my body to fight this disgusting Necrolla Carne disease. No way was I going to take the chance of getting some retched flesh-eating organism.

I was thankful for the comforts of the ambassador's house right now. It was Friday, my last day there, my last days living in the Aboves. Over the weekend I would be set up in my new habitat in Seneca. It was surreal, to say the least, to know that I was moving to a location below the surface of the Earth. Permanently.

It was no sweat off anyone's back that I wasn't making it to that Friday's sessions. I guessed this vaccination was something every citizen of Seneca went through, and my reaction was no different than anybody else's.

There was a light tap at my door and Jennifer Wallingsford poked her head in. It was the middle of the day and the mansion had been so quiet that I thought I was alone.

"Hi there." Her face bloomed in sympathetic recognition, "Oh, the Necrolla Carne vaccine. Isn't it *the worst?*"

"I just feel like death, but other than that, no big deal."

"Seriously. Well, it's worth it for a day of feeling like death over a permanent *real* death."

"No kidding."

"I have the day off to pack for my family vacation to Cape Cod. Do you want me to get you anything before I go?"

"No thanks, no appetite."

Jennifer was in sweats but still managed to look extremely put together. Like she was in a catalogue for high-end varsity athletic gear. It stung me in the gut when she said she'd be with her family. It not only made me jealous, but I felt cheated too. How come she could be with her family, but I'd been forcibly separated from my mom– especially while I was still dealing with losing my dad? My stomach was crippled with queasiness, not just from the shot, but also from the thought of not seeing my mom again.

A deep voice called up from downstairs. "J. Wall?!"

"I'm upstairs," she hollered back down. "My twin brother. Time to go."

Her twin brother: G.W. Wallingsford. From what I had always heard, the Wallingsfords were related to the first president of our country, George Washington. And so the first initial of his name was for George after the most famous George of all, and the middle initial, W, was for William, his uncle. G.W. had been in the news a lot because he had gotten busted at a party in Georgetown with a bunch of Mojo'd-out teenagers. The whole thing was pushed under the rug faster than a BoomJet as G.W. suddenly started speaking out on behalf of the anti-Mojo movement. He'd become their poster-child.

The Mojo Stick was a nano technology that rendered all other recreational drugs obsolete. Now you could just inject a micro-computerized version of your drug trip of choice straight into your bloodstream. There were cocktails of every variety, you name it. Anything from a light buzz to being completely out of it. Since there was no chance of overdose, people who wouldn't normally try drugs, did. I had never tried it, and never would because there was no way I was sticking a needle into myself for fun. The government was trying to block Mojo Sticks because even though you wouldn't die from using them, they were turning people into drugged-out zombies. There was an absurd demand for these things. A multi-trillion-dollar industry had grown up overnight.

G.W. poked his head in the doorway. You could tell in a second that they were twins, because like his sister, he didn't look like a teenager and his voice was deep like a *man* man. A head full of thick, blond, men's shampoo commercial hair and light blue eyes made me want to believe anything he was about to say. Perfect white teeth, just like his dad's, and athletic gear from head to toe that looked like it was fresh off the production line. He was not my type, but for almost every other girl, he was exactly the type, and I could understand why.

"Hey!"

"Hi, Georgie. I just have a few more things to pack. Want to hang with Dorothy while I finish up? She just got to Seneca and had her Necrolla Carne vaccination today."

"Oh, man. I feel your pain."

"Thanks." He seemed like a normal enough guy. Not so consistent with the bad boy image that had gotten so much press last year.

Jennifer sashayed out of the room and G.W. plunked down on the foot of my bed.

"So, where you from?"

"LA."

"Nice! I love LA."

"Me too. I miss it already."

"Come out sometime with my crew and me, you won't miss it anymore. We have some serious fun in these parts. It is possible, trust me."

"Cool, okay." I never trusted anyone who said "Trust me" and I wasn't going to start with the notorious son of a congressman. On the other hand, I was definitely down for experiencing a good dose of his lifestyle, if only to see what it was like and tell Julie about it later.

"Feel better. I'm gonna hit the loo and head out for a weekend of hobnobbing with pops and the rest of the corruption contingency. Wish me luck I make it through in one piece."

"Luck be with you."

"Nice to meet you. Dorothy, right?"

"Doro."

"Doro. Cool. That's slick."

He jumped up and whistled his way out the door. Too bad for him I didn't believe in luck.

11

SUNDAY NIGHT I was back to my sleepless self. Tossing and turning, hoping each one would be the last and I'd finally doze. Maybe that shot wasn't so bad after all, considering I managed to get some rest, for once, right after I'd had it. The weekend was all about getting settled into my new digs. This place was pretty darn bizarre. It might be cool and all, but it lacked the comforts of home and I just couldn't grasp how it could ever provide that. I longed for a welcoming lick bath from Killer, to get home from school and have my mom grill me on test scores. It was the little things that I would never experience again that I missed most.

Believe it or not, the noise from the double decker 405 Freeway that hovers below our 14th floor digs and bled through the double-paned windows and walls that might as well have been made of rice cakes. That is how we lived in Culver City, California. Not just us. Everyone.

When the California Gray Party jumped ship from the national agenda five years ago, and the Federal Government turned the other cheek, so began the official decline in Los Angeles civility.

Truth be told, it was already headed in that direction, but the rogue state government definitely sealed the deal. People stopped paying taxes and there was nobody to regulate a thing. At first, with the disappearance of building codes and regulations in the interest of raising money, ambitious architectural projects sprouted up across the city. But when the money dried up, and it dried up quick, we were left with a landscape of sophisticated and new mixed with unfinished and broken down. Our building fell somewhere right in the middle because our landlord had owned it since it was built twenty years ago, and he took great pride in managing it. I missed that building.

I was alone now in my golden room. My new home. A twelve-by-twelve cube with sleek lighting and texture just like the hallway at S.E.R.C. and, in it, all of my necessities. My bed had no frame, just a single-sized mattress that emerged from the wall when I commanded it to. It would soften, harden and adhere to my temperature preferences. I shared a wing with six other girls my age, also in the S.E.R.C. program.

In anti-contamination efforts, I was given a three foot by three foot cube which could be filled with any personal belongings that I wanted to bring from the Aboves. It all would have to go through a weeklong sterilization process in the Quarantine and Cleansing sector. According to Reba, humans went through a heavy-duty decontamination "zap" inside the dome that brought us down from the Aboves. "The Aboves" was a term I came to know well, as everyone in Seneca referred to the surface of the

Earth this way. I was no longer an American. I was a Senecan now, spending every waking second learning new things about my new life in this new world.

I'd just fallen into a catnap when Monday morning intruded as my flexer blurted that it was 7 a.m. My first session of the day would begin in an hour. I rolled out of bed, put on my Seneca blue robe and flip-flops, and headed to the restroom designated for my wing.

I had met a few hallmates while I was getting settled in, but had only exchanged small talk. I didn't know anything about these girls other than their names. Everyone seemed nice enough and welcoming. They all had been newbies just like me not too long ago.

The restroom was golden, like everything else. Sterilized to the max. There were UV self-cleaning mechanisms in place and smart automatic dispensary nozzles for water in the showers and sinks. I was super fascinated by the waterless toilets. They had a special red liquid that transported the waste away for conversion and gasification. We each had our own cubby that opened by flexer identification. Inside it we kept our shampoo, soap and mouthbrushes, Seneca's own version of toothbrushes. During my visit to Claytor Lake, not only did I get my Necrolla Carne vaccination, but they also swiped DNA samples, drew blood, did a full body scan and took a mold of my mouth, which they used to form my mouthbrush. It fits like a mouth guard and has five hundred tiny, powered bristles that, in ten seconds, does a better job brushing my teeth than I could in two minutes. I've always been a huge fan of efficiency, and in Seneca efficiency is scripture.

I got ready in a rush, and then took a one-minute ride in a super-speed acoustic carrier from the youth residential sector into S.E.R.C. It was my first time being transported through the air by sound waves. I feel like they should be called "non-sound" waves since the frequency is too high for us to hear anything at all. Quiet, quick, safe and devoid of harmful emissions, acoustic carriers are the only mode of transportation within Seneca City. It's a technology that people in the Aboves recently started to experience commercially on a limited basis. In Seneca it was completely normal and it made me feel like I had stepped into a new life in the future.

My goal was to get to S.E.R.C. early and be on the lookout for Blue Combat Boots. I'd thought about him a lot since I'd seen him last. My dad had always reminded me that I had important things to do in life and said that focusing on boys would just interfere. He said he was the only guy I needed, at least for the time being, but I didn't have him now, and the way Blue Combat Boots made me feel was out of my control. If my dad could know what had happened to me over just these last few days, I was pretty sure he would understand. I truly aspired to be everything he wanted for me. But I wasn't the first, and I wouldn't be the last girl to be swept away by a mysterious guy with electric eyes. I wanted to know so many things about him.

Where was his golden living cube? How long had he been here? How did Seneca find him? He was apparently involved in Seneca's advanced medical arena, but what exactly was he doing?

I posted up in the hall and waited... and waited, and waited. It was three minutes before session.

"Campbella!"

I let out a sigh.

"Oh sorry, not the person you wanted to see first thing on a Monday?" Reba's sincerity brought me a dose of warmth I'd been missing. I hugged him and could tell he was pleasantly surprised.

"No, no, I'm sorry, Reba, I just– it was a long weekend. The vaccination kicked my butt. You know how it goes."

"Do I ever. I told you it wasn't going to be pretty."

"You weren't lying."

"Chica, Puerto Ricans never lie."

"And what about Senecans?"

He raised an eyebrow and grinned. "Touché."

I looked up over his shoulder, trying to focus on the spot where I'd last seen Blue Combat Boots in S.E.R.C. Reba could tell I was pre-occupied.

"Well, glad to see you survived. Better safe than sorry. Who wants their face eaten off by a flesh-eating parasite, right?"

There he was. He was probably fifteen yards from the location where he'd entered his session last week. I had to get to him before he went inside. At least get close enough so that he would notice me. I ducked out from my conversation with Reba, "Gotta go, see you later?"

"Sure, okay. Lunch!"

At any other time I would have loved chatting with my new friend, but this mission was top priority. Our eyes had to meet again. I didn't take mine off of him. He stopped a few steps away from the door and took a look at his flexer. It was black and blue and wrapped around his wrist. I slowly moved in closer. I felt my temperature rising, my breath quickening. Every face in my periphery was blank except for his. I studied him. His serious expression, the way his sideburns faded into the stubble that traveled down around his chin and over his top lip. He was the perfect mix of babyface and rugged. I wanted to know him so bad. He was still, while everyone around him was in motion. I started in his direction, trying not to be obvious.

In the blink of an eye, I felt myself twirled around, a door opened in the wall and I was moved through it by another body. I was in the dark, with someone else's breath closing in on me. I stood stock-still.

And then we were illuminated. Blue Combat Boots and me. His flexer lit the room with its screen. Not a room, but a small closet, with walls lined in liquid mercury control panels.

"Who are you and why are you following me?"

"I'm sorry, I was just– I wasn't following you."

"You were. I saw you last week. Friday you came outside my first session and now you're back."

Busted. We stared each other down, each one having a completely different reason than the other.

"Tell me what you want."

He looked paranoid, guarded and intent on getting answers.

"I am so sorry, I think you have the wrong idea."

"I don't have any idea. I just see what I see and want to know what's going on."

"I totally get that and I realize how this might seem. Wow. I'm totally not spying on you or anything crazy. I'm Doro. I'm new here."

"Uh huh..." It wasn't enough.

"I just thought you looked... interesting."

"Interesting?"

Okay. I had dug myself into a hole. At this rate, things were not looking good. If I wanted to save face, my only option was to go with honesty. "I saw you on my first day and thought you were..." Wow. No matter what I said next, I was destined to sound like a fool–

"Handsome."

He breathed a sigh of relief. I allowed myself a bashful smile. He squinted but didn't blink. I welcomed the way his eyes pierced right through me. His paranoid, guarded, intent gaze morphed. He squished his lips in thought, trying to get a read on me, I could tell. Although these weren't ideal circumstances for a first meeting, I was glad that it looked like he believed me.

"You just sent me into code red, you know."

"I know. Bad move. I really didn't mean to cause you any–"

"It's okay. We're good."

He said we were good. I was closer to him than I could have imagined on this mission, and we were speaking, one on one, with no one else around. I could get used to this.

Suddenly, our flexer notifications went off at the same time. It broke the tension and we both laughed. Session was beginning.

"Dang." He muttered as he turned, flexer raised. The golden door opened, and he was gone.

12

AS THE WEEKS went by, I started feeling kind of down. Becoming acclimated to Seneca was a thrill and there were no dull moments, but I missed my family to death. If family was everything, then I had nothing. It wasn't enough that they were in my memories and digital images tucked away in the depths of my Veil— the virtual location in which all of a person's important data resided. I needed my mom. I was sixteen and I had lost both of my parents. I couldn't accept it. Somehow, I had to find the way to fight for the one parent I had left.

I sat on the floor of my room scrolling through old pictures: the Campbell family joking around, our house and yard in the Glendale 'burbs, the lemon tree my mom and I used to make lemonade from. My dad would come home from work right before I went to bed and tell us stories about what had gone on in his lab that day. He said goodbye to me in the morning and goodnight to me at bedtime, but other than that, during the week, all he did was work. His company was subcontracted by the largest particle collision research and testing facility in the world. The last thing he and his partners had created before he disappeared was an element. He told me he'd call it Doromium and that it was the thing he was most proud of in life besides me. But on weekends, there was no talk of work. We'd pack up and drive to Joshua Tree, where we'd spend all day collecting rocks and eating PB&Js with bananas. Then, when Mom and I slept, he'd stay up all night to work.

The hole in my heart wasn't going away. It was growing more and more raw by the hour. It was beginning to feel like I'd better do something fast, or eventually there would be no heart left to beat.

I had to find a way to let my mom know what was going on. Even more important than that, I had to get my mom into Seneca. She deserved this better life too. As a matter-of-fact, if we are all equal like I've always been taught and I truly believe, then what we were creating in Seneca belonged to everyone, not just to some elite selection of quirky geniuses.

It was Sunday afternoon. I'd spent the last sixty-two hours alone. If I had to endure one more, I'd go clinical. I flexed Reba. He picked up after one ring. "Campbella!"

"Hey. Busy?"

"Never too busy for my main California girl. Que pasa?"

"Just thought you might want to grab a late Sunday brunch or something."

"Pick you up in five!" He was at my door in four.

"Thanks for coming over."

"What are you in the mood for? Eggs, pancakes, a chocolate milkshake?"

"Chilaquiles." I was homesick like nobody's business and needed a plate of queso-drenched chilaquiles like a medical emergency of the highest order.

Ten minutes later we were seated in the best Mexican restaurant in our sector. Food was not a problem in Seneca. Top chefs and culinary gurus from across the globe were among those being recruited, as well as botanical and farming experts. If there was an expert for something, you best believe they were being recruited to Seneca. We had the best hydroponic and organic produce and meats, prepared in the most brilliant ways. New citizens were in for serious palate thrills when they got here.

After salivating at the amazing aromas, I had no trouble gorging on my favorite spicy delights. My eyes were closed, as they always were when I wanted to hone in on a particular sense, except sight of course. When I opened them, Reba was sitting in front of his untouched plate, just smiling, watching me.

"What?"

"You're a funny eater, Campbella."

I launched a tortilla chip straight at him. He picked it up and ate it. It was good to have a real friend here. Someone who would eat food off your plate, meet you for lunch on a minute's notice and maybe even give you the details on Blue Combat Boots. I still didn't know his name.

"Sooo... I was wondering."

"Uh-oh."

"What? I haven't even said anything."

"You've said enough. I liked it better when you were throwing food at me. How about that kernel of corn?"

He always brought such a great energy to the moment. I had completely forgotten the creeping depression that had been taking me under less than an hour before.

"Look. I saw who you were checking out. On the first day, and the day when you first got back from getting your Necrolla shot."

"Well?"

"Well."

I could tell that this was not what he wanted to be talking about. But I knew he had the dirt, and the anticipation was building. I flicked a sour cream-covered corn kernel and it hit him square in the forehead.

"Yeah! That's my girl."

"So, what, you don't want to tell me? I have to find out for myself, is that the deal?"

"Okay. What exactly do you want to know?"

"Everything."

Reba sat back. He was going to give me the info I wanted because he'd known all along that this conversation was inevitable... and that it was going to go down with a patch of sour cream between his eyes.

"Dominic Ambrosia."

"Dominic." I softly repeated his name like it was the finest name I'd ever heard.

"Look. I know he's got some weird magnetic thing about him that girls are really into. Trust me, I get it. But he's not good for you."

Didn't Reba know that telling a girl a guy isn't good for her can make the girl want the guy that much more?

"Yes. I know I've just made him even more attractive, but I'd like to think that you would trust me on this one."

I waited to hear if he had a good enough reason for me to disregard the laws of attraction.

"Dominic came into Seneca at the same time as me. He's a loner. Always keeps to himself, and is *always* under some sort of investigation with S.O.I.L."

"What is S.O.I.L.?"

"Seneca Observation and Intelligence League, aka, a much more hardcore version of the F.B.I. They know everything."

"Sounds like Big Brother."

"S.O.I.L. is like Big Brother's older, smarter, cooler, stronger and much more ruthless brother."

"I see."

"You start down the path of interacting with Dominic Ambrosia, and you're just asking for S.O.I.L. to be all over you like white on rice, for the rest of your life."

I wasn't so interested in my chilaquiles anymore.

13

THE ACOUSTIC CARRIER dropped us off at S.E.R.C. Monday morning. I wanted to dodge Reba so he wouldn't ask me what I'd decided about Blue Combat Boots. *Dominic*. I scanned my surroundings as I stepped off the carrier. I was in the clear.

"Campbellllla. Just who I was looking for."

Well, lots of things were unavoidable around here. "Hey Reebs."

"Listen, about our conversation yesterday."

"What conversation?"

"Exactly. Can we keep it that way? Dominic isn't a bad guy. I just want the best for you is all."

"You trust me, I trust you. Sounds like we have a pretty solid friendship."

Reba smiled. "Be careful. That's all I ask."

I nodded. He knew what I was up to. This kid seriously had some incredible intuition going on, and the nose of a bloodhound. There was no pulling something over on him.

"Lunch." He put his fist up for a bump, and I bumped him

back.

With five minutes to kill before first session, I booked it to the hallway where I invariably ran into Dominic. I waited until twenty seconds before my flexer session notification was set to go off, but no sign of him. I was royally bummed. Did Reba know Dominic wouldn't be around today, and that's why he was cool with me running off to find him?

I sat through my first few sessions that day completely unimpressed, even though what we were doing in them I normally would have found fascinating. Then, in Seneca Civics and Ethics we had a guest speaker. Seneca citizen, Julian Hollenbeck, was not only the head of America's top television network, but he also owned news outlets and multi-media distribution networks around the globe. I was more than surprised to see him since, according to reports in the Aboves, he had died of brain cancer a few years back. According to Mr. Hollenbeck, he had been given the opportunity; if he stayed for good in Seneca, to instantaneously eradicate his terminal cancer, and then go on to develop media distribution channels for this new, advanced society. He gave a really inspiring speech about why Seneca is the place where you can carve a promising new future with other likeminded individuals. He reminded us that we were empowered here, unlike anywhere else. Now, more than ever, I wanted to align with the people who could help create a positive change in our world. I had an overwhelming feeling that Dominic would be one of those people.

My last session of the day was quantum computing freestyle. I was exhausted but pepped up when we were given a project. My session mates and I were each assigned a different country and given two hours to bypass international government agency defense systems to extract intelligence on American nationals who resided there. It wasn't merely for the sake of taking a quiz. This was legit undercover operative stuff, and S.O.I.L. would use our information. There were twenty-two of us in the session. Whoever came up with the correct results first would be awarded an escorted trip to the Aboves with their guest of choice.

In seventeen minutes and six seconds flat I cracked the Iranian Ministry of Intelligence, a supposed zero-knowledge proof system. The session leaders reacted as if it was the greatest achievement since the inception of quantum algorithm freestyle. My session mates cheered like I was the quarterback who had just thrown a winning Hail Mary. This whole situation couldn't have been more different from Mr. Malin's calculus class back in LA, but the greatest thing of all was that Saturday afternoon I would get to visit Great Falls Park. Somehow, between now and then, I was determined to locate and invite my boy in blue combat boots.

14

TUESDAY, WEDNESDAY AND Thursday all came and went. Every morning I scoped out Dominic's first session, but he was nowhere to be seen. By Friday, when I stepped off the acoustic carrier, I was convinced that this day wouldn't be any different. I hadn't seen Reba all week either. He hadn't shown up at our normal meeting spot for lunch, nor was he at the arrival pad when I came in the mornings. I'm sure he was disappointed that I was pursuing Dominic. Part of me felt bad, but I knew I wasn't doing anything wrong. I was just following my instincts, which were just about all I had left from my former life in the Aboves.

I had a funny feeling and as I looked up, Dominic was there, exactly where I was hoping to catch up with him. When he saw me standing there, we stared each other down. This was my only chance. If I didn't approach him now, I wouldn't be able to invite him to the Aboves. He turned away and started along the golden wall towards his session. I booked it after him.

He lifted his flexer, and as the doorway began to open up, I did the only thing I knew would get his attention. "Dominic!"

He put his arm down. The door glazed back over as he pivoted slowly. I strode right up to him, having no idea where I got the nerve.

He looked me over. It was a "you again" sort of look, only this time, he wasn't paranoid and guarded at all. I didn't know how to begin, so I just went for it.

"Hi."

"Hi."

"You haven't been around the past few days."

"Nice of you to notice."

"You didn't catch the Necrolla Carne did you?" I thought I was being pretty freaking funny.

And there it was. His lips finally formed what everyone else in Seneca had given up so easily. A smile. My heart melted. I felt it drip down inside my chest. My knees almost buckled, making it an effort just to stand up straight. I hoped he couldn't tell.

He leaned in and whispered into my ear, so softly I could barely hear him but I could feel his warm breath and it gave me butterflies. "You don't believe that, do you? I was under the impression that you were smarter than the rest."

I wasn't sure what he meant, but I didn't want to get into that at the moment. Once again, our next sessions were starting in a second or two. "Look," he said, "I gotta get to session. I can't be calling any more attention to myself than I already have." He turned away from me.

It was now or never. "Hey! Listen. I was awarded a trip to the

Aboves because of a thing I figured out fast in my quantum computing freestyle session... and I get to take a guest. I'm new here, don't know that many people and..."

"You're inviting me to go with you to the Aboves?"

"Well, if you're not busy Saturday afternoon and–"

"I'll meet you at the base of Sector Twelve at nine."

Without waiting for my response, he moved through the doorway that was open for a handful of others headed into session.

15

I LAY IN bed watching the news on my flexer projector at nine o'clock on Friday night. Not that I'm big on the news, in all honesty, but everything else was a rerun and I'm not a fan of media that isn't on its first run. It must be something about feeling up to date, not stuck in the past. Guess that crosses over to many areas of my life. Tonight's main story was focused on how the Seneca medical community should be commended for their record in containing 98 per cent of the Necrolla Carne cases. I was right there with them, silently congratulating and counting my blessings. At the same time, I was turned off by the amount of time and attention Necrolla Carne got in Seneca.

All in all, I couldn't complain about the variety of media available to us here. Virtually every song that ever had been recorded and every movie ever made were at my fingertips. Each Senecan had the same level of access, and it was free. Hollenbeck Media from the Aboves scored the exclusive deal to provide entertainment to all of Seneca and ran it under the "Big Bang Boom Media" banner. Otherwise known as B3, the symbol was just about everywhere you looked and constantly popping up on my flexer to let me know about some new offering.

A knock at my door startled me. Nobody ever knocked at my door and I wasn't expecting anyone. I got up and moved to the door, pushed my ear up against it. "Who is it?"

"Hi Doro, it's Ellen–"

"And Gregory!"

I commanded the door to dissolve. It was nice to see familiar faces. I hugged Ellen, then went to shake Gregory's hand, but he gave me a big ol' bear hug instead.

"Hey. This is a surprise."

Gregory barely gave Ellen a chance to speak. "We thought we'd stop in and see how you were taking to your new living situation."

"Not bad. The food here is ridiculous. And I have a couple new friends, so–"

"Great!"

"That's good to hear, Doro. I knew you'd fit right in," Ellen said sincerely as she checked out my room. "You look like you've settled in nicely."

"Yeah. Still doesn't feel like home, but I know that doesn't happen over night."

Gregory took a seat on my desk, feet up on the chair. "Better than college dorms in the Aboves. You should have seen where I lived when I was at the Naval Academy. I was in a sports dorm, too, so it was extra nasty. Compared to that, you're living in the lap of luxury."

Gregory and Ellen laughed.

"I can't complain."

Ellen looked genuinely happy to see that I was doing well. Every time I was around her, I felt like she had my back. She had shared some deeply personal things with me, and I knew that, above all the business and politics, she had that maternal vibe going on and it needed an outlet. At the same time, Gregory was over the top with his cheeriness and I had no reason whatsoever to trust this guy. I wasn't one to buy into that whole "any friend of yours is a friend of mine" boloney. No thanks. Plus, I wasn't thrilled with the way he always seemed to interrupt Ellen. And here he was again, trying to buddy up to me. "Any plans with friends this weekend?"

"Actually, yeah, did you hear about how I cracked the Iranian Ministry defense systems?"

"We sure did."

"Three levels."

Gregory put his hand up for a high five. I threw one up to him. Why not? Might as well play along with the whole "buddies" song and dance to keep my new status intact. The people here appreciated me, and it was a relief after the way things had been at school back in LA.

"As my reward, tomorrow I get a trip to the Aboves. I'm going to Great Falls Park."

"Great Falls is beautiful. It's one of the best-kept secrets in the area. You'll love it." Ellen said.

"I cannot wait to feel the sun on my skin. Even though I was never one for tanning and all that, it's definitely a 'you don't know what you got 'til it's gone' kinda thing."

"That it is. Well, soak it up. You deserve it." Ellen meant it. I appreciated her being proud of me.

"And what deserving friend will be accompanying you?"

I blushed. Now it felt like prying.

Gregory caught on. "Uh-oh, must be a love interest. Someone's cheeks are on fire!"

"It's not love. I met this guy Dominic at S.E.R.C. I don't know too many people and thought it would be fun to do this with him, so I invited him and he accepted."

Ellen didn't show much expression, just a little nod. "I know Dominic. I actually recruited him in one of my first ever on-location visits."

Ellen knew Dominic. Did everyone know Dominic?

Gregory chimed in, "Smart kid."

"That he is. He's also... Let's just say, be careful how much you share with him about yourself and what you're doing here. And take what he says with a grain of salt," Ellen said.

It was fascinating. Everyone seemed to have an opinion on this guy. Now, more than ever, I wanted to form my own opinion. His intrigue factor had grown exponentially with this visit from Ellen and Gregory and, for me, that's what caught my interest. Not someone's looks, their sense of humor or how kind they are to babies. The mystery of what was going on in his mind was a major attraction– the unknown, the element of surprise. But I had to reassure Ellen and Gregory that I'd heard their advice, so they'd quit worrying about it.

"I will definitely keep that in mind. Really. I'm just looking to enjoy nature and have a good time with someone my age."

Ellen nodded. "Perfect, and you should. You have my flexer if you need to talk. Anytime, day or night, I'm here for you, Doro."

16

NINE A.M. SATURDAY could not come soon enough. Especially since my eyelids refused to cooperate with my overwhelming desire for sleep. I lay there in complete silence and avoided my flexer because I knew giving in to it would squash any chance of slipping back to sleep. Who was I kidding? It was going to be another all-nighter whether I liked it or not.

All I could think about was Dominic. Why did Ellen seem anxious about our potential bond? I was beginning to wonder if she had stopped by because she knew I'd be with him on Saturday, and not just for a social visit. She could have asked me how I was settling in anytime. Something was up. I might have been new to Seneca, but in real life I was no spring chicken.

I was relieved, to say the least, when my flexer finally signaled eight a.m. Unlike the Aboves, where the sun would come out and tap into your natural biorhythms to get you going, here we had to rely entirely on artificial light and flexer notifications to know the difference between night and day.

I was anxiously waiting for Dominic at 8:57. It seemed like

light years later when I watched my flexer switch to 9:00, and there was a tap on my shoulder.

"Ready for our big date?"

I felt my face flush. Oh no, please let him think I'm just a rosy skin-toned person. I really had to get this thing in check.

"Hi, Dominic."

"So formal."

"Who me?"

Dominic looked around as he squished his lips together. I loved it when he did that.

"I don't see anyone else here in this conversation."

"Sorry, I didn't get much sleep."

"Hey, no worries, you can be formal all day long if you want, but I'm on vacation. Hope that's okay with you. I haven't seen the sun in over seven hundred days, so this is a *pretty* epic day for me... And by the way, you can call me Dom. It's what my friends back home all called me."

I was blown away. Seven hundred days? Really? Even though I technically knew what was in store living here without sun, I couldn't comprehend being in his shoes. Or, rather, his blue combat boots.

"Oh, for sure. I'm dying to get out of here for a breather, too. It will be good to get a reality check."

"*Reality*. Funny thing, ain't it?"

Dom made some odd comments. Ones that made me wonder what he really meant. But I still wasn't ready to ask.

"We don't have to be at the entrance point until ten. Want to get some food first?"

"Doro, let me tell you something about me–"

Um, yes please, I thought...

"I'm *always* ready to get something to eat."

Ah, how refreshing. Dominic Ambrosia was handsome, witty, unequivocally mysterious, and a good eater!

17

THE RESTAURANT DISTRICT was a dreamlike version of a place I remember visiting as a kid. The sun beat down on me, interrupted only by rustling leaves from tall oak trees. I looked up, squinting to see how this could possibly be. The soft, cornflower blue sky blew me a kiss as a sweet floral breeze swept my hair across my face, tickling my nose. It reminded me of the outdoor mall near the beach in Santa Monica. Birds chirping, kids laughing, babies crying. All kinds of people and every kind of food. I heard murmurs of different languages–Mandarin, Spanish, Russian... Incredibly, I almost forgot I was with Dom, my attention was so absorbed by all the mouthwatering aromas around us. Dom didn't seem as mesmerized by this place as I was. He cut into a doorway and I followed, looking back over my shoulder.

We were at a sushi spot that he said he went to every weekend. We sat at the sushi bar. I thought it was funny that we were having sushi for breakfast, but fresh, edible, wild fish had not been available in my lifetime, so this was a mouthwatering treat.

Salmon, halibut, cod, and assorted rare fish and seafood were transported here on BoomJets from places that had the remaining clean water on the planet. They had also been testing new ways to replicate wild breeding here. Senecans were the only population with the privilege to enjoy these delicacies as regular eating habits. I could seriously get used to this.

Our first time eating together wasn't as carefree and lighthearted as my lunches and brunches with Reba. I didn't ask a lot of questions, but when I did, Dom answered with a question in return. He was obviously still vetting me. Could I be trusted and what was my motivation? Not the typical form of assessment I was used to from my peers. Usually it was questions about what musicians I like or if I got invited to some popular kid's party last Saturday night.

This morning I learned one thing about Dom. He was fluent in Japanese, and best buds with this restaurant's 28-year-old sushi chef, Ty. Ty had been recruited to Seneca because he had started a highly addictive sushi franchise that spread across Asia, Europe and the Middle East. It was literally the fastest growing food chain in world history. Addiction was an understatement. Ty knew exactly what Dom liked, so I went ahead and tried it all. No exaggeration, these were hands down the most explosive bites of food I'd ever tasted. Dom slowly savored each bite as he explained to me that in Seneca Ty was pushing the envelope of sushi preparation in a way he never could in the Aboves. He took the most ideal, fresh cuts of fish, and through the use of nanocapsules, he matched them with flavors of the customer's choosing. Ty's menu had everything from kumquat to truffle, which was injected into the fish for a timed release to deliver an eruption of flavor in your mouth at just the right moment. There was no question about it– I would be back for the jalapeno lime-infused halibut cheek.

Ty spoke English pretty well. When he and Dom flipped to Japanese, I sensed that they were talking about me. It seemed to be in a good way, though.

"You will take Dom to see the sun today. No wonder he likes you."

Please don't blush. Please don't blush, please, please, please... I took a huge gulp of water. Dom didn't notice– he was meticulously cleaning his vintage wooden chopsticks, which he obviously cherished like I did my vinyl LPs.

Dom grinned. "Don't get ahead of yourself, Ty."

"Enjoy for me too. Maybe next time I be your guest?"

"Whoa there, buddy. This is *my* gig!"

Finally, things were lightening up around the dark and mysterious Dominic Ambrosia. It was nice to see him become a little possessive about his guest spot on my Great Falls Park excursion. Whether it was because of the sun, or because of me, it's where he wanted to be and that was all that mattered.

We left our sushi breakfast feeling incredibly good. I could see why this was Dom's favorite eating establishment in Seneca. Ty was cool, and his otherworldly food increased his cool factor tenfold. I'd definitely be back... but first I had to take Dom for chilaquiles.

18

AS WE WALKED to the point where we would be joined by the men in blue for our ascent to the Aboves I tried to imagine what was on Dom's beautiful mind. I watched from the corner of my eye, knowing he was deep inside his own head. He scrunched his lips a lot. I didn't want to disturb him, so I decided to let him be the one that broke the silence this time.

One man and one woman in blue awaited our arrival. Without speaking they joined us in the dome, and up we went. What was normally a one-minute ride lasted forever with these mutes. It couldn't have been more awkward.

I wanted to catch every emotion Dom showed once he was at the top, truly experiencing the Aboves' daylight, after so long. He was so absorbed in the moment that he never even noticed that I was staring at him.

We came to a stop and he closed his eyes as the golden dome opened up to Virginia's blue gray sky. I watched him turn his face up and welcome the cool filtered light of the autumn sun onto his milky skin. He may have wanted to hide what he was really feeling, and he might have fooled the other two, but I could see an emotional meteor storm erupting behind those gripping eyes of his. Dom's reaction to the world he hadn't seen in two years was fascinating, heartwarming and sad to me all at the same time.

The sun shone down between streaks of cirrus clouds that were scattered high up in the sky. It was an ideal day for our visit. A small flock of birds flew over us, migrating south. Dom locked eyes on the flock. I could hear him breathing deeply, absorbing the real, if somewhat polluted, air of the Aboves. I didn't want to disturb his moment, so I climbed into the flighter that was waiting for us. He would come when he was ready.

Twenty minutes later, the flighter deposited us in a desolate area of Great Falls Park called Difficult Run. There wasn't a sign of anyone else anywhere around us. I wondered if this section of the park had been taken off the public access maps and repurposed for Seneca's use only. Actually, I would've been surprised if that weren't the case.

"In two hours we will depart." Those were the first words uttered by the folks in blue. They weren't messing around.

Dom wasted no time. He set off through the treed area, on a path towards the water. I followed. Finally, we were alone, without what I'd come to think of as our handlers. His pace grew quicker the closer we got to the water and I found myself practically jogging to keep up. We came to a point overlooking the Potomac, its powerful rapids mesmerizing. This was a force of nature that we both wanted to absorb in all its might.

The jagged rocks jetting out from the riverbed created a fast, intense flow of whitewater. A light, silky breeze contrasted with the dangerous rapids. I loved the sounds of the crashing water– so loud, but so soothing at the same time. Signs in various languages warned people not to try and swim in these uncertain waters. I hadn't planned on swimming anyway.

"Come on, let's go down by the water." Dom had a vibrant energy about him, instigated just by being in the great outdoors. This new side of him, just as much as his intense, mysterious persona, was exciting to be around. We trekked down a steep path to a small pebbled embankment on our side of the river.

Dom sat down and took off his blue combat boots. I was surprised at how meticulous he was with his laces, carefully undoing each one and then winding them up with precision and placing them inside his boots. He set them down next to each other, in complete alignment, pointed directly at the river. He indicated that I should do the same. Was he planning on getting in that water? Hadn't he seen the warning signs? Then he removed his flexer from his wrist and nodded to me, as if to say, "You do it, too."

I was apprehensive, but didn't want to appear weak or unwilling to try new, exciting things. Hey, I was the queen of trying new, exciting things. This was not the time for me to chicken out. Shoes came off, flexer out of my pocket. I looked at him, ready for the next dare.

Dom thrust his hand out. Better than a dare, this was a waking dream come true. I took his hand. He grasped mine tight and looked me in the eye. This wasn't a sweet, romantic, handholding moment like in the movies. This was a sudden, intense connection unlike anything I had ever imagined. It was just the two of us, together, against the raging river. His strong gaze spoke a thousand words. I knew what we were about to do, and discretely took a deep breath.

Dom stepped onto a huge rock a couple feet out into the water, then turned around to help me join him on it. Was this as far as we were going? No. He turned to take another step, higher, to a series of extremely steep rocks. Now I wasn't just intimidated. I was scared out of my mind, but tried my best to hide it.

It was frighteningly windy here above the rapids. My hair blew across my face, my teeth chattered a little bit. Dom's eyes were filled with determination. I fed off of it as we crossed a few more rocks. He let go of my hand and leapt to a higher rock, then turned back to me and reached down for me to jump up to him. I hesitated.

"I won't let you fall."

In a complete lapse of self-control, I trusted him. And for some dumb reason, I closed my eyes when I jumped.

I landed on the rock! My foot slipped, scraping my shin– there was blood, streaks of deep red against my pale skin. My foot plunged into the freezing cold water, sending all of my senses into overdrive. Dom grasped my hand tight and didn't let go. He was unfazed, and pulled me up onto the rock with him. There wasn't much space to stand. We were as close as we'd been in the closet at S.E.R.C. Closer. Only this time, we were out in the great wide open, not squeezed inside the darkness of closed walls and a closet full of chemical controls.

He let go of my hand and jumped down from the rock. I was on top of the world. The crisp water that penetrated my bones brought with it a surge of strength from another dimension. Dom turned and reached his hand up for me. This time I didn't take it. I didn't need him to help me or show me the way. So far, on this little day trip to Difficult Run, he had taken the lead. But this was my excursion and he was my guest. I needed to prove myself. It wasn't just about showing him that I was some badass chick. He was someone I needed to align myself with for so many reasons beyond even those that I was aware of. I needed to assure him that we were, indeed, cut from the same cloth.

And then I jumped. Something outside my body had taken over. After falling for what seemed like forever, I plunged into the only calm pool of water within sight. Under the freezing cold water, I welcomed the adrenaline rush like a long lost friend triggering the memory of my flighter heist with Julie and the exhilaration I'd felt then. I opened my eyes and surged back up into the humid Virginia air like a rocket from the river. I let out a wild scream of excitement and flung my hair out of my face just in time to see Dominic leaping off the cliff, the look of elation on his face during that free-fall something I'd never forget. He cannonballed and hit the water with a spectacular splash.

We surfaced and dove like porpoises, shouting out in pure euphoria. We didn't need Mojo Sticks– all we needed was each other and this sickening landscape.

We both bobbed up and down, doggy paddling, laughing and splashing around. My intuition had served me well. Dominic Ambrosia and me in a whole new world... it was going to be a wild ride.

I noticed an opening in the rock structure that formed against the river's edge, and swam that way. Dom came after me. We swam into a small cave that had its own natural skylight. The water was only waist deep, and the wind created a beautiful echo. He splashed water onto his face and then rubbed his eyes, before he opened them. Once he did, he didn't take them off me. The stillness in the cave enshrined the moment.

He smiled, and I smiled back. "You can trust me."

Dom moved in to be right in front of me, tucked my hair behind my ear and moved in even closer to whisper, "I know."

I could tell he didn't want to ruin the vibe of the moment, but he had something that he needed to share with me and it was time.

"They listen to everything."

"Who?"

"S.O.I.L. Nothing you say or do is secret. They know everything."

"How can they know it *all*?"

There was that paranoid look he had when I'd first met him, when he thought I was following him. Now, he looked all around, even up through the break in the rock structure, into the sky, scanning our surroundings like a raptor searching for prey.

"Our flexers?"

"Our flexers. Your blood."

"My blood?" I was baffled. How could they possibly listen to me through my blood? It sounded impossible, but then, why would he make this up?

"That shot you got wasn't for a flesh-eating bacteria. There is no such disease as Necrolla Carne."

I was dumbfounded. "How do you know?"

"I'll show you, but for now, just be careful. Watch every move you make. Don't trust anyone."

"Okay."

I thought about what Ellen Malone had told me the night before, and I felt conflicted. I had started to trust her as much as I could trust anyone, but here, in this moment, I trusted Dom the same, if not more. He looked back at me with those intense eyes– one hazel and one blue. He didn't blink. I felt him peering into my soul. Searching. Understanding me.

I wondered why he had decided to share this with me.

"You're different," he whispered. His hushed voice was melodic against the howl of the water rushing through the cave and the angry waves that smashed into the rock wall outside.

"So are you."

"That's why we are here together, right now."

I wanted to know everything right then and there, but I could tell that it wasn't the time to press. I was willing to wait, happy enough with this moment being just the way it was.

19

I DARTED AWAKE and grabbed my flexer. It was three thirty-three a.m. I'd slept for just over three hours– the longest stretch of sleep I'd had since right after my Necrolla Carne vaccination– or whatever that thing was. I couldn't wait until the next time I saw Dom, though we hadn't set a specific time. We didn't even have each other's flexer info.

I flipped on B3 and scrolled through the stations. The news was on with the same newscaster I'd seen the other day. She was an America's sweetheart type to a T. Light brown hair, and bangs that framed her lightly freckled face. Soft blue eyes the color of dolphin skin and a button nose people pay good money to have done with plastic. Becky Hudson.

"An outbreak of the VCF2 virus is creating a frenzy in the metropolitan D.C. area and the department of health is warning of its high level of contagiousness. This is on the heels of the third strain of bird flu to cause over two thousand deaths on the eastern seaboard this past summer."

Video images played of people sick in hospitals, wearing

facemasks in public places, from the mall to the post office. Kids were being removed from schools on stretchers, crying parents– the whole nine yards.

"Seneca Senate spokesperson, Terence Murray, issued this statement from the capital: It is in the best interest of all Senecans to avoid contact with the American population until the Center for Disease Control has declared this disease contained. Any Senecan who has been in contact with anyone or anyplace these diseases have been present, will be placed in the Quarantine and Cleansing Sector, and potentially removed from the Seneca Society. Rest assured, we are taking these matters seriously to ensure the safety of our citizens."

I flipped the channel. After what I'd heard from Dom I didn't know what to think about all this. I forced myself to push it out of my brain altogether. Nothing good was on B3, so I hopped out of bed and squatted down next to my record player. I pulled my Michael Jackson "Thriller" L.P. from the stack and sat back to crank some Billie Jean– one of my favorite songs of all time. I closed my eyes and enjoyed the warmth of the crackle on the vinyl. It always soothed me, and reminded me of my Mom. It was the one thing we loved doing together while we waited for my dad to get home after work. Sometimes he would come in the door and the two of us would be having the best dance party. We always danced like nobody was watching. Here, it seemed, maybe they *would* be watching. I wondered if I would still dance the same, knowing that. I thought I would.

20

THERE WAS NO sign of Reba at our usual meet-up spot when I got off the acoustic carrier on Monday morning, en route to first session. I was starting to think something was up. Was he mad at me for something I'd said or done? For a guy, he was pretty darn emotional.

After my first couple of sessions, it was time for lunch so I hit the monster of all meal halls. Pristinely white with long stainless steel tables and chairs, everything was perfectly symmetrical. The ceilings were about sixty feet high and lined in grids of tubes through which food was delivered. You ordered and it popped up directly on the table in front of your seat, and it was removed the same way.

I went to the table where I'd had lunch with Reba almost every day so far. He wasn't there. I walked up and down the aisles of tables hoping I would find him somewhere, but I couldn't spot him anywhere. I was starting to get to know who the cliques were at S.E.R.C. In this one way, at least, S.E.R.C. was just like my school back home in LA.

"Looking for someone?"

I spun around. Reba was there, sitting at a table with his back to me. He was eating a tuna fish sandwich on a French roll. There was a peanut butter cookie on his tray. It's what he had every single day.

"Hey, Reebs. I've been wondering where you've been."

"I've been around."

I eyed the seat next to him. "May I?"

"Please."

I knew by the tone of his voice that there was something going on. His usual peppy inflections were uncharacteristically subdued. He didn't even bother to look at me.

I took my flexer out and connected it to the port on the end of the meal tube. I placed my order for a cheese quesadilla with spicy salsa on the side.

"How was Great Falls?"

I hadn't even seen him since I'd earned the opportunity to go there. He must have heard through the grapevine. I guess the gossip mill is another similarity, between Seneca and my old school. So this was about the fact that I had invited Dom and not him. I definitely didn't want to rub it in that it had been unbelievably awesome, that I'd had the time of my life. That it had been a day undoubtedly I'd never, ever forget. "It was okay."

"You really expect me to believe that?"

"Are you mad at me? Because if you are, just tell me."

"Not at all. Why would I be mad?"

"Exactly."

"Exactly."

My quesadilla arrived. We ate in silence. He was clearly mad, and he shouldn't have been, but for some reason I still felt guilty. I didn't want his feelings to be hurt.

A deep voice boomed from behind me. "Doro from LA."

I twisted around in my seat to see G.W. Wallingsford. His arm was draped around an emerald-eyed brunette who managed to emit a high sense of fashion even though she was decked out in the same blue outfits as the rest of us. On his other side posed a beefcakey guy with dimples and a faux hawk.

"This is my girl, Brittany, and my boy, Mikey. Brittany, Mikey– Doro from LA." Brittany bent down and kissed my cheek, cooing, "Hey. I love LA."

"Thanks, me, too. This is my friend, Reba. He's from Texas via Puerto Rico."

"What up, man?" G.W. put his forearm up to bump Reba's. Reba pepped up, "Nice to meet you all."

Mikey eyed Reba's peanut butter cookie. "You gonna eat that?"

Reba handed it to him. "I can order another one."

"Sweet, thanks bro."

G.W. elbowed Mikey. "Come on, man, you just ate."

"Yeah, but not a peanut butter cookie."

Mikey inhaled the cookie as we all watched. G.W. shook his head, then put his hand on my shoulder. "Listen, Doro from LA,

Brittany's parents are headed to South America for two weeks. She and her sister are going to have the place to themselves, and this Friday night we're going to throw down hardcore. LA style. You should come. Both of you."

Brittany nodded in agreement. "For sure."

"Most definitely, we'd love to."

"How will we get there?" Reba was hesitant. I have no idea why.

"Don't worry, Puerto Rico. I got you covered, my man."

G.W. bent down to my level and tapped on a sleek black headband that was holding his abundant blond hair back. It was his flexer. I pulled mine from the meal port and put it to G.W.'s. My life was no longer my life. I was definitely living someone else's. Even Reba watched in amazement.

"Y'all kids enjoy your grub. I'll flex you with the transpo deets Friday, Doro from LA. Just remember, mums the word on this jam. The only people that need to hear about it need to hear about it from the right place. Know what I'm sayin'?"

"Of course."

Reba motioned that his lips were sealed. G.W. threw him a fist bump. The three said their goodbyes and then strolled off, turning heads all the way down the meal hall like a row of falling dominos. It irked me that their connections allowed them to traverse between Seneca and the Aboves, but I kept it to myself. If Reba felt the same way, I couldn't tell, because he acted as if it was nothing. He didn't even seem interested in the party. "You sure you want to go? You don't seem so into the idea," I asked.

"Yep. It's nice of them to extend the invitation."

He didn't seem sure at all. Like something other than the Dom-in-the-Aboves thing was bothering him. I wanted things to feel right again. "It'll be fun. I'm glad that we're going to a party together."

The corners of his lips tilted up. There was a smile breaking through. The freeze was over, thank goodness.

21

WHAT WAS IT with the men in my life? Or should I say men, dudes and for the most part, boys. They were all so elusive and unpredictable. From my dad's disappearance to Reba's avoidance of me, to the constantly unknown location of Dom, I was always left wondering where someone was physically or where he was at in his head. And if any of it had something to do with me.

I hadn't seen Dom since our surreal Saturday at Difficult Run. It was pretty strange that we hadn't exchanged flexer contacts. Which made it extra strange that I had both Jennifer and G.W. Wallingsford's. I wanted to see Dom more than ever, but I couldn't flex him. The initial crush had blossomed into something so much more. We hadn't even hooked up or anything, but we had such an intense mental connection that my thirst for what could follow was left completely unquenched.

An internal battle began to brew. My curious, determined heart kept luring me to follow it and try to track him down. My logical, but much less persistent, mind, told me to chill. Back-off. Don't chase the guy. Let him chase you. Besides, it would be a tumultuous road that could only end in either eternal love or heartbreak. It was a classic scenario, and my first foray into the trials and tribulations of heart versus mind.

My mind folded; my heart won. I went to Ty's sushi joint. Sessions had ended for the week and I couldn't go on leaving our next meeting up to fate. It was on the early side for dinner and the restaurant was already packed. I wasn't surprised. I made my way to the bar and found Ty, hamming it up for a group of four women in their mid-50's. Beneath the blue they were all ravishing and elegant. Social status bled through their pores. Their laughter was contained, but genuine. They savored this sushi and praised Ty. He soaked up the accolades, and when he caught me watching he enthusiastically waved me over.

"There she is!"

"Hey, Ty, nice to see you again. How's it going?"

"Bad bad bad. American bad. I'm bad, I'm bad, I know it, I know, woo!"

"M.J. Nice. Love the reference."

"Back for the jalapeno lime halibut cheek?"

"I'd love some yes, but actually, I was looking for Dom. I haven't seen him in a while and thought I might catch him here."

Ty leaned in onto the counter with a mischievous grin. "Ah ha. You are here for my friend, not my halibut. I see how it is."

"Well, both. I'm here for both."

"Give me a minute."

Ty spun around like M.J., and disappeared through the back

door. As I waited, I did some people watching. Clusters of patrons were eating sushi as if we were all within heaven's gates, where angels sprinkled a little bit of dust on each bite. Welcome to heaven via the Sushi Seneca gate. I chuckled to myself. And then I remembered the main reason I'd come there. Would Ty be able to work some relationship magic just the way he was able to take people to heaven with sushi?

Ty came back through the door with a grin. I liked the look of it.

"Doro Campbell, today is your lucky day. First, come, come."

I darted to the sushi bar and stood just behind the group of women. Anticipation felt so good. Ty moved behind the bar like a mad scientist with a ballerina's poise. In no time, a plate of jalapeno lime-infused halibut cheek was placed on the bar. Glistening and chanting my name like a choir. Two of the important women parted like the Red Sea so that I could reach between them and retrieve my passage to nirvana. I wanted to be polite and sophisticated and savor these two delectable pieces of Ty's food art, but I couldn't. The moment this sushi touched my tongue, the intense flavor triggered the bliss I had experienced the week before, only this time it was even more potent. I chewed fast, eyes closed, swirled my tongue around to get every bit of flavor onto every millimeter of taste bud inside my mouth. Time stood still. And then I swallowed, and snatched up the other piece from the plate like a toad taking in a fly with its tongue. The intensity amplified with the second piece. I finished.

I opened my eyes. Ty was a prophet.

"Come, come." He waved me to follow him and, before I'd even taken a step in his direction, he disappeared into the back.

I skipped around the sushi bar like a bullet, feeling high from the halibut. Everything about this felt like a holy privilege. How could this be allowed? I pushed through the swinging doors into Ty's kitchen, where the magic happened. It appeared to be just like a kitchen in any sushi restaurant in America, but like everything else in Seneca, there was more to it than met the eye. Ty made a little link with his elbow and motioned for me to lock arms with him. Wherever we were going was cool with me.

We made our way through the main part of the kitchen where sous chefs arranged plates of robust vegetables, and fileted unfathomably gorgeous cuts of fresh fish. We passed enormous steam ovens where rice and fish were cooked. We turned sideways and squeezed ourselves through a small, suffocating path between the shelves of cans, jars, bags of fresh limes... at the end we came to a door. On it, a sign: "Employees Restroom Only." Ty winked, and motioned for me to be his guest and use the restroom. I coyly opened the "Employees Restroom Only" door. Ty gave me a light shove inside and pushed the door closed behind me.

I was not in a restroom. The guy inside was not an employee. Dom stood up from behind a microscope. Across a kitchen counter just like the one the sous chefs worked on in the front of the kitchen, medical lab supplies were neatly spread out where you'd expect to see knives, chopping blocks and mixing bowls.

"Did you miss me?"

Dom looked surprised but pleased to see me.

"Actually, I just came to get some sushi, and then Ty mentioned that you might be here so I thought maybe I should say, "hi."

"I bet. I'd give you a hug, but I literally haven't showered since I saw you last. All I've been doing since Sunday is working, eating sushi, and going to sessions in between."

Dom wanted to hug me! He said some other words too, but that is all I heard. I played it cool.

"No worries. What are you working on?"

"Food science."

Hmm. Not what I expected him to say.

"For Ty. That's what we do here."

He pulled out a stone tablet and a pen. Wrote on it: *Give me your flexer.*

I did.

Dom took it and left the room.

I sat there and looked around, beyond curious. I still didn't know exactly what Dom did with that brain of his and was prepared for him to deflect the subject if I pried.

He came back in without my flexer and sat in his chair.

"Plug your nose. Come." He scooted over and patted on the other half of his chair.

Inside I was all lit up, but I strolled over nonchalantly and planted my butt next to his. Nose plugging was unnecessary. It was the first time in my life that I fully realized the alluring qualities of muskiness— Dom was definitely a little musky, but that was fine. Mighty fine. I felt my thigh tingle when our legs pressed together, shivers shooting up my ribcage in waves. On the outside I kept it cool, but on the inside my heart and soul were warm like a freshly baked buttermilk biscuit.

"They recruited me two years ago for molecular nano-biotechnology and genomics. Before I came to Seneca, I was imprisoned as a minor in Japan for injecting whales and dolphins with a synthetic cellular rejuvenator that rendered all the catches of the Japanese fishermen inedible."

"Whoa."

"Yeah, I know. Let me back up. I was just a science dork in New York with super liberal parents who became involved in the anti-whaling and dolphin hunting movement when they were in college. As I grew up I got passionate about it, too. I became a foreign exchange student in Wakayama, Japan, under the guise that I wanted to experience culture. It ended up having a huge impact on my life. I loved Japanese culture, learned Japanese... I met Ty. He's the nephew of the family I was staying with and he hired me to become a sous chef in his sushi franchise before he launched it. He was just as fascinated with American culture as I was with Japanese. We became great friends. It was a wild ride for both of us. His sushi franchise became the hottest thing in the eastern hemisphere, and, while I wasn't working or going to school, I was investigating a way to stop the whalers. What started as an experiment became a full-force mission. It was working. I was reckless, though, and the Japanese National Police Agency went after me. I wasn't as invisible as I felt. I got busted. They threw the 'no mercy, you silly American' book at me. It was... I can't even... Doro, I was treated like a caged animal. They wouldn't even let me talk to my parents. It changed me. I'm no longer the guy I was before that. After a month in lock-up, Ellen Malone came along and offered me a life ring. Seneca. Coincidentally, or not, Ty and I were both recruited at the same time."

"Ummm, well, that's just... let's just say that your story is a lot cooler than mine."

"I don't know about cool. Cool is swimming in crazy whitewater rapids. This is real."

"I'm really glad you're sharing your reality with me."

"You're the only person who knows other than Ty, the Seneca Senate, and S.O.I.L."

"Thank you for trusting me."

"Yeah, well that's just the backstory. Are you ready for the *real* real deal?"

"I've been ready."

"Take a look here into this microscope."

I was bent over Dom's workspace and peering through that eyepiece in less than a millisecond. Had no idea what I was looking at, but it appeared to be cells with little robotic tails.

"What you're looking at is a slide of my blood."

I hated blood, but I loved computers, and this appeared to be a fusion of the two. My bottom lip dropped. I'd never seen anything like this.

"A few months ago, when they started administering the Necrolla Carne vaccine, I didn't feel right. Something felt seriously off, at a molecular level. I wanted to see the breakdown of the virus they had injected me with, with my very own eyes. There had to be a reason it was making me feel so horribly sick."

"Right..." He couldn't talk fast enough. A whole new level of whoa was unraveling right before my eyes.

"What you're looking at, the thing that appears to be a microscopic swarm of bees, is actually a cluster of hollowed out viruses. Inside each one are nanobots with tails that are attaching to red blood cells, propelling through my blood."

"This is crazy."

"What's crazy is what it implies. The only reason a nanobot would be put in our blood to begin with is to communicate with the receptors in the brain. I think they've hacked our minds, monitoring our conscious thought and recording our thought patterns directly through the neocortex."

"So they're listening to us right now? They know we're in here doing this?"

"No, that's why I took your flexer. That's the only way they can really listen to our dialogue. But this blood thing is much more complex. It's access to our minds, not the words we speak.

I don't know the specifics of the data they collect. And who the bots are communicating with, I haven't figured out. I haven't figured any of it out, but I'm trying. I have to."

"My god."

"You're telling me."

I sat back in the chair, trying to wrap my head around the implications. It was beyond comprehension. Dom rubbed his head and squished his lips together as I attempted to take it all in.

"Watch this." Dom picked up a small device that looked like a needle with a syringe inside it. He looked through the microscope and extracted some of the sample, then carefully shifted over to another small box-shaped device that fit in the palm of his hand. It was dark gray metal with a very fine beam of light inside it.

"It's kind of primitive but I built this hyper-spectral nano scanner to determine what the contents of this virus are."

He carefully injected the sample into the device, then held his flexer to it and punched in a few keys. A ray of blue light linked the flexer to his nano scanner, which triggered the beam to cross the blood sample, and sent an instant reading back to the flexer screen.

"See? Nothing. I can tell that these are fully functioning nanobots and not, in fact, an actual virus, as they want us to believe. Problem is, it looks like there's some heavy-duty quantum encryption. And there is just no way for me to get past that."

I felt a rush like I was back atop that cliff at Difficult Run, about to launch myself into the rapids. "I bet I can get in."

Dom squinted, looking me straight in the eye to gauge if I was kidding around. "Don't mess with me."

"I'm serious. Give me a little time with it and I may be able to tell what it's computing and what it's communicating with... if anything."

Dom's eyes lit up, he threw his arms around me, squeezing me tight, then jumped up out of the chair we'd been sharing. His weight suddenly gone from the other side of the chair, the imbalance toppled me off to the ground.

"Doro!"

I just laughed. I was fine. Dom reached down to help me up, "I am so sorry!"

Instead of accepting his help, I yanked him down onto the floor. We laughed our faces off. It was a breather we both welcomed after such an intense mind trip. This next level of cooperation between us was bound to be exhilarating and terrifying at the same time. The pit of my stomach turned like a dryer with a load full of clothes. I so badly wanted to get into this now and could stay up all night deciphering the entire thing. But I couldn't just yet.

"I'm meeting a friend in an hour, so why don't I come by and we can work on it this weekend?"

"Tomorrow morning?"

"Tomorrow morning."

Dom was so happy. I wished I didn't have to leave, but I couldn't possibly stand up Reba *and* G.W. Wallingsford.

22

I DIDN'T REALLY even want to go to this party, but it was important to Reba. It was also a good idea to show my face and stay in G.W. Wallingsford's good graces. He was a strong ally to have. I didn't tell Dom about the party because GW had asked me not to talk about it, and I'd always prided myself on my ability to keep my word. So I couldn't invite him even though I really, really wanted to. To be honest, all I wanted to do was start thinking about all the work I'd have to do the next morning to get into those microprocessors flowing through Dom's blood. If he was right, then most likely, they were in all of our blood.

But, first the party. Not long after I got back to the residences, there was a knock at my door. It was Reba, dressed to the nines. He'd even taken a brush to his normally unruly hair. "My Senorita Campbella bonita. You look great."

I really hoped he didn't think this was a date. "Thanks. You too, *buddy*." I was bound and determined to make it clear that it was indeed not a date. We were just two friends, hanging out. "G.W. has a flighter escort waiting for us with S.O.I.L. officers at the Ascension Point," I told him. I had received the flex about an hour before.

Reba's face lit and his posture powered up. "We have our own S.O.I.L. escorts?" That kind of attention made him feel important. I got it, but I had so much more on my mind that being treated like a celebrity really didn't do it for me like it would have a couple of weeks ago. Everything was different now. Regardless, I smiled and went with the flow. "Yep."

We traveled parallel to the Potomac along Georgetown Pike, headed east into Washington, D.C. I couldn't help but think about my mission for the next day. I just wanted to get this party out of the way. Reba could tell something was up.

"This isn't as fun for you as it is for me, and I can't quite understand why. Don't you realize how cool this is?"

"I just have a lot on my mind."

"I get it, Campbella, but loosen up, chica. Enjoy yourself. Other teenagers where we come from don't get to do this. Seriously, nobody in Texas would believe this is happening to me. All I ever got called was 'freak.' Nobody in my town called me by my name except my family. I heard 'freak' so many times that I responded to it like it *was* my name. And now, 'freak' is going to a party that he was personally invited to by none other than G.W. Wallingsford."

Despite the tension and chaos raging inside, I made a conscious effort to absorb some of Reba's enthusiasm.

The navy blue night swallowed us. A full moon cast a glow on the river, serene and hypnotic beneath our cruising flighter. I should have been on Cloud Nine like Reba, but my nerves kept getting the better of me. The smooth ride transitioned us from the natural Virginia landscape into the distinguished Georgetown cityscape. Across the river, the edge of the Capitol glimmered in a welcoming amber light. Even though it was well past rush hour, the Key Bridge was smothered in bumper-to-bumper traffic. One thing I didn't miss at all was sitting in traffic. Who would? We breezed right over it, brushed with sympathy for the poor people below.

When I had first arrived in Washington D.C., Ellen Malone had told me that the Key Bridge was named after Francis Scott Key, the man who wrote our National Anthem, *The Star Spangled Banner*. A few weeks ago I wouldn't have been able to imagine a world in which America was no longer the land of the free, the home of the brave– a world leader in all ways. But now I knew that a time was coming when the U.S. government would be overtaken by Seneca. I reminded myself that, by agreeing to remain in the Seneca's Society, technically I was no longer American... but in my heart that wasn't going to fly.

Our ride took us up M Street, through the heart of Georgetown, a polished and inviting historic district of D.C. A spectrum of high-end, cutting edge and old faithful restaurants speckled along both sides of cobblestone streets, where conservative glamor could mix seamlessly with youthful trendiness. Our flighter made a wide left turn and we ascended slightly, parallel with the gentle, hilly street below. The further away from M Street we got, there were fewer lights and cars on the streets, and the houses became bigger and bigger. It went from apartments, to townhouses, to well-kept homes, to majestic city estates. Its Federalist architecture was completely different than the weathered stucco and modern metals I was used to in LA. Georgetown had a charm and elegance to it that I appreciated. It was no wonder that the legendary Bill and Hillary Clinton once had called it home.

The flighter landed in front of an imposing mansion with four colossal white pillars framing the doorway, and above it, a black wrought iron balcony. The home was perfectly symmetrical, with ornate white moldings framing large, gleaming windows dressed in grand draperies that must have been worth more than the entire building I lived in back in LA. It was exactly the type of residence I imagined senators and congressmen would live in. Definitely not the type of place I expected to go for a raging high school party, that was for sure.

A giant music sound system's bass vibrations radiated through me as we got out of the flighter and walked up the smoothly paved driveway. I was dwarfed by the entryway staircase, and felt like a tiny figurine. I glanced over at Reba who exuded enthusiasm from head to toe. This guy was seriously feeling it. Two men in blue were standing on both sides of immense glass French doors. Still as statues, they didn't even acknowledge our arrival. It was pointless to knock or ring a doorbell. Nobody could possibly have heard it with the loud music, so we let ourselves inside.

A cyclone of debauchery vacuumed us in. I assumed the extremely dim lighting was designed to try and keep the faces of the privileged from being captured and plastered on social media by moles. Flashes of light that pulsated from a DJ booth set up in the foyer were all that helped us see where we were going. We made our way inside through throngs of people. There must have been a hundred teenagers, if not more, upstairs and downstairs, too. A molecular mixologist was serving up beverages from high-end bottles of liquor which were being consumed as quickly as they could be created. Moderation wasn't in the cards tonight.

It was so loud in there that Reba and I didn't bother to try talking to each other. Reba's eyes were bigger than his head. I, on the other hand, was not fazed by all of it. It was just like an LA party, with more money. Ultimately, teenagers partying were teenagers partying and there was nothing more to it. One difference I noted between LA and here, though– the array of art on the walls. This stuff was truly classy, and obviously of such tremendous value that it could only clash with the brazen consumption ritual G.W. had arranged.

Hot and heavy make-out sessions seemed to block our way every ten feet or so, more for exhibition's sake than from honest passion. Still, I'd be a hypocrite not to admit I'd engaged in a few of them before myself. I couldn't picture Reba making out, though. He was starting to feel more like my brother than just some guy I hung with.

I didn't see G.W., or anyone else I knew. A few people looked familiar, when I got close enough to them to see. I turned around to look for Reba but he was gone. He must have followed his curious nose in another direction. I decided I would just wander and we'd catch up later. I noticed a sliding glass door to a back porch and, thinking I could get a break from the head-pounding sound, I headed out that way.

Illuminated only by the half moon and flickering candlelight, it was really dark out there. Just enough light to recognize that a few people on lounge furniture were injecting themselves with Mojo Sticks. I felt a tap on my shoulder.

"Hey, Doro, right?"

"Hey, yeah. Brittany."

"You made it."

"Yep, thanks for having me. Fun party."

"Eh, yeah, if this is your thing, I guess."

"What, it's not yours?"

"Me? No way. I can't wait for it to be over."

"But isn't it your party?"

"Theoretically. Really, though, it's for my boyfriend. G.W. likes his fun in all forms, what can I say? My idea of fun is an afternoon on horseback in the foothills or popcorn and a movie." She grinned. "Shh, don't tell anyone."

"Your secret's safe with me. Maybe you should date a jockey."

"Not a bad idea!"

Brittany and I laughed. Apparently she wasn't the vapid, entitled daughter of a politician that I'd expected. Just another lesson in not judging a book by its cover, something I would probably have to remind myself of until the end of time.

And then, in the candlelight, I saw something that nearly made me hit the wooden deck. One of the people on the lounge chairs was Dom. He laid back, his head in a girl's lap. He couldn't see me from there, but I squinted, trying to see who the girl was. Once I recognized her I literally could have spewed my insides out. McKayla Gordon.

"You okay?" Brittany took my arm.

"I'm fine." I wasn't.

"Want some water?"

"No, no, I'm good."

I took a step back behind Brittany, making sure to obstruct Dom's view of me. I could see him perfectly, though I so deeply wished I couldn't. His eyes flickered open and closed, and kept rolling back behind his eyelids. He was unquestionably out of his head on something. On the table in front of him there was a bowl of Mojo Sticks. The icing on the cake was McKayla Gordon seductively rubbing his head, leaning down and whispering into his ear. He didn't respond to her, he was just lost in this Mojo'd out state. I was shattered.

This wasn't the intelligent, alert Dom I'd been with just hours before. Dom was different than these insipid Mojo Stickin' types.

I didn't understand. We'd experienced such powerful moments in total clarity. He didn't need Mojo Sticks.

And McKayla Gordon. She was horrible. Why her? He must not have felt what I was feeling. My entire world was crashing down on this deck. The stars above us were still twinkling so I knew that it wasn't officially the end, but it sure felt like it.

"You've got to be kidding me." Brittany lunged to the edge of the deck and hit the solid wooden railing circling it.

A flighter pulled up alongside her and hovered in the air as the tinted passenger side window lowered. G.W. was piloting– he leaned forward, peering across a giddy Mikey, in shotgun. "Hop in, Brit! Come do some loops at the bridge with us!"

"G.W., no way! I told you, my dad will lose it if he finds out you were piloting his flighter!"

"Don't worry, baby, just a quick spin."

"G.W., please, just put it back in the garage, before anything happens."

"Relax. Ten minutes!" Mikey stuck his tongue out, and with that, the flighter popped off into high speed, leaving a small trail of white steam behind it. Half of the people on the deck who weren't too Mojo'd out to realize what was happening jumped in excitement, cheering on the speeding flighter.

Brittany rubbed her temples with her fingers and clenched her teeth. It obviously wasn't the first time something like this had happened.

"Now it's my turn to ask. Are you okay?"

"I can't even watch this." She turned her back to avoid seeing the flighter. And I was avoiding Dom. What was supposed to be a fun party had turned into a night of torture for the two of us, flung together in an unlikely connection.

"There you are!" Reba came running out the back door just in time for the spectacle. "Campbella, chica, I couldn't find you anywhere!"

We had sweeping views of the river and the Key Bridge all the way to the Washington Monument. Cars and flighters were abiding by traffic laws for as far as the eye could see, but one lone flighter was twisting and turning as it gained speed towards the bridge. The cheers on the deck became wilder and more intense as everyone watched G.W.'s antics. Amidst the escalating jubilation, Brittany actually started to calm down, visibly attempting to block it out. I tried to do the same with the horrendous scene on the lounge chair.

Reba had grabbed a cookie from a nearby tray and nervously chomped at it as he watched the flighter. Through no fault of his own, this guy hadn't gotten out in a long while and he was soaking up every minute of it. I actually think this was his first high school party ever, and what a first it was. The chomping was too much for me, though; I was already way over the edge. I elbowed him in the side.

"Ouch! What was that for?"

"Chew with your mouth closed."

He gave me a hurt look but dutifully closed his mouth. I felt bad. I was taking things out on him and he didn't deserve it. I shouldn't have hit his positive vibe with my negative one. "Sorry," I said.

I was trying to think of a way to explain my reaction when his face changed completely, as if something had possessed him. His eyes glazed over in a controlled stare toward the bridge. The Reba I knew was gone. He started to hum anxiously and rock back and forth. I didn't care that his mouth hung open with chewed up cookie inside. I was just worried about him. Something wasn't right.

Just then the cheering thundered with elation as G.W. looped the flighter three times around the Key Bridge. People jumped up and down to the music's thumping bass... and then the flighter went for a fourth loop... and did a nosedive crash into the top of the Key Bridge!

A billowing cloud of purple flame burst into the sky. The hooting and hollering suddenly changed to complete silence. The music stopped. Everyone was pressed up against the back of the deck, mouths agape. The boom from the crash reverberated through the sky.

Brittany let out an agonizing scream and dropped to the ground. After a brief moment of silent shock, complete chaos hit the back deck. Everyone scattered, even the Mojo'd out ones fumbled to bail. Everyone was aware of the consequences to come and nobody wanted to be anywhere near the scene that had started it all.

Reba stood, frozen, holding the last little bit of cookie up to his quivering lip. Sirens blared in the distance, and we could hear the muffled sound of a helicopter. I looked down at Brittany on the ground, alone and completely destroyed. With one hand planted on the deck, she lifted herself just enough to look up at the clouds of smoke invading the clear sky. She wailed in desolation, at the same time gripping a hand over her heart and pummeling her chest over and over. She hit herself so hard I could feel it vibrate across the wood planked floor we shared. As the rest of the guests fled, I bent down and wrapped my arms around her. What she needed right then was the one thing I could be– a friend.

23

S.E.R.C. RESIDENCES WERE on lockdown all weekend long as the flighter crash investigations went down. Men in blue were positioned everywhere to make sure nobody tried to go anywhere but their residence, the bathroom, or meal hall. We weren't allowed to go to each other's rooms, only our own. I knew that if I flexed Reba, the communication would be traced. I didn't even know what I would say. I was creeped out big time. It felt like he had known somehow that the flighter was about to go down, but how would that be possible? I didn't know what Reba's role was here in Seneca, but it seemed like his uncanny premonitions had something to do with it.

I was so consumed with comforting Brittany when the party broke up and the feds arrived at her place, that I never saw what happened to Dom. He'd been in no shape to drive, so I had no clue how he'd gotten out of there. I was so angry I didn't know if I even cared. Scratch that. I did care. As much as it had pained me to see him like that. But all I could do now was sit tight.

I flicked on my flexer. B3 News. Becky Hudson was reporting

from the studio, as footage from the scene of the crash played on a screen behind her. *"Three people dead, six in critical condition, all of them remain unidentified."*

No way anyone could have survived that crash. People don't walk away from crashes like that.

"Officials are still unclear if the crash was due to pilot error or a flighter malfunction, but sources say the flighter was taken that evening from the home of Senator Walton Gilroy, where his daughters, Brittany and Samantha, were hosting a party. We expect a statement from Senator Gilroy this evening. Mojo Sticks are believed to have been a contributing factor. The alleged source of the contraband has been identified and is currently under investigation. Officials are asking that anyone with information please come forward."

My flexer buzzed. It was Reba. I flipped off the news and accepted his FigureFlex. A six-inch hologram of Reba, sitting in his room, appeared in front of me. It was my first FigureFlex since I'd come to Seneca. "Reba."

He was so relieved that I picked up. "Hey! Are you okay?"

"Yeah, what about you?"

"I am now."

"What was up with that? Did you know that crash was about to happen?"

Reba blinked about a mile a minute and then took a deep breath, before changing the topic. "They're saying that Dominic Ambrosia brought the Mojo Sticks to the party."

"What?"

"I know for a fact he didn't, though."

"How can you be so sure?"

"I just know."

"Well, then someone is lying."

"Someone's gotta be the scapegoat."

"Not Dom."

"He's being taken to the Aboves, and, if S.O.I.L. has it their way, he won't be coming back. Soon, he won't even remember having ever been here."

"They can't do that!"

"They can do anything. And they will. You know that."

I didn't know what to think, what to do. True to form, Reba's eyes glimmered with optimism. "You can save him, you know."

"You don't care about Dom."

"I care about you... and I care about the future."

"Thanks for the info, Reebs. I owe you big time."

"No you don't. Just be careful, Doro." And with that, hologram Reba dissolved into the disinfected Seneca air.

24

I HAD TO find a way to get out of the S.E.R.C. residences and into Dom's secret sushi lab. Usually I was good on minimal sleep but now it had been two whole days, going on two nights with only a few hours under my belt. My brain was fried. I was borderline delirious, operating on adrenaline fumes. There was no way I was getting past the men in blue so I buckled down, brainstormed and began to devise a plan.

An hour later Ellen Malone showed up at my door.

"Thank you so much for coming, Ellen. I'm sure this isn't how you want to spend your Saturday night."

"Of course, Doro, are you kidding? I can't imagine how you must feel after witnessing something so awful. This is such a tragedy."

"I know. It's so surreal. One moment they were laughing. Right there, a few feet in front of me, the next..." I replayed the crash in my head, Brittany's scream, the chaos on the porch, Reba standing there with the chewed-up cookie in his open mouth. The visuals were burned on my mind like a brand on cattle. I knew it would be with me forever. "I wish that whole night never happened."

"There are a lot of people who feel the same."

I hung my head. Ellen patted me on the back. "Don't worry. Everyone is going to go through their own grieving process after what happened, and things are going to be tense around here for a while, but they will brighten up. Just know that, okay?"

"I hope so."

"So, how about those chilaquiles?"

I smiled, but not fully. I was dying for some Mexican food, but hated that I was pulling one over on Ellen. There'd been no other way. I figured that, if she knew what was really going on with Dom being thrown under the bus, she'd have understood. Either way, I had to make the decisions that were in the best interest of Dom, myself, and as bold as it sounded, the entire Seneca Society.

"I am so ready. The meal hall is great and all, but I need a change of scenery."

"You bet."

Ellen Malone and I strolled right past the men in blue, who didn't question us. Few people in Seneca could get away with questioning Ellen Malone. Congressman Wallingsford was out of the picture, I assumed, consumed with the well-being of G.W., who was in critical condition at an undisclosed location. I really hoped he'd be okay, and was sure he was receiving the best possible medical care, but I'd seen that crash and I knew it would take a miracle for him to walk away from it the same way he went in.

Ellen didn't ask any questions and thankfully she didn't try to make conversation for the sake of avoiding silence. She was comfortable just being. There were so many things about her I really respected. She was one of the people I looked up to most in Seneca, one of the ones who gave me hope that, although there were some shady things going on behind the curtains, there was also limitless possibility.

At Dia De Los Ninos, my favorite Senecan Mexican Restaurant, the hostess was happy to see me. It made me feel good. I was regarded as a regular in a spot that not so long ago had felt so strange. Seneca was starting to feel like home, or at least a home away from home. I still missed my Saturday night excursions to Highland Park for driveway pupusas with Julie and our moms and I always would, but this helped fill that hole inside me as best it could. The hostess walked us to our seats and looked back at Ellen, "Trajiste a otro amigo que chilaquiles."

"Sí, nunca los ha tenido tampoco," I replied.

The hostess gave Ellen a playful 'shame, shame' wave of the finger and then handed us our menus as we took our seats. Ellen didn't know what we said, but she went right along with it. A waiter brought over some chips and salsa and I dove right in. There was no holding me back from chips and salsa.

"I didn't know you spoke Spanish. That's something I definitely should have known, considering."

"Everyone in LA knows Spanish."

"Makes sense. Silly me."

It was pretty funny that she knew about my quantum computing skills and offshore financial activities, but had no clue that I was fluent in Spanish.

The waiter came and took our order. I asked for two of the same dish– went for the verdes because I knew that would be easier on Ellen's undoubtedly sensitive palate than my go-to chipotle.

I gathered my nerve because I was about to lie to Ellen's face. Something I really wished I didn't have to do. I felt the guilt building from my toes to my fingertips. She'd been awfully nice to bring me out, and I did appreciate it. I hoped she would never find out about this.

And here it came.

"I don't feel so hot."

"Oh no. What's wrong?"

"My stomach. Ugh."

"Nerves?"

"No, more like *sick* sick."

"We can have them pack our food to go if you want–"

"No, no. I'll be fine..." I hesitated. This was tougher than I'd thought. I hunched over a little and feigned stomach cramps. The guilt running through me was ridiculous. "I think I might vomit."

"We'd better get you home."

"You know what, I'll be okay. I'll just head back. You stay and enjoy your meal."

"Doro, I can't just leave you."

"No, really, I'll be fine."

The way Ellen looked at me so caringly jabbed me with little needles all over. I felt like such a deceitful person. I second-guessed myself, wondering if I should have concocted another plan.

"Why don't I just walk you back, and then I can take my food home with me?"

"Please, Ellen, I really want you to have the full experience here. I'll be fine." I stood up and hunched over, rubbing my belly.

"I don't know—"

"I'll flex you later to check in."

I could tell Ellen just felt bad for me. I had to drive this home. She was insisting, but I had to insist more.

"I'd hug you, but I don't want to get you sick."

"Okay, I want to hear from you before you go to sleep, understood?"

"Yes, I'll flex you."

Ellen watched me go. Emotions of every variety rushed through me as I walked out into the bustling restaurant district of Seneca City. People in blue streaming through the halls, coming and going on the acoustic carrier. But I didn't have time for anything but the mission at hand. I was in a race against the clock.

25

TY WAS HUSTLING behind the sushi bar at the peak of dinnertime as I darted in through the entrance. He locked eyes on me while continuing to work his culinary magician's hands. He didn't need eyes on what he was doing, he was that good. I knew that, when he saw me, he hoped I knew something more about Dom.

I wiped my sweaty brow with my shoulder and kept going straight behind the bar. Ty and I had an unspoken understanding. He knew that I was here to help Dom. I went directly through the double doors, through the kitchen, past the claustrophobic aisle of supplies, and straight to the door marked, "Employees Only Restroom."

Before the S.E.R.C. residences, I had programmed my flexer with a hardcore multi-level quantum encryption so that any activity I engaged it in could not be read anywhere else. Still, I knew that the potential for tracing my whereabouts was there, since I had yet to tap into the microprocessors in my bloodstream. I assumed that physical location was one of the bits of information that was definitely being traced. I didn't know how much time I had. I had a massive feat to accomplish before I was caught, or Dom would forever be just a memory to me... if even that.

I took a seat in the chair I'd shared with Dom only the day before. Then, the vibe between us had been full of exuberance, optimism, teamwork and what I thought was mutual attraction. But now it was all urgency, a crazy fast learning curve on things I knew nothing about, lying to one of the only people I trusted and a whole lot of nerve. I had no partner this time— whatever happened seemed to be down to me alone. This wasn't easy. It wasn't easy at all.

Dom's lab was foreign to me. First I had to attempt to do what I had seen him do. His equipment was all in the same place I'd seen it last. I powered on his makeshift hyper-spectral nano scanner. I looked across the table, in drawers, all over the place trying to find his blood sample. Not a trace of it anywhere. I spotted a needle and syringe. I felt weak, then shook it off. This wasn't the time or place to feel freaked out over needles. I was much bigger than that needle. My dad had always said that to me about me and spiders.

Without Dom's blood sample I was going to have to draw my own blood and get down to business. I had seen my mom do this so many times when I'd gone with her on house calls to her private geriatric patients. Still, everything about it made me squeamish. I told myself this wasn't about me. I had to move out of body now and make things happen. Easier said than done. I felt the blood leave my face, my palms become clammy, my feet scorching hot and, although the room was silent, I could hear every single sound. My hearing became wolf-like. The buzz of electricity, water flowing through pipes, forced air and the slight hum of the scanner all played together in perfectly organized chaos. I focused in on the noise like it was an orchestra, playing to calm my rapidly swelling nerves.

I pushed the sleeve up on my left arm to look down at the crease on the inside of my elbow. Doctors always made the comment that my veins are good. The thought of forcing a needle through my flesh into my good blue vein was dizzying. When had my mouth gotten so dry? I had forgotten to drink water, with everything else going on. You can't draw blood if you're dehydrated, my mom had repeatedly told her patients. There was a half-full glass of stale water on the table. What the heck... I gulped it down and grabbed a rubber band on the desk. Snapped in half, I could cinch it tightly around my arm just above the crease. I took a few deep breaths as I opened and closed my fist and watched my vein bulge. It *was* a really, really good vein. I made a mental note to myself that the next time someone asks me that strange question: "What quality of yourself are you most proud of?" I should say, "My veins."

I wasn't afraid of heights. I imagined that the way I felt when I looked at that needle was exactly how someone with acrophobia felt when they inched towards the edge of the Grand Canyon. Just as they had to get over the fear just long enough to see that gorgeous expanse below them, I needed to overcome my own fear, just long enough to accomplish something that was desperately important to me. This needle wasn't going to kill me, I hoped. Did I know that? Could I guarantee myself that? I wasn't sure. No, wait, I *was* sure. This little needle was not going to kill me! I clutched the thing, and stuck myself in my flawless blue vein. I let out a sound that was as much a moan as an exhalation, while blood filled the small glass tube. When it was full I pulled the needle out, grabbed a tissue and pressed it down over the tiny incision. I finally caught my breath. Smiled. Blew out a "whew." That was intense. There was no time for patting myself on the back. I'd have to remind myself to do that later.

I turned to the centrifuge that Dom had lifted from one of his sessions. It had an S.E.R.C. emblem on it. I placed the tube filled with my blood into it, closed the lid and peered at the dials. I would have bet my life that Dom had the numbers set to where they needed to be, so I pressed "start" and waited for it to finish spinning. This was definitely working. I was starting to feel a lot less like a teenage girl, and a lot more like a professional scientist. If only I had a white lab coat. Maybe next time.

The spinning stopped. I opened the lid, carefully removed the vial, and used a syringe to take a sampling of the same heavy particle part of the blood that I had seen Dom extract yesterday.

Next, I turned to his hyper-spectral nano scanner, to pull out the glass plate that rested beneath the beam of light. I slowly pushed down on the syringe, watching my blood sample drip soundlessly onto the glass.

I took my trusty flexer from my pocket, held it up to the device and issued the communicate command. A beam of blue light linked my flexer to the scanner device. The beam of light spread across the blood sample and sent an instant reading back to my flexer screen. Here we go. My flexer picked up on signals being emitted from the nanobots Dom had detected. There was no question. I tried to access the communications. I was blocked.

Bring it on!

My hands danced across the flexer screen like an accomplished pianist on a baby grand. I was in the zone. I had passed the challenging part and was in my element now. Nothing could stop my ferocity towards these nanobots that were squatting in my blood.

I was on the verge of something huge. I felt it as the equations and formulas surged through my head like the rapids of Difficult Run. This gush of numbers, symbols, solutions, resonated deeper within me than any equation I'd ever pursued... and BANG! The nanobot I cracked revealed its quantum state– I could instantly tell that it was part of an entangled quantum system. I sprung from my chair, my body electric with delight, but I kept my victory dance muted. I dropped back down to the seat even though my heartbeat flew through the roof. I had to keep my eyes on the ball. On the screen: charts, graphs, neurological statistics and biometrics. I couldn't decipher what it all meant specifically, but I knew it was a biological spying mechanism.

The implications were almost both too vast to wrap my head around and horrifyingly clear: A literal, duplicate copy of the inner workings of my brain was tied directly to a mainframe elsewhere and being manipulated... affecting my mind right here and now. Not if I could help it, and I knew I could.

As the reality of this set in I became furious. I felt so violated it was as if my skin crawled with armies of fire ants. Someone was literally inside my head without my permission. I didn't know the extent to which my thoughts had been tweaked or traced so far, but I wasn't going to let it happen any longer.

My dad had always said we were here for a reason. Now I understood. I was brought to Seneca for a reason, I met Dominic Ambrosia for a reason, I was sitting here faced with this problem for a reason... and problems are meant to be solved.

My fingers moved maniacally. They were possessed. I was possessed. I couldn't stop until I found the opening at the end of the maze. I moved through every twist and turn, holding my breath, not blinking, until finally– "Ha!" I leaped from my seat in victory. I'd broken the quantum entanglement. Whoever, wherever was not inside my head, anymore. I was uncoupled from their manipulation, but they would still think they had me, because when I'd run the break I had simultaneously synched my mainframe ID to a random Senecan's nanobot data.

Oh, but there was so much more to figure out! I quickly returned to my seat and wiggled my fingers around the flexer frame, stretching in preparation for round two.

Now I had to figure out who was controlling the mainframe to which we were all tied. Was this an official Senecan plan or were some outsiders infiltrating the Senecan population? If Dom hadn't trusted me, I might never have known about any of this. And what about everyone else? This was bigger than Big Brother. Just like he'd said.

I began to run equations to help tap into the system I was tied to. Who else controlled it and what was it doing? Cranking away I realized that this part was much more difficult, with thick layers of encryption. Encryption I had never faced before. I rubbed my chin, closed my eyes. Maybe scrunching my lips like Dom did would bring me some new ideas.

The familiar white noise that had formed the symphony of background sounds while I'd worked suddenly changed. My eyes flew open when loud footsteps trampled in my direction, stopping just outside the door.

Boom! The door splintered off its frame. As I jumped out of my chair, two men in slick blue guard uniforms stormed towards me.

"Don't move!"

I didn't budge a centimeter. Didn't make a single sound, not even a breath.

One of the guards scanned the lab while the other released a silver liquid cuff around my wrists that hardened in two seconds flat, just like a soft-serve ice cream cone dipped in chocolate. I hadn't seen handcuffs like this before, didn't even know they existed.

A female S.O.I.L. officer entered the room next, along with a man who held a suspicious-looking case. He placed it on the table and opened it, revealing a variety of vials filled with viscous fluids.

"Please don't, please! What is that? What are you doing?!"

The man was unruffled and methodical. Void of expression, he operated like a robot and didn't even make eye contact with me. The S.O.I.L. officer came within inches of my face, staring me in the eye. "Relax, and this will be easy. Resist, and you will be in pain. Make a choice, make it fast."

"Please don't–"

"Just do as you're told and you will be fine."

I didn't resist. I was petrified. I whimpered and shifted my eyes to the man who must have been a doctor. He moved towards me with a syringe. My god, not this again. He squirted a liquid through the needle in typical preparation for an injection, then lifted it to my shoulder. I squeezed my eyes shut, felt a pinch, and opened my eyes. Everything was distorted for a few seconds and then black.

26

MY NECK CRACKED as I awoke and jerked myself up to sitting position. My head was foggy, my body stiff and achy. I tried to move, but that wasn't happening. I realized I was in a chair, paralyzed from the neck down. I was alone, in a pure white room wrapped in mirrored blue windows. Two empty chairs were positioned six feet across from me. A flat glass monitor took up the entire wall I was facing. It powered on, as if triggered by my gaze.

A striking woman with light, almost albino blond hair gelled back into a bun and wearing a blue suit, sat in front of a gold wall displaying the Seneca Society emblem. The emblem itself was a little creepy: Two gold eyeballs inside a black oval, one with an infinity symbol in the pupil and the other with "Dm" inside. I wondered what "Dm" was. Department of Military? Demobilization? That was probably it considering S.O.I.L. had definitely demobilized me.

"Hello, Dorothy Campbell."

I opened my mouth to speak, but couldn't because of the

paralysis. My tongue felt like Velcro as it separated from my upper palate.

"Your motion and speech will be restored momentarily. For now, I just want you to listen closely."

I was pissed, but even more frightened. First my mind had been invaded and now my body.

"Would you like some water?"

I nodded my head.

A doorway opened in the wall and a Seneca blue uniformed guard brought in a glass and put it up to my mouth. I gulped it down unceremoniously.

"You can speak now."

"Thank you." The words crackled from my throat as the guard left the room.

"You're welcome, Dorothy."

This woman wasn't the typical, smiley type of my initial Seneca experience. Her face had no lines to betray expression. Her eyes were the crystalline green I'd seen in pictures of the Caribbean Ocean. Her teeth were perfectly white like Congressman Wallingsford's. Oddly, though, with all this perfection, one tooth in front was very crooked.

"We have a few things to go over with you. Are you prepared?"

"I think so."

"What were you doing in Dominic Ambrosia's food science laboratory?"

I didn't know what they knew. Signals from my brain were registering elsewhere up until the moment I broke the entanglement, but just how detailed was their analysis of the data? Did they have access to everything I knew? I didn't want to answer a thing.

"Can I speak with Ellen Malone?"

"Dorothy Campbell, it is my duty to inform you that this is an official Seneca Observation and Intelligence screening. You are required to provide truthful answers for all of the questions you are asked. You may not divert or deflect questions. You may not ask questions. Is this understood?"

This woman meant business. I nodded my head, figuring it was in my best interest to play by the rules here, or find myself in the kind of trouble I couldn't even imagine.

"Very good. Again, what were you doing in Dominic Ambrosia's food science laboratory?"

"Nothing really, I... was just messing around. I didn't know what happened to Dominic after the party and when I went by and he wasn't there, I just started playing with things."

The silence that followed was filled with the tension of a fully stretched rubber band, aimed directly at me. Whether it was released or eased up entirely depended on the believability of my explanation.

"You will now be joined by two members of Seneca's Observation and Intelligence League."

My heart skipped a beat. There was no way that this sixteen

year old Southern California girl was going to fool the likes of the most powerful intelligence league on the planet. I couldn't comprehend what they were capable of. I had seen portrayals of the C.I.A. in movies, and, if S.O.I.L. was more powerful than that, this definitely wasn't the time or place for me to try and pull one over.

A doorway opened on the golden wall, and in walked Gregory Zaffron and another man, maybe 60 years old– dark brown skin, distinguished, shiny bald head and a goatee so impeccably shaved it looked like it had been drawn on with black magic marker. The man took a seat but Gregory remained standing. They both wore crisp, tailored blue suits with Seneca Society emblems shining from small gold medallions on their lapels. Gregory definitely did not look as easy-going and casual as he had the other times I'd seen him.

"Dorothy."

"Gregory– this is all some huge misunderstanding."

He flashed a pompous smile. "Ah, well now, we don't meddle with the behavior of Seneca's citizens over a simple matter of misunderstanding. I think everyone here is very capable of complete understanding."

Gulp.

"Don't worry, sweetheart. We're going to sit down and work it all out now. That's what we all want, right?"

I nodded in agreement. I did want it worked out. I never wanted to experience paralysis again. And I didn't want to be on

Gregory's bad side either.

"This is Lieutenant Marcus Otis. My boss."

Lieutenant Otis sat back in his chair, studying me. I needed to change any negative first impression he might have of me as soon as humanly possible.

"Hello, sir. I'm really sorry to be taking your time with silly little issues. I promise I won't be causing any more disturbances."

Lieutenant Otis was a man of few words. And by few, I mean none.

"Lieutenant Otis just wants everything cleared up, Dorothy. We can handle that, right? You and me?"

"Yes."

"We know that you've interfered with official Seneca security. We don't want to believe you meant it maliciously, but we have to handle this the same as we would with anyone– in the interest of security for the entire Seneca Society. You understand?

"Yes."

"We've been watching Dominic Ambrosia for some time now. He was tampering with Seneca security operations and he was warned not to. Mr. Ambrosia continued to disobey this one, simple official S.O.I.L. request and, because of that, he has been dealt with accordingly."

"Where is he?"

"As anyone guilty of the same actions would be, he has been removed from society."

"He's dead?!"

I felt the oxygen vacuumed from my lungs.

"Mr. Ambrosia was put through standard Senecan reversal procedures and was re-established in the Aboves."

My Velcro tongue inflated like a pufferfish in my throat. I could barely breathe. Heat swelled behind my brow bone. My eyes stung. I fought to keep my cool as tears began to well up.

"We don't want that to happen to you, too, Doro."

"I don't want that." I couldn't let that happen. Even though I was experiencing the dark, oppressive side to this society, I still felt in my heart that all of us in Seneca had been given an opportunity to make a difference in the world. If I were removed from Seneca, I would never be able to be a part of that. And I'd never get my mom here. I would be put back into the same old dull school curriculum with the same old herd of sheep. I wouldn't remember Dom. It hit me hard to think that right now, Dom didn't know me. He didn't remember our first time in the closet at S.E.R.C., our day at Difficult Run or our epiphany together in the lab. He was alone out there. Seneca was dead to him. I was dead to him. And I was alone in here.

"Good." Gregory turned his wrist up and pulled his cuff back to reveal a flexer. He tapped at the screen and it lit up blue. FigureFlexing activated and Dr. Ashvind Kulkarni appeared in hologram. "Dr. Kulkarni, please administer the Vigilogstimine on Miss Campbell here."

Dr. Kulkarni's six-inch hologram approached me. He seemed

like a kind man who wouldn't harm me. There was a depth inside his eyes and his walk was smooth, not intimidating at all. He maintained eye contact and a warm smile. A needle emerged from the back of my chair, on a robotic arm. At that point I was willing to try anything to regain body movement.

Gregory patted my shoulder. "Let's get your motion back up and running, what do you say?"

"Please... and thank you."

"Thank *you*, Dorothy."

Dr. Kulkarni nodded to me, as if to say, "Here I go." Then he engaged with the robotic arm and gave me the shot. I didn't feel it at all. Either FigureFlexing was the ultimate way to get vaccinated, or I was becoming an old pro.

"Thank you, Doctor." Gregory pulled his shirt back down over his wrist and the doctor was zapped out of the office.

The tips of my fingers and toes fired sparks into the rest of my body. I wiggled in my chair and felt my legs and arms loosen up. In seconds, I was completely back to normal. Not an ache in any inch of me.

"How's that?"

"Much better," I said, with the greatest sense of relief. I felt as though I'd just made it to the bathroom after holding a full bladder for hours on a highway with no exit. "Much, much better."

"Now, let me be very blunt. I want to like you, Doro. We all believe you can be a major asset to this society, but we can't tolerate any breech in security– at all. I know that sometimes you teenagers feel curious and become compelled to explore areas that are out of your depth. But I want to make sure you are totally clear on what will happen if you do it again."

I was absolutely not going to question Gregory. Swimming upstream against the rapids would be a foolish decision, and I, Doro Campbell, was no fool.

"I would like to think that you don't want to go the way of Mr. Ambrosia, or the dozens before him that have met the same fate."

"Of course not." I was heartbroken for Dom, but I had to deliver a persona that Gregory would start to trust again, no matter what.

"I know some of these actions taken against you might feel scary or over-the-top, but it is important that you realize, they are designed for the safety of our society as a whole. Understood?"

"Completely."

Lieutenant Otis stood up and spoke for the first time. "Miss Campbell. I hope we don't have to acquaint ourselves with one another again, unless of course it is on much different terms."

"Yes, sir."

Gregory bowed lightly. "Lieutenant." Lieutenant Otis turned and left, not interrupting his confident stride to allow for the door to appear, he made his way through it just as it opened. And then it closed.

"Don't make me look bad, Dorothy. I put myself on the line

for you."

"I get it, Gregory. I'm sorry I made a problem for you. It won't happen again."

"That's what we like to hear. Your future here is bright. Don't go and turn out the lights now, you hear?"

"Loud and clear."

"The next few days might be filled with surprises for you. As a beholder of confidential Seneca intel, your lips must remain sealed. What you hear is the word of truth. I'll leave you with that, kiddo."

27

MY PILLOW WAS soaked from balling my eyes out all night long. I hugged it tight. My face was swollen and warm, lips salty from the canal of tears that had streamed down my cheeks for hours. I blew my nose and breathed a deep long sigh that comes at the finale of one seriously marathon cry.

My life as a normal teenager was over. I didn't have parents around to protect me. Of the only friends I had here, one had been banished to the Aboves, and the other had some weirdo psychic thing going on that I hadn't figured out yet. I didn't know who he really was. I didn't really know who anyone was. I felt ill with worry about Ellen Malone. Did she know what I had just been through? Did she see what happened with Gregory? I had no idea how much she knew. How could I trust her, and would she ever trust me again after I had manipulated her interest in me to pull this last stunt?

It was around 4 a.m. on Monday. I contemplated how I was going to go to session and not look like I'd spent the night flipping out. Even looking like I'd been crying would be so embarrassing. I had to remain cool, calm and collected– Ellen Malone style. That would be easier said than done.

Lockdown was over. I understood that much of it was about Dom and me, and what we had been doing in the lab. Now that S.O.I.L. had removed Dom and had me conforming to the system, they'd determined it was safe to lift my lockdown. S.O.I.L. wanted to control the situation before anyone else in Seneca got wind of it. They knew that we'd been meddling in their top-secret procedures, but they mustn't have realized the scope, or they wouldn't have let me go. They most likely hadn't measured my computing distance and were unaware that I had placed a block on the quantum entanglement in my own blood, thus creating a virtual immunity to mind monitoring within myself. If they had known, they would have forced me to unblock it. But nobody could detect what I did. They would need *me* to do it because, as far as I knew, there was nobody else on Earth that *could*... at least not yet.

With four hours until session, and most people in the residences still asleep, I got up and took an acoustic carrier ride to a twenty-four hour market in the restaurant district to pick up a cucumber for my eyes. I had to make an effort to appear normal. My goal from now on was to fly under the radar with my eyes wide open.

28

MY RIDE IN for my Monday morning session was the same as it had always been– quick and smooth. Not nearly long enough to rehash the longest weekend of my life, but I didn't need to. I was determined to act as though everything was completely normal. It kept getting further away from normal each day I was here. When I stepped off, there was Reba, who was in chipper spirits considering what we had just seen. "Campbella, there you are. Long time, no see."

I was thrown. We had just FigureFlexed less than two days ago and attended the infamous flighter crash party together Friday night. I hoped he wasn't getting so clingy that he needed to keep tabs on me every day. "We just saw each other, dude."

"If you consider last Wednesday as 'just saw,' then okay." He winked and started down the hall. I was completely stumped and frozen in place. Last Wednesday? I didn't get it. He turned back to see why I wasn't walking with him. "Coming?"

I caught up to him. Why would he say that we hadn't seen each other since last Wednesday? Maybe he was trying to purge the party from his memory. This wasn't the aura of a guy who had just witnessed a massive flighter crash on the Key Bridge, but I decided not to pursue the conversation. Maybe I was being overly cautious about saying the wrong things, but I knew I was being watched one way or another. *We* were being watched.

We reached the entrance point to my first session. He kept walking but turned to face me and smiled, "Lunch?"

"Lunch."

He spun back around and skittered off.

I sat through my sessions in a daze. Not a single person mentioned the flighter crash, which was evidently taboo. By the time lunch rolled around, I felt like a caged lioness that hadn't been fed in days. The only thing I'd had to eat all weekend was half a cucumber. The half I hadn't used to relieve my puffy eyes.

I hustled to the meal hall but Reba wasn't at our normal spot yet. I was too starving to wait for him to order. It felt like eons passed before my quesadilla popped up through the meal delivery portal, but when it did, I ravaged it.

"Somebody likes quesadillas, wowza!"

That deep voice was familiar. I stopped mid-chew and looked over my shoulder. It was G.W. Wallingsford, and Brittany Gilroy. I could feel the color in my face disappear and a surge of unease spread through my limbs. I was speechless.

"What's up, girl, don't remember me? G.W. Wallingsford, Jennifer's brother?

"No, no, of course I know who you are." I stared at him like he was a ghost. He was flawless. This was not a guy who had just been involved in an explosive crash.

"Okay, good. I was gonna say..." He palmed my shoulder like we were old pals. "This is my girl, Brittany. Brittany, Doro from LA."

Brittany bent down and kissed both of my cheeks. "Hey. I love LA."

"Me, too," burst from my mouth, exactly as it had when we'd had the same exchange the week before. I barely knew what to say to these two. How was G.W. alive? How did he look like this? His flawless presence defied reality. How could they be acting like the party never happened? Brittany and I had bonded. I knew she liked to watch movies and ride horses. Now she smiled blankly, as if we were two strangers meeting for the first time. This was deja vu of the most distorted variety.

"Cool, well, you look like you're crazy busy with that quesadilla. We'll leave you to it. Just saying what up."

I went with the 'play it cool' approach. Question nothing out loud. No way was I going to stir this pot after what I had been through this weekend. I appreciated having a range of physical motion and the ability to speak. "Good to see you, G.W."

Brittany had a fleeting look, like for a split second she remembered me. "It's really weird, you are so familiar, but you just moved here, right?"

"Yep. I know. It's weird. Happens a lot though. I guess I just have a familiar face."

"Well, nice to meet you, Doro from LA."

"You, too, Brittany from Georgetown."

She gave me another funny look. And then I realized she was probably confused as to how I knew she was from Georgetown; if, according to this new reality we were in, that party at her house never had happened.

"See you around," she said with a flicker of curiosity in her eye.

"See you around." I gave a flicker right back.

"Later, girl."

G.W. and Brittany strolled off in perfect harmony, looking like a billion bucks. I looked back down at my half-eaten quesadilla but had managed to lose my appetite. I was in a daze. Is this what it felt like to be a conspiracy theorist? I so did not want to become like that. I pictured a pale, skinny guy with terrible hygiene in a small, messy room, posting wild speculations online. Never sleeping or eating right, never interacting with people, except for maybe a cat whose litterbox is never cleaned. His only stimulation in life looking out the window at passers-by or watching fetish porn. Oh god, I didn't want my mind to be consumed with conspiracy theory. Just as I was moving into a good anxiety jag, Reba's backpack hit the table and then his butt hit the seat.

"Was that G.W. Wallingsford and Brittany Gilroy just talking to you?" He was reacting like a kid who had just seen Mickey at Disneyland.

Did none of these people remember the party?! Then it hit me. The memories of that night must have been blocked wholesale from their minds. Their brain synapses had been reprogrammed directly from the mainframe to which the nanobots in our blood were entangled. My memory had stayed untouched because I had broken the entanglement in my bloodstream. But of course I couldn't let on. "Yeah, crazy, right?"

Reba wasn't buying my B.S. "Doro, what's going on? Something doesn't feel right here."

"I'm not sure what you mean."

"What you're saying, it doesn't feel genuine."

Reba was about to screw things up royally, maybe beyond the point of repair.

"Of course it is. Everything I ever say is genuine."

"It's not, Doro, come on."

I couldn't let this happen. I knew there was something up with him, that he could sense things, and if I didn't do something to break free of him immediately, S.O.I.L. would figure out exactly what I had done. I was left with no other choice.

"You know what, Reba, it's no wonder the kids where you're from called you "freak"– because you are. So stop freaking me out, stop following me around, just stop, okay? Just leave me alone!" It killed me. His permagrin disappeared. All the muscles in his face dropped. I couldn't bear the sight of him feeling so sad. I stood up and turned away. I had to. There was no other way.

"It's better that we don't talk anymore."

"Doro? Where is this coming from all of the sudden?" He was so confused.

"It's not all of a sudden. You're making me really uncomfortable."

"What your saying isn't consistent with what you're feeling. I can tell."

"Stop! Just stop with all this psychobabble. If I say it, I mean it. So let's just get this out there in the open now, because it's long overdue. I don't want to be your girlfriend."

I didn't have to see his face to know that I had just stabbed him in the heart.

"I don't want you to be my girlfriend either, Doro. Because I have one."

Well now I really felt my foot stuffed into my mouth.

"Yeah, you're surprised I can tell... but you know what, Doro, you never asked. I know you just assumed because I was nice to you that I wanted to be your boyfriend. But that's not what I wanted. I just appreciated that you were real... and I thought we could be real friends."

I wanted to know who his girlfriend was, but I needed to move away from this situation as soon as possible. Somehow he must have read my mind.

"Lindsay."

The way he said her name was just so genuine and filled with pain that it made my heart sink. He might love her, but there was some kind of problem there. I felt his heartache inside my own. I wanted to give him a hug, but I didn't.

"My first and only love. We were both recruited but she chose not to stay. She got sent back to the Aboves. We never broke up. We never even said goodbye, which was fine with me because I know we are meant to be together. She's still my girlfriend, Doro. She's still in my heart and I know I'm still in hers. So I'm sorry if you mistook my friendship for something more, but that's exactly what it is. I felt like we had become real, true friends."

I beat down my emotions. Smothered them. Gave him my best apathetic facade.

"If you want to throw it all away, well then that's your prerogative. It was nice while it lasted."

I could see in his eyes that he wanted me to apologize so things could go back to how they were. But they couldn't now. I didn't respond, because I had to let him think I was a jerk. Clearly I didn't have a hard time playing the part. And before the silence moved past awkward to deadly, he turned his back to me and walked away without looking back.

My heart was broken.

29

I HAD NO one. Not a soul. Only when I closed my eyes could the ones I loved visit me, the ones I had left behind for this. But it wasn't all peaches and cream, these imaginary visits. My mom. Julie. Killer. My mom's sweet patients and the people I knew from Café Firenze who always wanted to hear about my day. I pulled their faces to the forefront of my memory and it stung like a hard shower beating on a fresh sunburn. This wasn't a life worth living if they weren't in it. They wouldn't take me back now. Nobody here cared about Doro Campbell, except for Reba, and I had sabotaged our budding friendship.

Exhausted, I'd fallen into a deep sleep right after I got home from sessions around five and now it was midnight. My schedule was way off. The lack of sunlight totally messed up my biorhythms. The normally dark circles under my eyes were pitch black, as if colored with chunks of coal. This wasn't a look that cucumbers could fix.

I clutched my flexer like a security blanket. Flipped on B3, only to land on the news, of course. My parasocial relationship with Becky Hudson would grow tonight as all of my real relationships had been squashed. The lower third of the screen read, *"Previously Aired."* I was surprised that the video of the crash was playing. If nobody seemed to remember this crash, how could it be that it was still being reported?

"Following the fatal flighter crash at the Key Bridge in the Aboves Friday night, officials are cracking down on the escalating Mojo Stick problem. The Seneca Senate has introduced new measures at the recommendation of the advisory committee which, if sanctioned, will mean that a zero-tolerance decree for Mojo sticks will go into effect by the end of the year."

Seneca didn't have jail or prison, which were at odds with the utopian, 'one world' system of government the founders had envisioned for this society. Instead, those found guilty by jury for engaging in criminal activity were banished to the Aboves, permanently. Nobody wanted to mess up. There was an extremely low crime rate here. Of almost one and a half million Senecans in Seneca City hubs worldwide, there had only been two dozen banishments to the Aboves. Not even a fraction of a fraction of one percent. Those chosen to be here were in many ways a self-selecting group, and once we had tasted the Senecan life, we simply didn't want to go back.

My attention had veered away from the B3 News, but snapped back when the screen that contained crash footage was now filled with a photo of Dom.

"Officials have identified the stolen flighter pilot's body as that

of Senecan Dominic Ambrosia. B3 News can confirm that Ambrosia was flying recklessly under the influence of a Mojo Stick, and will be held accountable for a total of six deaths. Two more are still critically injured. Congressman Frank Wallingsford had these words: "Our prayers are with the families of the victims. These were utterly senseless deaths that Senecan leaders will tolerate no longer."

I was enraged, full throttle. Sickened. I smashed my flexer down into the bed. Burying my head in the pillow, I screamed my face off, and kicked my legs wildly. When I pulled back from the pillow, I could barely breathe. I stood up on my bed and threw the pillow across the room. I jumped down and crouched with my knees on the floor, to pull out my record player and turn it on. Fingering through a stack of records, I stopped on Nirvana– *Smells Like Teen Spirit.*

I hadn't listened to this record since I'd come here. Now was the perfect time. I put it on, cranked the volume all the way up. For some reason, this song always riled me up more than any other. Right now was no different. I was already provoked. Now I was really getting amped. This was my own form of mojo. I jumped back up onto the bed, grabbed my flexer and commanded it to a microphone. I belted out *Smells Like Teen Spirit.* This wasn't just karaoke. This was my anthem.

30

ALL I WANTED to do was purge on the outside the rage I felt on the inside, but for now it only could happen in the squared-off, golden boundaries of my room. My music blasted in an effort to drown out the thought processes of my battered mind. I didn't want to think anymore. I wanted to be a part of the "ignorance is bliss" camp. But it was too late. I was in way too deep. I wondered if it would be better to go down with the sinking ship along with everyone else on Earth or be here, in this idyllic place, but miserable and alone. Yet, from somewhere deep inside there was a speck of hope prodding me. This speck, a luminous underdog within, invisible to the eye, is a persistent little thing. It told me that if there was a real reason the facts had been hidden, covered up by blaming Dom for awful things that he didn't do, I would be the only one who could uncover them. There were answers, and I had to find them.

I was out of breath, lying on my bed, chest pumping up and down after that intense release of everything I had in me. Moving from chaos to a meditative state was not so simple a process. I had to get out of here.

I tried to use S.E.R.C.'s bustling morning rush to drown out the automatic thinking inside my head. The acoustic carrier was packed with people headed to session. I wouldn't be able to concentrate on mathematics applications, quantum computing or anything else for that matter, but I had to show my face.

When I hopped off in S.E.R.C., Reba was there. I was surprised. How could he not hate me? We locked eyes. I was ashamed. He didn't appear upset. He looked resolved. "We have to talk."

"Not now."

"Yes, now."

This wasn't the sweet, playful Reba I was used to. He was assertive, refusing to leave this alone. "You can't just blow off our friendship like this. I know you don't mean the things you said."

I started walking towards my sessions.

"Doro, stop! Talk to me."

I stopped. Spun around. My glare ripped into him, "You're putting us both in danger. You need to quit. Don't question this anymore, okay? You have to trust me."

"If I have to trust you, then you have to trust me. It's a two-way street, isn't it?" I stumbled for an answer, because I didn't have one. He was right, but I couldn't even begin to go there. My emotions went into code red. Just being there with him, with this conversation headed in the direction it was, put us both in jeopardy.

"Come on, Doro."

"You don't understand what we're dealing with!"

"Part of me does. My mind is telling me one thing, but my intuition is telling me another. It's tearing me apart. I've always trusted my intuition before everything."

"You need to just leave this alone now. Before it's too late."

"There's no such thing as too late. You may think there is, but, trust me, there isn't. *You* may not know it yet, but *I* know you have the answers... not just for me. For everyone."

I glanced around in a complete panic. The crowds of people headed to session moved around us as if we didn't exist, but even with all the noise surrounding us, I knew his thoughts were being analyzed in some way. I didn't want him to tap into mine. It must have been too late, though.

"We can't do this here." I walked away from him. He didn't chase after me. He knew that I would be at the meal hall for lunch.

31

REBA WAS THE only one I had left, and our relationship was hanging on by a thread. But it was all I needed. One human connection was all it took to believe I could get the others back. I couldn't believe I'd be disconnected from my mom, and from Dom, forever. A strong, loving, lifelong bond and a fresh new one, overflowing with possibility. I wanted them both so badly.

I sat in first session, daydreaming, and it hit me. This was a sickness of the soul I was feeling. I was love sick. Dominic Ambrosia had intercepted my heart in these golden halls, and having him ripped away from me had spun my world out of control, in complete disarray. It was one thing to accept the progress of life and technology, but it was quite another to give in to the man-made dictate that Dom and I were to be separated. If Reba could fight for our friendship, and not let me give up, then I could fight for everything I had that was right.

My session leader said my name at least three times before I heard it and it registered that my brain had checked out of there long ago. Everyone was staring. I blamed colitis. I didn't have colitis, but it seemed like the best excuse in the moment. Unlike school back in LA, where Mr. Malin always thought I was up to something, my session leaders in Seneca respected me. I had proven myself here. I don't mean to be creepily boastful, but my math and tech capabilities made my session leader's own abilities look elementary. I was lucky that far from crushing his ego, it garnered me a certain level of respect from him. So when I complained about a stomach problem he simply believed me and dismissed me from session.

I knew my time to act would be limited. There would be a point when they would catch on to me, no telling when that might be.

I charged through the doorway to my room that opened as I approached, and immediately threw on a record. I needed to get in the zone. I popped a square of cacao into my mouth and dove headfirst into my flexer screen.

I had to access my Veil– all of my online endeavors in offshore gambling and financial accounts were running there. I knew that S.O.I.L. had a trace on it because that's how they noticed my mathematical skills to begin with, so first things first– I had to place an encryption there. I coded it so that they would only be retrieving randomized repetitions of what they had already seen, and not any new activity. That would keep me under the radar at least for a while, and it was simple to accomplish. Done.

Next was the hard part. I had to trace the flow of data transfer from Great Falls, which was directly above the main Seneca City hub of the region, to determine where the bulk of it was going. That would lead me to identify and enter the mainframe that all the nanobots flowing through the blood of Senecans were entangled with. I ran equations until my fingertips were completely numb, but just kept coming up with dead ends. My hands couldn't keep up with my head, as if these two body parts were on two separate entities. I would go down one path that was seemingly effective, but then, bam, dead end again.

Time for a new approach. I had locked my entanglement to my flexer and had it under unbreakable encryption, by today's standards. I bypassed the encryption and followed the entanglement to an IP, which contained map coordinates that placed me right at the physical Latitude, 37.057372. Longitude, -80.627394. Claytor Lake. I ran a test to measure the data input and output there. It was astronomical. This was it. The mainframe was located in the hub below the incredibly inconspicuous Claytor Lake.

I crept into the mainframe through my own entanglement, and now had remote access to every nanobot with which this system was entangled. My body buzzed. My fingers were dead. My eyes numbed by the data in front of them. It wasn't just data, it was life. Identical versions of the neurological processes of every single citizen of Seneca were right there. I was blown away by the magnitude of what was at my fingertips. I paced circles around my square room, shook my hands to loosen them up for round two. The challenging part was over. I was in. Now I just needed to find Reba's brain data in the mainframe and break his entanglement, so that any communication between us would be undetectable.

We were categorized by name, DNA and Senecan ID #. I ran a name match search. Bam! There he was. Timothy John Reba.

My next step was to remove the block on Dom's memory and make sure his entanglement was also cut, but, before I had the chance to dive into that process, I received an incoming flex from Reba. S.O.I.L. was headed my way.

Even though I had blocked the data output from my blood and piggybacked off of another Seneca citizen's data, I was not completely in the clear. S.O.I.L. had probably analyzed Reba's data from our time in the hall at S.E.R.C., and determined that my thought process, which they got second hand as it was communicated to him, was a threat to the system. I wasn't surprised that they had analysts on top of this data twenty-four-seven. I had to get outta the hot zone. I flipped the needle off the record and bailed.

As I jetted down the hall to catch the acoustic carrier back to S.E.R.C., I reprogrammed my flexer to appear as if I was in the restaurant district. They already thought I was skipping session, so I was going to try and send them on a wild goose chase. I needed to buy time. Judging by Reba's flex, this wasn't too serious, yet. They were just taking precautionary measures by monitoring me. Still, it was best I didn't underestimate S.O.I.L.

32

I FOUND REBA at our usual meeting time and place. Once Reba and I were seated at our regular spot in the meal hall, it was safe to release my whereabouts. That way, S.O.I.L. would come find me here and see that everything was all fine and dandy. I lifted the block on my flexer. If it's all smoke and mirrors, I was puffing the biggest Cuban cigar in front of the wonkiest funhouse mirror of them all.

I bit into my quesadilla and noticed several S.O.I.L. guards walking nonchalantly through the hall. They had eyes on me. I had more than just eyes on them. I savored this Jack cheese. My appetite was back. Reba was chomping a mouthful like he always did. He wasn't acting like I was the presumptuous jerk who'd told him I didn't want to be his girlfriend. What a good guy. I was fortunate he could see past my imperfections. He was antsy, though. I could tell he was desperately waiting for me to let him in on what I'd been doing. But he was going to have to wait. He was going to have to give something up first. How had he known that S.O.I.L. was on to me? How did he continually answer my unspoken thoughts?

Chomp, chomp, chomp– it drove me insane! Couldn't this guy eat with his mouth closed?

"What? You don't like to see my food break down?"

Wow, okay, there he went again with that answering my thoughts stuff.

He chomped again and I finally grasped how this was going to be. This was going to be a T.M.I.-loaded relationship. Here we go.

"I like it so much actually, so much..."

"I can tell."

"Okay listen. You want me to come clean with you on some things, then first, I want you to come clean with me."

"Chica, I'm cleaner than soap."

"You'd tell me anything?"

He hesitantly made the decision in that moment that indeed he would. "Anything."

"Tell me why you're here."

Reba sat back, chewing the rest of his mouthful slowly, with his lips pressed closed. I found relief in that.

He swallowed dramatically. "What does it matter?"

"It matters because I feel like you expect me to show you all my cards... but you. *You* remain a mystery."

"Hmm... then you're saying I'm dark and mysterious."

"No. Just annoying."

"Ohhh."

"What's your story, dude?"

Reba pushed his tray full of half-eaten food into the tube. "Alright. But if we go down this path, there's no turning back. So let me go ahead and prepare for your reaction." He pushed the button and his food was retrieved.

"Do you know what my reaction is going to be?"

"Surprisingly, no. But I have enough experience with everyone else to know how this plays out."

"I'm not everyone else."

"Fair enough."

Reba fidgeted in his seat. I wanted to lighten the mood so I took a bite of quesadilla and chomped it. Smacked at that scrumptious Jack cheese. I watched his face warm up, his cheek muscles tightened, prompting a little grin. I think that although he was intimidated by opening himself up to vulnerability, there was also an impending sense of liberation in coming clean.

"Spit it out, freak."

"Okay, okay..." He lowered his voice, "Ever heard of an Intuerian? Well, that's what I am."

I stood up, feigning horror. "Oh, my god. I have to go now."

"Okay, come on. Stop. Sit down."

I sat. We needed to align and take some time to understand each other on a deeper level. I placed my almost finished food in the tube and sent it back, giving him every particle of my attention.

"When I was four years old, my birth parents started to notice that I was different than the other kids. I wasn't interested in normal kid things like playing in the park. I was always tuning into someone around me. I would alert them to things that were about to happen before they actually did. Little things, like a woman about to stumble on a crack in the sidewalk or that my dad's boss was about to flex him. My dad was freaked. My birth parents are super religious so they took me to the church looking for answers, solutions, anything. They were worried that somehow this could be the work of the devil."

"That's so messed up."

"Yeah, well, that's basic human error for you."

"Can't argue with you there."

"But hang on, because there's the other side to that. There's always the other side."

I nodded in agreement, wanting to show him that this didn't freak me out in the least bit. It actually made me appreciate him more. I could tell that he felt more comfortable as he got into it and stopped worrying about the people around us. They weren't paying attention anyway.

"They tried to have exorcisms performed on me, but my abilities only grew stronger. I tried to hide them because I thought they were bad. I have an older sister. We're fifteen months apart so we were super close. They started keeping us separate. I became really depressed and didn't want to eat or go to school. My premonitions became stronger by the day. I wanted them to stop because I thought it was why my family hated me."

"Wow, Reebs. I am so sorry."

"Don't be, please. I don't want you to feel sorry for me, Doro. I just want you to understand. Then you can decide for yourself whether or not you want me in your life. I understand either way, I really do. I know this isn't normal."

"What is normal anyways? I don't think I'm normal."

"True."

I smiled. Felt our connection grow. "So, then, what got you here?"

"After my birth parents tried everything that the church had advised, and I was still me, they decided the only thing to do with me was send me into foster care. I was placed with a family who raised special needs kids. They embraced me, while everyone else in that small town community didn't want anything to do with me. I wasn't allowed to play with anyone's kids. By the time I got to intermediate school, I was bullied and beaten up so many times that my parents had to home school me."

"Your parents or your foster parents?"

"My foster parents *are* my parents. They gave me the love and support that parents are supposed to give. Without them, I never would have survived. They were a blessing. And then along came Seneca."

"The juicy part."

"Exactly. When I was thirteen, a woman was raped and murdered in my town. I started having these visions that I couldn't stop. They were so gruesome, Campbella, like nothing I'd ever seen in any movie. It made me want to kill myself. I fell so ill that it landed me in the hospital. I told a nurse that I knew what happened. The local authorities came to me, and then, the F.B.I. My visions were actual accounts of the murder. I knew who he was and where he was. I was brought in to help the F.B.I. uncover murders. Everything I gave them came from pure intuition. It was good because I was helping people, and that felt like the right thing to do, but it was bad too because those images stayed with me. Haunting me, keeping me up at night. Nobody understood what I was going through, until I met Lindsay. The F.B.I. had her there doing the same thing. We got each other like nobody else ever could. And then, when I was fourteen, Ellen Malone showed up at our house. My parents didn't want to send me away at such a young age, but I begged and pleaded. I had to get out of that town. I had to get away from the people who had persecuted me and the memories there."

"I don't blame you. I am so sorry for ever calling you... the "f" word, Reba, I had no idea. I knew you had the nose of a bloodhound, but I never would've really thought you were a full-on psychic."

"I'm no psychic, Campbella. I'm an Intuerian. I don't speak with dead people. I can't tell you if you're going to come into a windfall of money. I am driven by my intuition. I have premonitions and visions that tie in to the life force around me. None of it is controlled. It's all based on where I am at any given moment. People don't understand us in the Aboves. We are seen as either psycho or satanic. But here in Seneca I am appreciated for what I am. They have accepted me and applauded my value to this society. I never imagined that could happen. The past two years have been my first chance to really live. Seneca is a dream come true. I never, ever want to leave. Even if it means never seeing Lindsay again."

33

IN THE OLDEN days, people came to America to give their kids the chance for a good life they couldn't have in other parts of the world. Seneca was oozing with the same romanticism, only much more so. I left my lunch with Reba feeling a fire burning inside– a fire for my life at Seneca. I couldn't let S.O.I.L. extinguish it. I couldn't let them get away with expelling Dom and silencing me. No way. My new friends and I were on to something beyond major. I wanted to make it here so I could help clean up the planet, bring optimal health and wellness to those in need, extend a greater level of efficiency to the world at large, and open up a whole new approach to education. This was all way overdue, and now we were on track. Reba was absolutely right. These were undeniably terrific goals, and if I had anything to do with it, I was not going to let the manipulations of a few ruin the potential of my future here... or Dom's future. I had to fight to right the wrong that had been done to him.

It was no wonder they wanted to keep Seneca exclusive. After all, exclusivity is nothing new. But just like the American dream, the Senecan dream could only truly be declared by those who lived it most graciously and with liberty and justice.

Of course, there were minor bumps in the concept. For example, as far as I was concerned, my mom deserved to be here just as much as, if not more than, people like Gregory Zaffron or G.W. Wallingsford. There was no reason that she couldn't accompany me, if G.W. could be here with his sister and his father, Congressman Wallingsford, and seemed to be able to go back and forth between Seneca and the Aboves whenever he felt like it. I'd never liked the dismissive saying, "Life isn't fair." I believed in Seneca, but wasn't about to accept all of their arbitrary barriers so easily. This society was being developed, not just by the powerful, but equally by great minds of all classes and circumstances. Forward thinking was what really created the true potential of Seneca, not fear and power. No, fear and power just created unjust imaginary boundaries. Boundaries I had every intention of breaking.

That evening, after session, I decided to take a ride to the restaurant sector and pay Ty a visit. It was no different than any evening– his place was packed to the brim with elated patrons. There was just one empty seat at the sushi bar. I bee-lined for it, knowing it would be filled in a matter of seconds.

"Well, well, well. Look who's returned to the scene of the crime."

I knew that voice. Ellen Malone. Uh-oh. It was time to face up to the betrayal. "Ellen."

Ty leaned forward onto the sushi bar. "Hi Doro! You two know each other, yes?"

Ellen nodded as she gracefully nibbled at a piece of salmon wrapped around a melon spear.

"Very nice. Let me make your favorite."

"Thanks, Ty."

I didn't know what to say, but I needed to start somewhere. "You hate me."

"*Hate* is a strong word, Doro. I could think of a more apropos term to describe how I feel about what happened."

"I'm sorry, Ellen, I had to find a way. There are things going on that I had to try and get to the bottom of."

Ellen calmly sipped some tea. She wasn't someone I'd ever wanted to hurt and I hoped she would accept my apologies. I just hadn't been able to think of any other way to get out of S.E.R.C. while it was under lockdown.

"You know what, Doro? Friends don't take advantage of each other, no matter what the circumstances."

That stung. She was right. "I'm sorry for the way I went about things. From now on, I won't drag you into my shenanigans."

"You shouldn't even be into shenanigans here."

"I know. You're right. I really am sorry. I have so much respect for you and I just want to go back to how things were. Can we do that? How can I make it up to you?"

"Backwards is never an option for me, but going forward, of course I hope we can have a new understanding."

"We can." I don't know if I was more excited about the direction of this conversation or the plate of halibut that had just entered my line of sight. I pulled it from Ty's magic hands to the counter in front of me. He looked back and forth between Ellen and me, and then proceeded to say exactly what had been on my mind ever since that bogus B3 News report.

"What happened to Dom? I don't believe he would steal a flighter. Something's not right. One of you has to know something."

Ellen and I looked at one another. Who would be the one to speak? Ellen put her tea down and took a deep breath–

"Look, I know you two must be wondering what happened to your friend. I get it. This whole thing is a complete mess. But, as far as I know, Dominic was meddling where he shouldn't have been, and he defied multiple warnings. I only have a certain level of clearance so I don't know exactly what he was doing, but I do know it was big enough that S.O.I.L. saw it as an immense security hazard to the society at large."

Ellen couldn't have known the truth about why Dom was messing around in the lab, but I couldn't let this moment go without defending him. "I think S.O.I.L. is the one that creates a flaw in the Seneca Society security, not Dom."

"Well, unfortunately, Doro, you aren't the one running things around here."

"Maybe she should be."

"Thanks, Ty." I smiled.

"Maybe. But she's not."

Ty and I both hung our heads. Ellen was coming from a place of logic, and wasn't trying to convince either of us of anything other than the facts.

"*Maybe* doesn't run societies. *Maybe* doesn't make things happen.

Ty and I got it. Someone we both respected had given us a reality check.

"Look, I really like both of you. You are two of my favorite recruits of the thousands I've been responsible for. I hope you'll see Dominic as an example and not take the path he did. Seneca is a great chance for anyone to whom it's granted. Don't throw it away trying to prove something or uncover some conspiracy. It's not worth it, you guys. Once they deem you to be a greater threat than an asset, it's too late to reverse it."

I pondered that deeply.

Ty swallowed his dismay and slid on down the sushi bar to tend to others, as Ellen and I ate our sushi. As I took those last few bites, I was trampled by revelations— but not the ones that Ellen would have been happy about. I *needed* to get to the Aboves. I needed to get to my mom and Dominic. There was no more time for *maybe*. It was time for me to drop the maybe and take on the must.

It was time to make myself become the threat. The one they would never see coming.

34

LAST SESSION BEFORE lunch would be my launching pad. Seneca Civics and Ethics. It was life as usual for everyone else in the ethereal golden hallway at S.E.R.C. on this early mid-week afternoon, but not for me. I marched through the arched doorway and as the wall closed up behind me, I knew that it would be a long time before I experienced those amazing disappearing doors again, if ever.

My session leader was Richmond Shields. He, like our other session leaders, went by his last name. Shields had received his PhD in political science from Berkeley, and was later recruited to work in various think tanks on Washington, D.C.'s Capitol Hill before coming to Seneca to serve, not only as the civics and ethics session leader, but also on the advisory committee to the Seneca Senate. Shields told us he was originally from Utah, that he'd left behind the life he'd been born into, which (although he doesn't refer to it much) I surmise had been a strict Mormon upbringing. By the time I met him at Seneca he had catapulted himself to the other end of the political and spiritual spectrum.

The Shields we knew was a 34-year-old atheist bachelor who never referenced his life outside of S.E.R.C., no matter how much we hassled him. He had that crushable, boy-next-door quality and was super intelligent and nice, to boot. And, like everyone else at Seneca, he was flying with that element of the unknown.

I couldn't let my nerves get the best of me. It was all on the line. I sat down in my usual seat, next to Jennifer Wallingsford. It was the only session we had together. Her other sessions were ones that would send her on a leadership path. She and her brother were both being groomed to be Seneca Senators one day. I'd once thought it would be a miracle if G.W. lived to see the light of day, let alone the day he would sit on the Senate of the most powerful society on Earth. But given the series of events over the last couple of weeks, I realized that here in Seneca the phrase, "anything is possible," was, in fact, nothing short of literal.

Session filled up. Far different from the normal high school atmosphere back in LA, my peers here were a copacetic student body by anyone's standards. No normal teasing, jokey chaos and incessant rumbling of gossip. People simply took their seats, prepared for session, or whatever was in front of them. Part of the cooperation I saw within session walls stemmed from the fact that this wasn't just "school"– this was S.E.R.C. Being in Seneca was a privilege and that held a persuasive power which was applied to every facet of life here.

I was about to do something that would shake up all that calm and compliance. The only thing I could hear was my thumping heartbeat, resonating against my chest cavity. I felt like everyone else was in the pool, mindlessly playing Marco Polo while I was underwater. This was almost it. The moment when I would abandon "maybe." Drown it. Plunge to the surface with a fistful of "must."

Two dozen flexer notifications went off in sync. I sucked in a boundless breath. My lungs swelled with air like a helium balloon. I rose. My heartbeat dropped. Time stopped.

"You are all being controlled. There are forces at work here in Seneca that not all of us know about. They want us to believe certain things and they are manipulating our minds to think them. Untrue things, things that didn't happen. Dominic Ambrosia is not dead. He was not the one driving that flighter–"

Shields calmly inched towards me, "Dorothy, please take a seat. This isn't the time–"

"I'm sorry, sir, it is."

Shields was genuinely confused by my sudden eruption. I scanned the faces in the room. Everyone was. My gaze fell upon Jennifer Wallingsford. I liked her. I didn't want to hurt her. But, after Ellen Malone, she would be my next case of collateral damage.

Two S.O.I.L. guards entered the session room.

"G.W. Wallingsford was piloting that flighter!"

Jennifer's lips parted and her jaw fell. Her brow tightened. Her eyes shrunk. But with all that, she didn't look shocked. Her face splashed with fascination, like she sensed something was up but needed to hear more.

The two S.O.I.L. guards stormed in my direction. I put my hands up. That was all I needed to do.

35

I WOKE UP freezing cold in a white room wrapped in blue mirrored windows. Thousands of one inch white tiles made up the floor, and flat white paint covered the ceiling. No blemishes. It was just like the last time, only this time I wasn't alone. From my horizontal perspective, I spotted several figures. Everyone was blurry. Slowly, I craned my neck. While I was fully expecting to be paralyzed, I was pleasantly relieved to find my body fully functioning. They had only knocked me out this time. Thank goodness. I emerged from the brain haze and recognized that there were five... or six people present. I was on a hospital bed, in a hospital gown. Gregory, a couple of S.O.I.L. officers, two women I never had seen before in doctors' coats and... Reba?

Reba's eyes were pinned to the ground in front of him. I didn't allow my gaze to linger on him for too long because I knew what they had done. I had to go with the flow because they had tried to wipe out my memory. I couldn't let on that I knew who Reba was and it appeared that he was helping me do that. Normally I would have been shocked to see him here, but these days I was shockproof.

Gregory stood up. "Hi, Dorothy. I'm Dr. Wes Stanton. You have experienced a bad fall but don't you worry. You're going to be fine. You can go ahead and sit up whenever you feel ready. Everything looks good, so we're going to send you on your way, we just need to ask you a few questions to confirm there hasn't been any memory impairment. Okay, sweetie?"

I wanted to jump out of my seat and get right up in his smiling, lying face.

"Okay." Wow. They really had gone through with it. They were purging me from society. At least, they were trying.

I sat up. Looked at Reba. He was watching me intently, but quickly shifted his eyes away to avoid eye contact.

"Dorothy Campbell?" One of the two women I had never seen before wore eyeglasses that she focused with a tiny nob on the side as she looked up from a tablet in her hands. Her lenses reflected a charged silvery glare from her screen so I couldn't see her eyes.

"Yes."

"Do you know where you are?"

I swallowed. I swallowed my pride. I swallowed my fear. I swallowed my sense of rebellion. "No."

She smiled sympathetically, "You were on a trip to the Capitol with your second cousins from Ireland. You slipped on a candy wrapper and hit your head pretty badly. You are in the infirmary at the Smithsonian."

The woman next to the interviewer typed feverishly on an identical tablet. She didn't even look up. They both had their hair in buns. They could have been twins, except that only one of them wore glasses.

The interviewer cocked her head and spoke in a warm, relaxed tone. "Dorothy can you tell us where you are now?"

"The infirmary at the Smithsonian."

"Good."

Gregory looked to Reba.

Reba's whole body was tight like he was under a dentist's drill. He blinked about a mile a minute. "Affirmative."

This was unreal. They used *Reba* to determine truth in exit interviews for exiled Senecans.

Gregory nodded to the interviewer.

"Dorothy, can you tell us the last person you saw?"

I squinted and rubbed my forehead as if trying to think through the pain of my fall at the Smithsonian. "Well, before my cousins, it would have been my mom and my dog."

Gregory waited on Reba. "Affirmative."

Reba knew that the brainwashing was not working on me, but he provided an "affirmative" for every answer I gave. For two hours we went through a list of things that I'd supposedly done. The interviewer planted in my mind bits and pieces of facts from my alleged travels with my second cousins. The twisted part was, they knew all about my second cousins. Even more than I ever did. The woman next to the interviewer worked the tablet like a stenographer. I knew exactly what she thought she was doing. She *thought* she was re-calibrating my neurological processes via the mainframe to which I was supposedly entangled. They were attempting to implant false memories.

Reba was so focused on keeping his gaze locked on the floor, he could have burned a hole in it with his eyes.

Gregory approached me and patted my shoulder, just as he had when he and Ellen had stopped by to see me with the Dominic warning. "The gentlemen and I are going to be going now. This nice woman will help you get dressed in the clothes we found you in. You go ahead and make yourself comfortable here, sweetie. Later this morning, these two nice Smithsonian liaisons will be accompanying you on a flight back to Los Angeles."

Smithsonian liaisons! Gregory was proving himself to be quite a piece of work.

"You'll be home with your mom by dinnertime."

"Thank you." I purred pathetically, like an injured kitty to a pro-bono veterinarian. And, voila, my work here was done.

36

WEDGED BETWEEN TWO civilian dressed S.O.I.L. officers on my flight back to LA, I sweated buckets and fidgeted the whole time, unable to find any sort of comfort as the searing heat in my feet radiated up my legs. People think I'm a chill person. I do a good job of radiating that vibe on the outside, but I have the tendency to be high strung. They, on the other hand, were as static as a dial tone the whole time.

We landed at LAX. As we made our way into baggage claim, we were welcomed by a chauffeur holding a "Dorothy Campbell" sign. He was a middle-aged, Iranian gentleman with a thinning hairline and deep wrinkles in his weathered skin. He quietly offered to get my bags, but I had nothing and was unsure of what had happened to the case of belongings I'd had at Seneca. I just kept the hope alive that one day, some way, somehow, my vinyl and I would come back together.

As we moved with the crowd across the dull cream and gray speckled tile, I soaked in the airport arrival atmosphere: people calling out to one another, kids on the loose, business travelers looking distracted, elderly folks being pushed in wheelchairs, lovers hugging, laughter, tears, sneezes, teases, happiness, frustration, tattered and bourgeois luggage side by side on squeaky conveyer belts, the buzz of outdated, unflattering lights, the faint smell of cigarette smoke and exhaust fumes wafting in from outside the automated sliding glass doors.

Ah, the airport. On this late afternoon at LAX, it all made me feel somber. Saddened by the naïveté of everyone around me. My heart palpitated, conflicted. Joyous and excited to see my mom and Killer, troubled in the realization that all these people who surrounded me would not be afforded the same opportunities as those in Seneca. I saw a man in a wheelchair missing his leg from the knee down. Shouldn't everyone have access to regenerative medicine? A Senecan education? Clean air? The duality disgusted me. I felt helpless. I hated that feeling.

It was a relief to be back in a car. I hadn't been in one since I had left LA, months before. Traffic on the 405 had never felt so good. Northbound, amidst an ocean of road-raged Los Angelenos, I finally felt content. The setting sun bathed my left cheek from the west. No matter how chill I tried to be, there was a hint of nervousness underneath, but dang, it felt good to be back in my city– The City of Angels.

A twenty-minute ride and we pulled up to my building. Everything felt right. S.O.I.L. shadowed me up to my apartment. When we got to the front door, there it was, music to my ears. Killer's yappy bark. I crouched down in anticipation of his welcome. The muffled sound of the 405 and my mom's hurried footsteps. What a precious symphony. And then she opened the door. Like a jack-in-the-box, Killer sprang into my arms. His tiny, wet tongue pelted my arm like a cyclone as he squealed with happiness.

"Killer! My baby, my love, I missed you so much. I'm so sorry I left you for so long." Finally. I squeezed him against my heart. My hands disappeared into his soft black fur.

Tears of happiness streamed down my mom's cheekbones. I stood up, cradling Killer with one arm, and threw the other around her, burying my face into the nook between her shoulder and neck. She held the back of my head. "Doro," she whispered. I never wanted to let go, never again. Neither did she. I clenched my eyes shut, letting the aroma of roasted coffee in her hair bring me back. There's no place like home. But it didn't matter where we were. It was all about *how* we were. Together. The S.O.I.L. officers stood silently by, erect like metal flagpoles, but it didn't matter to us. Nobody else was there.

We stayed like that for a long time before they interrupted us.

"Ma'am, we're going to need you to sign here, acknowledging your daughter's arrival, and then we'll be on our way."

My mom didn't want to let go of me, but she did, reluctantly, when they handed her a tablet. She glanced at it, signed with her finger, and with that, S.O.I.L. was gone.

I was back in the Aboves with my mother. When you live in Seneca's idyllic halls it's easy to think of the Aboves as a disease-ridden, dismal place. In that moment, though, it was everything I wanted and more, and it won the applause of my heart.

Sadly, that bliss didn't last long. The pressures of reality tiptoed back in. Dom was in a different world, my mom and I were destined to a life on a planet devoid of hope, while a wicked bunch known as S.O.I.L. destroyed the great hope of the Seneca Society and would alter human history with the ultimate manipulation of all time. I was seeing things more clear than ever as I slowed to the end of this roller coaster ride. One minute I felt trapped and manipulated in Seneca, the next I was fueled by the opportunity there. I realized that it was S.O.I.L. that kept me on that wicked ride. But the truth is that what Seneca has to offer is mine for the taking and not S.O.I.L.'s to take away from me. The pressure for me to turn things around loomed as ominously as an offshore hurricane.

37

MY MOM HAD take-out waiting from my favorite neighborhood taqueria. Carne asada tacos, a cheese quesadilla and the best salsa verde in America. I vacuumed it. Barely chewed. It was too good. She updated me on her regular patients that I'd grown close to and all the people from Café Firenze, but mostly we just enjoyed the heavenly food and each other's company. She loved watching me. She knew how much it meant to me. Even though I was in the dire Aboves, I felt safe again. There was nothing quite like being with my mom, who loved me unconditionally and did things for me out of the goodness of her heart. I'd really missed that. And then I wondered... "Aren't you going to ask me about my trip?"

"There will be time for that. I know all of this took a lot out of you, and I just want you to have a breather. Relax on your first night back and don't think about any of that."

There was something slightly off. My mom was being so vague— with no mentions of reform school, Seneca, Ellen Malone, or anything about where I supposedly was... at all.

"Okay." I wanted to tell her everything, but I also knew that they could be listening. Let's not be naive, they were *definitely* listening. My mom's flexer wasn't safe. She was right. There would be time for that, but right now I had some important stuff to do. First things first, I had to find Dom.

"Crazy long day, Mom. I'm beat."

"Of course you are. Why don't you get some sleep, and when you wake up, come by Firenze for a mocha?"

Even thinking about that brought the comfort of a long, warm hug. For a split second I could smell that Café Firenze mocha. Then I thought about Ellen Malone. I wondered how much she knew about what had happened to me. If only she had the chance to reunite with her little boy, Connor, just like my mom and I were doing now. It didn't make sense to keep people who loved each other apart. There had to be a way to make space for that, even in a place like Seneca. *Especially* in a place like Seneca.

"I love you, Mom."

"I love *you*, Doro. You have no idea how happy I am that you're home."

"Me, too." I wanted to tell her my plan to take us to Seneca. That this wouldn't be our home much longer. But for now, I stayed mum on logistics. All we needed was love.

"Sweet dreams and I'll see you in the morning... or afternoon."

Man, was my room a sight for sore eyes. My mom hadn't touched a thing. Everything was exactly how I had left it. Killer was on my feet like socks. He wasn't going to let me out of his sight. My eyes lit up when I saw the seat at my desk. *My seat.* I'd spent many a late night planted right there. I ran my finger along the smooth plastic arm, and shoved it just enough for it's wheels to roll a few inches. This had been my dad's office chair when I was a little girl. I used to go bug him in his office, beg him to push me around in it. Nostalgia always took me away to another place, no matter what was going on.

It was already nine o'clock, midnight on the east coast. I took a seat. I hadn't lied to my mom— I was beat. But sleep is for the weak, and my night was just getting started. I had to stay strong. S.O.I.L. had confiscated my flexer. Even if they had tracked my Veil and tried to take the whole freaking thing down, they would have had their hands full. I had location scramblers out the wazoo on that thing. Good luck to whomever would have been given that challenge.

I powered up my computer, while simultaneously counting my blessings that the F.B.I. hadn't confiscated it. The sound of electronics coming to life set off a familiar excitement in me and pumped energy into my veins. Like a fan in the stands at a packed stadium, the rush of what was to come surged through me. The darkness of my room soon shifted to my favorite brilliant blue glow. I was in my element and ready to rock out. One thing was missing. I scooted across the room in my seat and flipped through some vinyl. I was in the mood for something that screamed victory with beats. Heart pounding, deep bass beats. Slipping my headphones over my head, I hit spin and lightly dropped the needle on the Endless Horizon record.

A few minutes short of a couple hours later, I'd done what I'd set out to do. I'd located Dom in a neighborhood in Manhattan, set up a nice little virus on the Seneca mainframe that would trigger on my command, and checked on my Cayman Islands accounts.

I was tickled green. While I was away, I had become a billionaire– a 2.3 billionaire, to be exact. It didn't fully register. How could it? It wasn't like I could use this money in Seneca. They were on a completely different system that wasn't exactly monetary like America per se. They'd described the economic structure of Seneca in my Seneca Civics and Ethics session. The opportunity to live safely in the lap of luxury with everything your heart could desire was not granted free of charge. Scientists, doctors, business people, inventors, you name it, signed over patents, licenses... entire companies to Seneca's corporate wing, Senecanomics, in order to be granted citizenship. For example, B3's Julian Hollenbeck had provided libraries of media content dating back well into the last millennium, and signed over all of his licensing revenues from the Aboves. This cash flow made it possible to do everything in Seneca from maintaining agricultural productivity to providing citizens with toiletries.

Even with this unique economic structure in place, something else was the source of power in Seneca. Something bigger. I knew it wasn't a system of pure equality, no matter how much certain people wanted us to believe that. It was true that we all had access to the best of everything. The best food, the best entertainment, the best health care, you name it... but at what expense? There had to be a trail back to a motivation beyond living the good life.

I wanted to hit the sheets before I hit the streets, but my mind was too far out of frame. No time for R.E.M. For a moment I wondered if the trinity of my mind, body and soul would ever be in sync, or if I was destined to a lifetime of serving one at a time, but never together. If I looked at my dad as an example of what was to come, my path would be the latter.

38

I HEARD MY mom tiptoeing around to leave for work at five in the morning. I waited patiently, and when the door shut behind her, that was my cue. I loaded my backpack with the essentials: toothbrush, a few pairs of underwear, some Mexican cacao and alkaline water. I paused to make sure I had everything. Oh, yeah, I needed a Vitamin E melt for the flight. No more split lower lip for this girl. Killer watched me like a hawk. I avoided eye contact because I didn't want to feel or feed his anxiety. I knew what I had to do so that we could be together again soon.

Some people had already been allowed to bring their animals into Seneca, but I'd never seen them because they weren't in the S.E.R.C., restaurant or youth residential sectors. It was said they allowed pets because of the great happiness they brought people, and that happiness, along with safety, health and peace were the ultimate goals of The Seneca Society. I bought into all of that but also believed it was only possible to have all those things in Seneca, if I was with the people I loved (and Killer, too, of course!)

To me, the one exception to Seneca's controlled population and DNA differentiation quotas was keeping people who loved each other together. Sure, they told us that, after a generation or two, the compromises initially made by the first Senecans would no longer be necessary. But this, in particular, was just not a compromise I was willing to make.

I was flexerless, so I scraped my secret cash stashes together to have just enough to cab it to my favorite little flexer store in Century City. I was there when the store turned its lights on. The bottom of the line version of my old flexer would be all I needed to enable retrieval of my Veil data and pull as much money out of the bank as possible.

Next stop— the bank. The bank teller was caught completely off guard when he saw how much money I had in my account. It wasn't every day they saw a teenage girl walk into a bank in a Nirvana t-shirt, backpack and headphones with over a million in her name. I had only wired that much in from my Cayman Islands account. Imagine the look on his face had he seen the whole two plus billion.

"Um, this needs my branch manager's clearance. I can't authorize a withdrawal of this size."

I had to get that cash, stat. I felt the beginnings of hot feet.

"No worries."

He walked over to a young woman who looked up at me and smiled as she came toward me.

"Hi there, Miss Campbell. We just want to make sure we take

appropriate care of your account, since you're such an important client. I'm sure you understand."

"Oh for sure, I get it. Thank you..." I eyed her name tag... "Sandra."

Her brows lifted as she scanned the numbers on the screen in front of her. "You must have quite the career going for you."

"I can't complain."

"My daughter wants to get into acting. Anything you would recommend so that she can find the kind of success you have?"

Okay. Time to play the child actor card without being a complete liar. Obviously that's the only way she could explain someone my age amassing that kind of money.

"Hard work and determination."

"Amen." She looked over my withdrawal information I had input via flexer. "You want to withdraw twenty thousand dollars, I see."

"Mmm hmm."

I downplayed it and crossed my fingers that she would just do it and stop asking questions.

"I can give you nineteen thousand and ninety-nine dollars right now, but if you want twenty thousand you'll have to wait until tomorrow since that's over the limit for a same day withdrawal."

"Nineteen thousand and ninety-nine dollars is good." My voice went a few notches higher than normal.

"Come over to the side and I'll buzz you in. We'll count this out for you and send you on your way."

I nodded, smiled, "Great, thank you."

Once she'd counted out my bills, she added, "If I could give you my daughter's e-mail address..."

I happily obliged and left with a backpack full of cash and the e-mail address of a twelve-year-old girl who wanted to be a famous actress. Next stop, LAX.

39

WITH ALL THAT money handy I could buy a BoomJet ticket to New York City, an expense my parents probably wouldn't have approved of. Still, I needed to use the short travel time for a catnap, and the economy cabin just wasn't the place for that, all claustrophobic and full of crying babies. Plus, this was no vacation— I was on a mission. My justifications for spending all that money played over and over like a broken record in my head as I waited to buy my ticket. Yet, somehow, I still felt guilty for being a spendthrift when there were billions of people in need out there.

I was over the guilt thing by the time I arrived in the Big Apple. It was late afternoon. I took a flighter taxi in, and landed on the Lower East Side. I had traced Dom to a small shop called Berserk Boots, at what was probably an after school job. The store appeared to be one of the last original spots still standing in a hood that had been thoroughly gentrified before I'd even been born. Chic, environmentally efficient construction was juxtaposed with classic pre-war architecture, giving off a polished noir feel. Manhattan was a ghetto for the rich; everyone with less than a million in the bank had been pushed off the island and into the outlying boroughs. Retail chain domination had finally laid claim to one of the last cool hoods in Manhattan. It was a miracle that a place like Georgetown had managed to preserve its classic beauty and charm.

People were packed into these streets like sardines. I wondered how, even if the progress developed in Seneca were to extend to the rest of the world, how the over-population situation would be handled. While everything I did in Seneca was about looking toward the future, standing there on the Lower East Side of Manhattan, my attention was on the now. Dom probably had acclimated nicely into an after school work routine, and I was about to flood that world like a tsunami.

I popped a piece of cacao and stopped into a corner café before going into Berserk Boots. I knew I was stalling. I was scared that Dom wouldn't recognize me, but realized it was something we both had to go through. It wouldn't have worked to shock him with a memory block removal while he was in the middle of a school day, at work with a customer, or enjoying a family dinner. My approach had to be responsible, clean.

I walked out of the café with my mocha, mesmerized by cinematic views of the Brooklyn Bridge nearby– such a stark contrast to the flat, beige cement bridges of Los Angeles. I stood there a while, across the street from Berserk Boots, slurping the last traces of what I'd begun to think of as my "security" beverage. It was November, and freezing cold in New York. After being in a controlled climate for the past several months and southern California my entire life, my thin blood wasn't prepared for the shock. Most of the people who walked by were too wrapped up in their own thoughts to notice me, but the few that did gave me the most hilarious range of looks for being out in nothing but a t-shirt.

"Hey." A woman approached me. Are you okay? Do you need some help?"

My teeth chattered. "I'm good, thanks."

"You sure? You look like you could use a hand."

"I just got here from Cali and I've never been here before so I didn't think it would be so flippin' cold."

She smiled, and then took off her jacket and a sweater from underneath. "You look like a nice kid. Take this. No point in getting sick on your first trip to New York."

"Oh no, you don't have to."

"Please." She pushed the sweater into my hands. Being cold sucked, so I took it.

"You just remember that the people of New York aren't the rude jerks we're always painted to be."

"I will."

She smiled, threw her jacket back on, and skipped across the street with three seconds left on the crosswalk sign.

"Thank you!" I called after her. She turned back, waved, then disappeared into the crowd.

It was always nice to be reminded by a random act of kindness that people were inherently good. I bit down on the lid to hold my coffee cup between my teeth while I put the sweater on. It was gray, long to my knees, soft like a teddy bear and warm from being worn. It smelled like the incense Julie's mom was always burning to cover up the smell of her weed so she wouldn't be a bad influence on us 'under-agers'. Little did she know that in our world of Mojo Sticks, the archaic Reefer Madness should've been the least of her concerns.

I was all warmed up now – the invisible force I needed to push me across the street. Through the store window, I saw the outlines of two figures. One of them was tall and built from dreamboat material. I literally sensed the handsomeness emanating from that simple silhouette. I'd found my guy.

I tossed my cup in the trash, pulled the door open without hesitation and stepped inside. A little electronic bell sounded. Dom glanced over his shoulder and spotted me, but didn't stop stocking boxes on a shelf near the back of the store. A short and stout man, about thirty, with a chunky, poorly groomed beard and matching meaty glasses, greeted me. "Welcome. Looking for a pair of boots or just some warm air?"

"Just looking."

"Name's Eric if you want to see something in your size."

"Thanks."

I pretended to look at some boots as I inched along the wall towards the back of the store. Of course I wasn't paying attention, walked right into a footstool and stumbled, nearly hitting the ground. Dom quickly dropped the box he was holding and rushed to help me. "You okay?" He bent down and offered his hand. For a moment, I froze.

Snapping out of it, I stammered, "Yes, sorry, I'm such a klutz," and accepted his hand.

"Don't be sorry. Someone falls over this particular footstool at least once a day."

We were eye to eye as he helped me up. Electricity gushed between my soul and his. I didn't want to let go of his hand. I was speechless, like the first time we had met.

"You looking for some winter boots?"

"Boots! Yes. Exactly."

Dominic Ambrosia may have ignited my heart, but ours wasn't a fairytale story– not yet, anyway. We were stuck in a no man's land, somewhere between blossoming young love and Shakespearean tragedy. My heart raced, knowing at the same time that his had flatlined. He'd been altered to forget everything we'd had. Everything *he'd* had in the past two years as a Senecan. That avalanche of bliss dissipated as anger stormed in and occupied the void. How could they do this to him? To us?

"Let me show you a pair I think would be perfect for you."

"Thanks."

Dom sidestepped down a few rows to a pair of saddle brown leather boots with intricate stitching. "A bit steep on the price tag, but you look like you're worth it."

Was Dom flirting with me?

"Hey, you poaching my client over there, Ambrosia?"

Dammit, here came the dumpy guy ready to crush my boot-buying moment with Dom.

"Me, poach? Never."

I rushed to Dom's defense, "No, no, I just asked him to show me these boots."

"I'll take it from here."

Dom gave Eric a little nod barely concealing his annoyance, and then turned to me. "You're in good hands with Eric here. He knows his boots."

And just like that, Dom turned his attention to stocking the shelves.

"What are you, a seven? Eight?"

"Seven and a half."

"Baddabing! Let me get you the right size. Take a seat here and I'll be right back." Eric disappeared into the back room.

Dom looked over at me and mouthed, "Sorry."

I mouthed back, "It's okay." Just being around Dom made me feel strong. Confident. I kept my eyes locked on his. The magnetism was just the same as the first moment I'd seen him. Then, I wanted to know him. Now, I wanted him to know me... again. He squinted a little and bit the inside of his lip. Our moment lingered, but then he went back to what he was doing without giving me a second glance.

I didn't know how much more of this I could take. I watched

him working diligently at his job. Whatever he did, he did with all of his heart. Not even a week ago, he was fully dedicated to the unearthing of an evil within our society and now, he brought the same concentration to meticulously stacking shoeboxes was his world.

Eric brought out the boots and helped me put them on. They were actually perfect. And Dom had picked them out for me. "I'll take 'em."

I left the store wearing the boots. Dom never gave me a wave or anything. It hurt, even though I knew it wasn't about me.

40

THERE WAS A bus stop with a bench a half a block down from Berserk Boots. I would wait forever if it took that long for Dom to get off work. Fortunately, I was comfortable in my new, old sweater and my new boots chosen by Dom but I was still pretty anxious. The bus shelter was packed, so I had to wait for the next bus to come and that crowd to go, before I could snag a seat. I sat there for two hours and didn't take my eyes off of the shop door. As the wind picked up, it howled between the skyscrapers like coyotes back home in the canyons.

I let my mind drift to the steep, dusty terrain at Will Rogers State Park, where my Dad and I used to hike together at sunset. Even though remembering my dad made me sad, it brought me fortitude. He always had inspired me to overcome my fears. He'd climb ahead up a steep trail and then turn back to help me up, not by offering a hand, but with words. He empowered me to believe in myself. "Turn your feet sideways as you climb and lean forward. Make sure you get a grip with your feet before each step you take." He knew I could do it before I believed I could. And then I would try. Before I knew it I was up. When we got to the top of the trail, we were rewarded with an unending panorama of the Pacific. The curvature of the earth grounded me. It made me feel alive and revived.

At seven on the dot, Dom came out. I jumped up and let out a yelp of excitement. A few people at the bus stop gave me funny looks, but I couldn't have cared less.

Dom headed south and I tracked him from the other side of the street. As soon as there was a break in traffic, I skipped across to his side. He moved fast, with a "places to be" sort of stride, but he couldn't have kicked me off his trail if he'd tried.

I was about fifteen feet behind him, clutching my flexer, eager and ready to make my move. I was in the zone. Even the chaotic urban soundscape didn't throw me off. In fact, it played to my energy. I was exhilarated. My new boots hit the sidewalk in sync with each heartbeat. The wind had picked up even more and deep-sea blue washed the salmon-colored sky away as twilight rolled in. The moon rose in the east as the sun slid beyond the skyline on the opposite side of the Brooklyn Bridge.

Dom flipped his hoodie up as he hit the walkways on the bridge. We trekked straight down the middle, elevated slightly above the automobile traffic. I picked up my pace, just a few people behind him now. My entire body vibrated, my vision blurred with each thump of my heart.

Dom stopped in his tracks. The flow of foot traffic kept up around him like he was a rock in rapids. I came to a halt. He spun around. I was busted. But I wanted to be. I needed to be. My muscles relaxed. Here we were. Car horns, engine noises, footsteps, the flowing East River, boats cutting through the water below us, a helicopter in the distance... it all faded away as Dom stared me down, taking a particularly long beat on my boots before returning to my eyes.

"It's you."

"It's me." I took a step towards him. He took a step back.

"Why are you following me?"

"I know this is going to sound crazy, but you and me– we actually know each other."

"No, not crazy at all." His words didn't match his body language.

I grinned at his sarcasm that I had missed so much and took another step towards him.

"Not another step!"

"Okay, understandable request– please just hear me out."

"Fine, but from right there."

It was as if the old paranoia I'd seen in the early days was still alive somewhere, inhabiting a different part of his brain.

"Your parents must love having you home. Are they still involved with the anti-whaling movement?"

His eyes and lips scrunched up. "What do you know about my parents?"

"I know they love you enough to let you go to Japan for school. I know they fight for what they believe in, and you get that from them. It's really admirable."

"Alright, you're *really* creeping me out right now."

There was a degree of humor to his confusion, while at the same time it really wasn't funny at all. And I was scared. Was my attempt at removing the memory block going to work, or would it all be a grand failure right here on the Brooklyn Bridge?

"I hope I can change that."

I slowly lifted my flexer. Dom watched me intently. His body tightened, on guard. My fingers were numb from the cold, but the rest of my body burned up. My feet tingled and itched, my legs shook. I could see my breath in the air, coming in hard, quick spurts. Dom's was much more controlled as he consciously breathed through his nose. The coding was set to go on my flexer. All I needed to do now was give the command, and the memory block that had been placed on him would be removed. I looked at my flexer screen and tapped the purple "enter" symbol.

My screen went blank. And then it read, "**command accepted**." I slowly looked up.

Dom's bottom lip hung slightly open. The awareness in his eyes, pinned to mine, deepened by the second. He tilted his head ever so slightly and pulled his lips together. They quivered. In my humble little existence, this felt like The Big Bang. It was as if I stood on the verge of a whole new universe being created. Would we inflate into a cosmic singularity or would everything vanish permanently into a black hole?

I didn't say a word but waited as something organic and true brewed before me in that one-of-a-kind spongy sphere located between Dom's two ears.

He was fixated on me as tears welled up in his eyes. Then he came towards me, and before I even had a chance to blink, his lips were pressed against mine. I closed my eyes and didn't move, paralyzed– in a good way this time, a *really* good way. The ruckus around us vanished. His cold hands tempered the heat that radiated from my face and I fell into a wave of electricity. This kiss was voltaic. My head spun. My stomach dropped. Energy traveled fiercely between our lips. But we were still. And then his bottom lip trembled against mine. I pushed in more, to comfort him. Our lips fused into one, and I was only reminded that we were two separate beings when his hands slowly spread wide across my face and slid down to my shoulders. He pulled me into his enveloping universe, his arms around me. The seal between our lips came undone in slow motion. My eyes were still shut, as I hung onto that moment with every piece of me. His breath was short and quick. I raised my hand up to his chest, our foreheads pressed together. His heartbeat was even faster than mine. I kept my hand there as it slowed. He moved his cheek against mine and he whispered, "Thank you."

41

THIS MOMENT WITH Dom and me on the Brooklyn Bridge was exactly why they say you should be in "the now." Neither the past nor the future mattered. But, moments like that, feelings like that, have to be fleeting. We couldn't expect the world to stop for our passions to unfold. So, it was time to tell him everything. I didn't know where to begin. He did–

"How did you find me?"

"After you were banished to the Aboves, I had to do something. I had to figure out what they were computing with those blood nanobots. I snuck back into your lab, and S.O.I.L. caught me, but not before I found my way into the mainframe. Not just to your data, but to everyone's in Seneca."

"You're incredible."

Dom wasn't shocked. He was impressed.

I started to blush as a new realization dawned on him, "My flexer."

"Don't worry, I re-routed our flexers to piggyback randomized flexers. We're good."

He looked over my shoulder. I saw a terror in his eyes, and turned to see two men running down the bridge, straight towards us. We weren't good. They weren't in blue, but we knew they were S.O.I.L. I looked back at Dom. He was peering down at the road below– two matte black SUVs were right below, trailing us. He grabbed my hand and we took off towards Brooklyn.

"Stay with me!"

I grasped his hand tight, weaving through throngs of foot traffic on the bridge. The SUVs cruised right alongside us. I turned to look behind us. S.O.I.L. was closing in. We were no physical match for what were probably two former Navy Seals.

"Don't look back! Just keep up with me, Doro!"

No choice but to rally my hidden inner-athlete. Wait, there wasn't one. I had to trust Dom to get us out of here. We were nearing the end of the bridge when he abruptly stopped. A matte black flighter hovered ahead of us. Dom looked back, the S.O.I.L. officers were twenty-five yards away, sprinting toward us at full speed. "Hold my hand, don't let go."

I looked down. It was a really long daredevil drop to the water. It seemed like our only option. Beads of sweat beaded along my hairline and trickled down my temples.

"Come on!" Dom hollered as he clambered up onto a steel plank that extended above the roadway below. "Watch your step." I followed, petrified. Now I was in a full body sweat. I had always prided myself on being gutsy, but this was way out of my league. If we fall, we die. I wasn't ready to die. "You got this,

Doro!"

We were directly above the Brooklyn Bridge traffic that moved at roughly twenty miles per hour. My heart raced, my adrenaline cranked.

"It's now or never."

He wanted me to jump.

"You're kidding, right?"

"Do I look like I'm kidding?"

I tightened my grip on his hand. The S.O.I.L. officers closed the gap, now ten feet away, "Stop where you are!"

"1-2-3 go!" He bellowed.

We jumped! As we crashed onto the road below, cars swerved to dodge us. Dom took my shoulders and forced me behind him, protecting me from oncoming traffic. I screamed bloody murder. Not in a million years, or even my craziest dreams, did I picture myself doing something this insane. I clenched my eyes closed as the sound of horns zooming by freaked me out. I desperately wanted it to end.

"I got you, Doro! Stay with me!" I put all my trust in him, but that didn't stop the sheer terror I felt. I could conquer any computation system, but this physical test was too much. I was standing in the middle of oncoming traffic, on top of a bridge, in the looming darkness. What was next? I couldn't keep myself from crying.

"Okay, focus! Look at me, Doro, look at me!"

I looked up at him through the haziness of tears streaking

down the side of my face. My mouth was dry and lips chapped from the force of wind. Dom darted his eyes to the plank where we had just stood. The S.O.I.L. officers weren't walking out onto it like we so recklessly had. Instead they peered down at us as they communicated to someone on a flexer.

Dom shouted so I could hear him, but he was calm. "Run as fast as you ever have."

"I can't!"

"You can! Just hold my hand and stay on this yellow line." His look channeled courage my way. I gritted my teeth, forced myself to stop crying and let out the most unattractive, guttural call for power. I heard my dad's voice reminding me I had this, and knew I could do this on my own. I didn't need his hand, but I kept our grip because I wanted him to know he had my trust. We ran full steam ahead between the lanes of oncoming traffic.

Cars screeched out of the way. People yelled from their windows, but nothing could stop us. An irate man jumped out from a driver's seat, "Are you kids insane?!"

I was riding my adrenaline now.

We ran the way we'd come, back into Manhattan. Dom slowed to a stop. He kept a hold of my arm. I was amped up. "Ahhh! That was the craziest thing I've ever done!"

"We're just warming up!" Dom's tenacity ignited me.

We both turned at the sound of wheels screeching. The two SUV's were coming back down the bridge against oncoming traffic, smashing into any car that didn't move out of their indignant path. The S.O.I.L. men on foot were trying to push through dense foot traffic to get back down the bridge too.

We scanned our surroundings.

The matte black flighter swooped in and hovered just above us. A suicide door lifted on the shotgun side. It was Gregory. Dangerously deadpan, he shouted out above the din, "You're wasting your energy."

My last meeting with Gregory certainly hadn't been the most pleasant, and now it couldn't have been more glaring that his mission was to mute us permanently.

"And *you're* wasting *your* time," I retorted, nudging Dom to follow me. I bolted down onto the bike and footpath that ran along the bank of the East River, and away from Gregory.

The rising lights of the city illuminated our path on the greenway. The trees still held just enough fall foliage of deep orange, magenta and maroon to block the flighter's view, and we had lost the SUVs– we thought. We hoped. One mile down, we panted for breath.

We reached a bumping barbecue of about thirty young professionals, eating, drinking and having a good time and tried to blend in with them— not the easiest task when you're in the fight of your life. The flighter was just overhead. In a desperate effort to camouflage ourselves further, Dom and I dove down and huddled beneath one of the recycled plastic picnic tables speckled along the river. The flighter continued along the path down the river. For a few seconds we thought we were in the clear, but then it stopped about a hundred yards down from where we crouched and just hovered there.

"Looks like we got us some underage party crashers!" Leave it to a drunk guy in a suit to call us out. We looked like a couple of jail-breaking orphans hiding under that picnic table. A few people laughed and offered us beers. Others told us to get lost.

The flighter busted a U, apparently figuring that we couldn't have made it in the other direction. It began to creep back our way.

I spotted a gas station through the trees across the street. "I have an idea, come on!"

Dom and I gave one another quick nods and climbed out from under the picnic table. He grabbed a freshly opened bottle of water right out of a guy's hand—

"Hey!"

And we ran.

We made it to the station. Sharing the water, we looked back to see the flighter landing alongside the barbecue on the riverbank.

Every pump at the gas station was in use. I scanned each one and picked up on the oldest car in the lot— a little white Toyota Prius from just after the turn of the millennium.

"Oh man." Dom said. His attention was on people from the barbecue who pointed in our direction. Gregory was there, standing outside the flighter, looking at the gas station through night vision binoculars. We ducked down behind the Prius.

"Psst, hey!"

A guy in his late twenties put the gas nozzle back on its pump. "Nope, sorry, don't have any money. Isn't that obvious?" He motioned to his old clunker. It was worth its weight in gold to Dom and me.

"Let me change that." I reached into my backpack and pulled out the wad of cash.

The stranger's eyes widened incredulously. "Whoa," he and Dom exclaimed in unison.

"What's it worth to you?"

"Well I paid almost a grand for it six months ago, and just spent three fifty filling up, sooo..."

"How's five grand?"

42

THANK GOODNESS THE car was automatic, because I'd only driven a few times before. With Dom in shotgun I pushed away from the gas station in an automotive relic that reeked of stale corn chips and dirty old coins. It was nowhere near as fun as piloting a flighter, but it was the perfect disguise for us. S.O.I.L would never imagine us driving at all, no mind in a vintage heap like this.

"Which way to the closest tunnel out of Manhattan?"

"Bust a right."

My vision was glued to the road in front of me and nothing else. I left navigation and S.O.I.L. lookout duty entirely up to Dom. He sat forward in his seat, rubbed at his buzz cut and examined the streets and skies in every direction. "They're tracking us, Doro. It may feel okay now, but this can't end well for us."

"Whoa, hold on. It's not over yet–"

"I wish I could believe we have a chance, it's just that I know what they're capable of."

"Don't worry, I have a plan."

"Oh yeah? You gonna share? Take a left."

I took a left into tunnel traffic stopped dead. I hit the breaks hard and fast. "Easy!" Dom smashed into the dash– he wasn't wearing a seat belt.

"Sorry. Just getting the hang of this whole driving thing."

"Awesome. Perfect timing for driver's ed."

"Right?"

He put his seatbelt on and braced himself in the seat with a smirk– an absolutely, mesmerizing smirk. As much as I wanted to get moving as fast as possible, being stuck there meant that my sore eyes could get a recharge on Dom.

Something in that moment felt so incredibly good. It was the first relaxed moment we'd shared since laughing together on the floor in his secret sushi lab. Mojo sticking might have its followers, but this was all I needed– just Dom, me, and a little bit of laughter. Oh, and another kiss wouldn't hurt.

There were no shady matte black flighters or SUVs anywhere in sight. That gave me the peace of mind I needed. For now. I stared down a square barrel of geometrical genius– the Brooklyn-Battery Tunnel. We inched our way in with the droves of gridlocked commuters. It was like entering a civil engineering time warp. Other than the cars that passed through it and the lighting power source, nothing had changed since it was built, circa the mid 1900's.

Dom and I settled into a much-needed shared silence, lulled

by the transitory effect of the cool, hollow tunnel vibrations. Neither of us spoke a word on the five-minute ride to the other end. I tried to process what had just happened and pondered what was to come. It hit me at every angle: external and internal, emotional, physiological and psychological.

We emerged into a gray rainbow stone landscape. Brooklyn, New York. Despite the absence of color, I started to feel revitalized. Manhattan might have had a glorious past, but now it just could not deliver the way it had in its heyday. Now the inimitable New York City energy had taken up residence in its boroughs.

We drove alongside an illuminated wall of speckled gray granite into which was smoothly etched the emblem of a robed young woman carrying a small bundle of sticks and the saying, "*Eendraght Maeckt Maght*". Above it, the American flag majestically flapped in the salient fall winds. "In unity there is strength," Dom enunciated in a tone just above a whisper. I wondered how many languages he could speak.

And then, without hesitation, he reached over and rested his hand on my thigh. A tingling sensation spread up and down my leg but I hoped it wasn't obvious. There was still some unresolved stuff with the whole McKayla-at-the-party thing, and I still didn't really know how he felt. The very thought of it stuck a fork in the tingle, which was good, I guess, because I needed to keep focused on my plan of action. I couldn't let this gaga-eyed side of me fog up the clear line I'd concocted to get us where we needed to go.

"We should be able to make it to Seneca by sunrise if we drive through the night."

"Seneca? That's your plan? To take us into the eye of the storm?" Dom was eons from sold. He pulled his hand back to his lap, and that mellowness he had acquired in the tunnel vanished just like that.

"I know it sounds crazy, but it's the only way."

"It doesn't *sound* crazy. It *is* crazy. We can't."

"We have no other choice. We can't hide. S.O.I.L. will find us. Now that you're with me and you know as much as I do, we need to get back inside Seneca City."

Out of the corner of my eye I could see Dom bite into the side of his lip.

"Let's hear it."

This was big, coming from Dom. He always followed his own plans, and nobody else's. It felt good that he would consider my plan.

"But, I'm only listening on one condition."

"What's that?"

"I drive."

So much for Dom feeling comfortable with me driving.

"Don't take it personally. I hate being in a car. If I'm not driving, I'll have even more anxiety on top of the anxiety I already have."

We pulled over and swiftly executed a Chinese fire drill.

Dom meticulously positioned his seat and mirrors for the long journey ahead. The immediate plan was to continue down through Brooklyn, across Staten Island and head south on one of the most traveled interstates in the United States– 95.

I pulled my flexer out. "Okay, first things first, I need to flex Ellen Malone. She's the only one I can trust–"

"Wait!"

Dom threw his right hand across me, knocking my flexer against the window.

I gasped. "What the–!"

"I'm sorry."

I didn't know what to say. I fished in the side door pocket where my flexer had landed.

"I'm sorry, Doro, that was a defense reflex. I didn't mean to scare you, but we can't trust Ellen Malone."

All along, Ellen had been nothing but good to me. She had earned my trust and I felt genuinely connected to her. She'd shown time and again that she cared for, and wanted the best for me. And from our conversations at Ty's sushi spot, it seemed Dom and Ty were on the same page with me on this.

"That night. The party..." Dom's voice started to shake, "I was invited to a party at Brittany Gilroy's place in Georgetown by this girl, McKayla Gordon."

My skin crawled. Sickness brewed in my gut, but I sucked it up and waited. I was glad he was opening up. The mystery of that night had plagued me since it went down. I wanted him to tell me everything, no matter how much it was going to hurt. He had no idea that I'd been there, that I had seen him... that I knew McKayla Gordon and couldn't stand her, even more so after I saw her clawing at him that night.

"We have session together and she's always real flirty."

My stomach turned with disgust, my temperature began to rise. I had to get these boots off or they would trap the heat inside and, next thing you know, I'd be all red and sweaty. Not good. I pried them off.

"I mean, I try to be nice about it, but that girl is persistent, let me tell you. I've known her since I came to Seneca and she's never let up. She even forced her way into being my lab partner in session."

"Obnoxious." I had to let that one slip.

"Pretty much. I honestly had zero interest in hanging out with her, but after the week I'd had, I thought getting to the Aboves would be a great escape from it all. I could have cared less about some party, I just wanted to breathe real air, you know? It's just so suffocating down there sometimes. As incredible as it is, I still can't wrap my head around spending forever there."

"I'm right there with you."

"Well, McKayla was the means to getting me to the Aboves, so I took her up on it. That turned out to be a terrible decision."

Relief flooded over me and I let forgiveness move in. I'd let what I'd seen that night at the party drive me crazy when I hadn't even heard the truth from Dom himself. My life experiences had conditioned me to brace for the worse as a defense mechanism. Maybe it was time I reprogrammed myself like I'd reprogrammed the nanobots. I made a silent vow to give people the benefit of the doubt, and have faith in possibilities.

"I was in a pretty desolate area of Japan when the whole Mojo Stick movement hit the big cities. I came straight to Seneca from jail in Japan so I was never around it. I'd never gotten into them in Seneca, and when I saw people doing them at the party and I thought to myself, "There is no way." I never even want to get drunk or anything like that because I just don't like the idea of not knowing what's going on around me. Turns out, I didn't have a choice. I felt a prick that instantly numbed my arm and that was it."

"Are you serious? Someone drugged you?!" Even though it completely sucked for him, I have to admit that I was relieved he hadn't made a choice to get Mojo'd out with McKayla. Part of me felt guilty for feeling that way, but I couldn't help it.

"Yep."

"I can't even imagine. Who was it, McKayla?"

"Thing is, I don't even know."

"That is so random."

"Something tells me it wasn't all that random considering whose house we were at."

"Brittany Gilroy?"

"Brittany Gilroy's dad used to be U.S. senator who's now the Seneca Northwestern hemisphere ambassador to the

Southwestern hemisphere. There are all sorts of crazy rumors about what's going on down there."

"Hmm. Okay. I still don't get why someone there would drug you with a Mojo Stick."

"You just never know the tricks these people have up their sleeves to keep everyone from asking too many difficult questions. All I know is that Mojo Stick prick ended with me being banished to the Aboves."

"Hmm, right."

I let it sink in. He still didn't know how spot on his suspicions were. It looked to me that he'd been labeled a troublemaker and set up with the Mojo Stick injection to get him out of Seneca.

"I'm not gonna lie, I felt insanely phenomenal at that party..."

And *I'm* not gonna lie, even though I felt horrible for Dom, my curiosity was piqued.

"I was flying. I melted into the air and rode the vibrations like I was on a magic carpet made of silk."

"I still don't see how Ellen connects to all of this."

"For a while I didn't have a worry in the world. It was amazing for all of an hour, two, shoot, I have no idea how long. But then a wave of chaos hit the party. I didn't know what was going on, I couldn't even move my mouth to form words. I seriously lost my mind, Doro. The last thing I can remember, was being rushed by McKayla into a flighter that was piloted by someone from S.O.I.L... and Ellen Malone was riding shotgun."

My stomach lurched. Ellen must have known Dom wasn't in

the flighter crash if she'd seen him that night after it happened. She definitely knew something about his disappearance, and she would have known it when we went to dinner in the restaurant sector during lockdown. Dom didn't know that they had pinned the flighter crash on him. In fact, he didn't even know about the crash at all. I couldn't bring myself to tell him. It would destroy him. I needed him to maintain any iota of optimism that he still had about Seneca.

"We'll get to the bottom of it." I tried to come across as resolved, but even I could hear the tremble in my voice.

I kept talking. "That's why I need your trust"

Dom took a breath. "Alright, boss... lay it on me."

I turned to face Dom as he drove. "Spinal flexer implants. You and me."

"No thanks."

"I've coded our flexer chips for connection to the entire Seneca network. If we become one unit with our computers, and our computers have the information that can reach every Senecan on the planet..."

Dom's posture tensed as he leaned towards the wheel, chewing on the inside of his bottom lip.

"You know how dangerous spinal flexer injections are?"

"I do."

"There's a reason they're illegal."

"I think we're past what's legal and what's illegal at this point."

"True."

Dom sat back and so did I. A spinal flexer injection wasn't something you did off the cuff. It was dangerous physically and the implications of it were far-reaching. I could see his mind sorting through all the logical scenarios, and saw the easing of his neck as he came to the same conclusion I had. "My family friend has a self-sustained farm outside Charlottesville. Completely off the grid. About two hours by car to Claytor Lake. If we can go see her, I think she'll be able to help us."

"Can we trust her?"

"Absolutely. Anika Clark, she saved my grandmother's life. Thirty years ago when the government started regulating the flex medical movement and renegade doctors started going underground, this woman was one of the first. She used cellular reprogramming and ancient Chinese medicine to cure my grandmother's breast cancer. And my grandmother is still alive at a hundred and one."

"Incredible."

"It is. My family is super tied into the whole hack doc community."

"So, does this mean you're with me?"

Next thing I knew, we were cruising down the highway, under the night sky, psyching ourselves up for the mission of our lives.

43

THE EASTERN SEABOARD had taken a beating over the past several decades, and until now I'd only witnessed it via the news. The most recent tropical storm, Hurricane Molly, had left the majority of the coastline from Maryland down through Virginia, the Carolinas, Georgia and Florida, in a state of emergency. This was the biggest storm on record since these parts had been settled.

The absence of moonlight made it harder to see the scenery along the highway, but I didn't mind, because it was such a nice contrast to the urine-colored blaze that had replaced LA's night sky so many years before. As the morning light began its slow fade-in, the weather-battered land became more and more evident. An overturned water tower nestled, abandoned, in a bed of weeds. A massive uprooted oak tree had taken out half of a gas station.

Only those places rich in private financial reserves had enough resources to repair the damage in the affected areas. And those communities were few and far between. The government had nothing to give and nobody to borrow from. And now I knew that the resources that could have saved these areas were being channeled into Seneca instead. My Country, 'Tis of Thee' was being left in the dust. It was depressing, really, but I tamed my emotion, and recognized that the cyclical nature of empires, and even species, were amply illustrated by the history of the rest of the world. Now it was America's turn.

After Maryland, we crossed through a cool, cobalt Washington, D.C., in its wee hours, and then on to Northern Virginia. We traveled against the flow of the morning commuters ascending from the exurbs in sync with the rising sun. Below a golden tree-tufted horizon, prisms of amber morning light bounced between the stream of flighters in the air and the cars moving slowly on the roads beneath them; the two socioeconomic groups were connected whether they liked it or not. Dom and I were starving now, our stomachs running on empty.

We pit-stopped at a gas station in Front Royal, Virginia to use the bathroom and grab a snack. This was a town stuck in the past. Strips of one-and two-story red brick office buildings and warehouses, dormant apple orchards and sprawling horse farms. Four lane roads. Old time yellow traffic lights on posts. Ironic as it is, Front Royal is Virginia's main Smart Road hub. Football-field size solar awnings covered the communication towers and generators that powered the automated vehicles.

At a classic, "you pump, you pay," gas station Dom and I

agreed to take turns waiting at the car to keep a lookout, just in case. Dom awkwardly danced his way inside, trying to withstand the pressure of a near-bursting bladder.

He came back, relieved. My turn. I thought nobody was in the gas station except the cashier but then I saw some old lady in the aisle reading the label on a pack of vita-melts. Ancient country music was playing. Patsy Cline. A muted monitor with the news was on behind the FlexPay hub. Local weather report– 30 degrees.

I hit the bathroom. As I headed back out, I looked straight at the cashier. There was just something about him. The guy was about fifty years old with thick gray hair, weathered reddish-brown skin, shielded by a layer of red-gray stubble. A toothpick dangled from his mouth. A dark blue and white striped button-up, sleeves rolled above his leathery elbows, this was a man who had clearly worked his whole life to provide for someone, somewhere, who loved him, like I loved my dad. There was a sparkle in his eye as he smiled and nodded at me. I grinned back.

Then, behind him on a screen, something snagged my attention. Side-by-side pictures of Dom and me, captioned with, "Runaway teenagers in extreme danger. Please report to authorities." I froze, tried to keep from choking and jetted out to the car, not giving a second glance at the cashier I left in my dust.

44

"GUN IT!" I was panting, but he was right there with me and didn't ask a thing until we'd peeled out of the station.

"What is it?!"

The Prius took off up the circular highway entrance ramp.

"The search– it's gone full force."

"How?"

Before I had the chance to answer, an ominous buzz rained down on us. Through the rear windshield we saw a swarm of twelve football-size helicopter drones headed straight for us. We hit the friction of the shoulder.

Dom whipped his head back around, gripped the wheel and swerved off the shoulder back onto black, nearly nailing a freight truck as we merged onto the highway. My head spun between hanging on as we wove in and out of traffic and tracking the swarm of drones that was closing in behind us.

Panic alarms were going off in my head, but at the same time I focused on my conscious agenda. I could run codes to change any quantum computing system in the world, and this was the time I needed to make it happen.

Game time.

"Gun it! I'll get us connected to these suckers."

"Doro–"

"Just drive, Dom, I got this!"

And he did, as I huddled over my flexer and locked into the zone. I smashed through screen after screen, feverishly drilling code into the communication-crowded airwaves, determined to access the network those drones were on. They had multi-layered shields on them, but I just kept pounding, trying every access code I could. Pain radiated up my forearm. I shook my right hand to ward off the burning onset of Carpal Tunnel.

Dom careened through cars and trucks doing about fifty now with the drones right behind us. Dizziness set in as my eyes went from the road to my flexer.

"Ughh." I squeezed the bridge of my nose.

"What, what?!"

"I'm just a little car sick."

Dom gave me a look that might have been comical if the whole situation hadn't been so crazy. He yanked the wheel to squeeze between two cars to the clear lane on the far right.

Pop! "Ahhh!" Dom shouted as one of our rear tires was shot out and we skidded back across two lanes. A horn blared as the truck it was attached to swerved to miss us. Dom tugged at the wheel as he gunned it. Sixty miles per hour and climbing, the awol tire's metal rim grinding into the asphalt.

The drones flew out in front of us. A red beam shot down on each of our faces. Dom tried to swerve out of the beam, but it was locked on us. I didn't take focus off my flexer, "Just a few more–"

"We don't have a few more!" Dom yelled.

Sparks spewed up from the tire rim.

Boom! I was in the drone network. "Got it!" I'd cracked their code, and reprogrammed them to take command from my flexer.

Pop! Another tire blew– the front left. The car screeched back across the highway and rammed the rail on the inner shoulder. Dom yanked the steering wheel the other way and the car fishtailed, flipped up onto its driver's side, slid about ten yards, then slammed down, landing on its roof and skidding about thirty yards more before coming to a stop, upside down in a ditch.

My hair swept the car's ceiling as I twisted my head to get my bearings. I peered in Dom's direction. He'd been super jostled by the impact, and had been knocked out but was coming to. "Dom! Dom, come on, we gotta get out of here!"

I scanned for an exit plan. The roof was flattened halfway, the windows all smashed. Dom's side was covered in blood, his head severely gashed by broken glass. Two cars of concerned witnesses pulled over to the shoulder and stopped above the concrete ditch we were in. I held my flexer to my mouth. "Activate sunglass flexer mode." My flexer blinked three times and morphed into black shades, I put them on, undid my seatbelt and tumbled out with a thud. It knocked the wind out of me, but I powered through it. Gasping for breath, I got up on my knees and picked broken glass out of my bloody palms.

"They got us, Doro. They got us!"

"No way!" I reached for his seatbelt. "Ready?" He painfully nodded.

Click. He dropped like a sack of potatoes.

I pushed at his shoulder. "Out the window!"

He groaned in pain and pulled himself through the crunched glass. I trailed after him. He collapsed onto the debris-caked cement. It stuck to his blood and sweat-drenched forehead.

"Y'all okay down there?!" A man called from just up the hill. He kept glancing from us to the drones above us.

"You shouldn't stay here," I yelled back, knowing that just being near us could put an innocent bystander in danger.

"We've flexed for help! They're on the way."

This poor nice guy. He didn't know there was no such thing as help right now, but he was definitely freaked out by the hovering drones.

Dom's eyes squeezed tightly closed, and he winced from the pain, using shallow breaths to control it. I wiped the blood from his face with the sleeve of my newly acquired sweater.

It was only seconds before the rumble of more airborne predators infiltrated our sound-space. Dom and I looked at each other. In that moment, without uttering a sound, we both knew this would either be our end, or a new beginning. Dom hedged his bets. "Doro, please, I need you to look out for my family, get them to Seneca..." He forced himself to his feet.

"Dom, what are you doing?"

He didn't reply, but for a guy who'd just had the daylights knocked out him, he gave off a powerful vibe. He turned and focused on the hard line that separated the road from its neighboring forest of half-naked November trees that ran parallel to the ditch as far as the eye could see. He pointed into the woods, "Go that way, and don't look back."

"Dom, don't you do anything–"

"You got this, Doro!" And with that, he bolted up the hill from the ditch and ran full speed, down the outside shoulder.

"Dom!"

He couldn't hear me as he ran straight into the oncoming enemy cyclone. This guy had a thing about putting his own life in harm's way to protect mine.

During my second week at Seneca I had practiced force field science in the defense-tech lab in mathematics applications session. I knew if I could transfer the energy from Dom's flexer with mine as the control center, I could utilize the drone network to form a shield over us. It was a long shot and time was running out. I ran up the hill and looked down into the oncoming traffic, in the direction of the drone fleet. "Activate virtual keypad," I commanded my flexer. Three, two, one, bam, the iridescent orange keys appeared and floated in the mist-thick, brisk air, two feet in front of my chest. I didn't miss a beat. Punching commands at the speed of light, I was rocking my coding maneuvers inside the drone network faster and harder than I even knew I could.

The deathly rumble closed in, rattling me from my toes to the tip of my head as cars whizzed by on the highway. It became a deep, wicked roar.

Dom must have tapped into some reserve adrenaline supply, because I could see that he made it far, fast. He looked back over his shoulder to me as he ran, and frantically threw his arms out to signal me to go into the woods, but I wasn't bailing on him. No freaking way.

I pumped the air buttons in one seriously hardcore last-ditch effort, commanding the creation of a shield formation over my positional coordinates, and covering one hundred yards to my north, which was how far away Dom was by then.

The vibrations from the imposing threat felt like an earthquake. Pieces of glass popped off the cement like Mexican jumping beans. The Ghost Barrel rotorcraft fleet were in view now, dwarfing the oncoming traffic to toy car status. Six Ghost Barrels– silver and black robot driven vessels with ten-foot wingspans capped in spherical propulsion fans, flew straight towards us from the direction we had just come. The big dogs had been called in. And my coding was coming up short. The drones weren't responding to my commands.

Dom abruptly stopped in his tracks on the road's shoulder. He threw his hands over his ears, as his clothing rippled from the sickeningly powerful mechanized winds. Something invisible slammed him to his stomach pinning him to the ground. One Ghost Barrel stayed on him, holding him pinned against the pavement, the rest kept on moving toward me.

Ghost Barrel fleets were known for taking out entire villages in an instant. They were built from weather and crash-proof superalloy materials, armed with the most extreme assault weaponry. They would incinerate us, destine us to air pollution duty, using our remains to quicken the demise of our dear Planet Earth. It could happen to Dom and myself in less than ten seconds. I dropped to my knees. Bowed my head in defeat, knowing I'd done all I could.

Suddenly the swarm of drones spread out into a dome correlation along the shoulder of the highway that extended from over my head to Dom's limp body. It created a whirlpool-like pull on us and all the debris nearby. Their bending light, sound and energy deflected all outside signals and materials. Through the blur of it all, I could see the Ghost Barrel fleet do a 180 in perfect formation, and fly back in the opposite direction. The shield I had created with the drones kept the Ghosts from being able to trace us. Their menacing purr made the hair on my neck stand up, sending shivers through my shoulders. And off they flew, hopefully right back to where they came from, with the message that we meant business, too. Was I excited? Sure. But I knew better than to celebrate prematurely. First things first. I had to get up from my knees and on to my feet. And then figure out what our next move would be.

45

THE GHOST BARRELS' grim aftermath filled my head with sludge—fumes that stank like burnt egg and gas, dirt and debris that were caked in my nostrils and my snarled hair. I realized that I was too exhausted to stand so I lowered myself to a rigid roadside seat. Hugging my arms around my shins I dropped my head to knees. Soon, the sound of my own breath overtook the distant pounding of the Ghost Barrel fleet. I rested my cheek against my thigh, and looked over in Dom's direction. He was still laid out flat, his chest rising and falling like a pneumatic drill. He finally pushed his body up to sit, looked back at me and softly shook his head in disbelief. It was a miracle we'd made it, but it wasn't over yet.

We were beaten up, but not broken down. His intense eyes found their way to mine and held on unwaveringly, re-igniting the conviction we felt and the stamina each of us needed to keep on.

He made his way over to me. "You're bleeding pretty bad," I told him.

Dom wiped his fingers across his temple and looked at his

hand, unfazed by the blood. He took off the t-shirt he had on underneath his hoodie, ripped it into a rag, and wrapped it around his head like a warrior.

My flexer was still in sunglass mode, wrapped around my eyes with coordinates pulled up for Claytor Lake in the upper right corner of the black lens. It was the only Seneca entrance point for which I had location data. This would be our one shot. My air keyboard still floated there in front of me. I stared it down, knowing exactly what I needed to do. "I'm locking our position to the drones, and we're outta here." Dom nodded, and let me do my thing without uttering a word.

I concentrated on getting the coordinates right. Within seconds, the hovering drones amped up, and buzzed back in the direction they'd come from. Just like that, nemesis was repurposed into ally. Whoever said mine were idle hands could kiss my butt. My shoulders loosened up. I cracked my neck. My tech work here was done... for now.

"Let's go." Dom nodded toward the southwest. I didn't question him. It was his turn to fuel this unpredictable ride. He started into the woods and I was right there, in mutual stride.

As we trekked along, the only sounds we heard were the crackle of twigs and rocks under our feet, and the faint howl of winter winds blowing in. We came to a stream, maybe four feet across, caked over in a thin layer of misty ice. Dom brightened up when he spotted it, and stomped a hole in the ice with his heel. "Ladies first." And they said chivalry died long ago.

I knelt down palming the cool, clay-colored earth, and lowered my face to the dark blue, rippled reflection in the freezing water. I could see the pain in the mirror image that stared back at me. I smashed into it with my fists, cupping the water back up to my mouth. I gulped and gulped with my eyes closed. I ran my hand along the ice and then over my face to wipe away some residual grit. Invigorated, I turned back to Dom. He was transfixed, watching me with those tiger-eyes of his. "Sorry, I'm hogging all the water."

"Girl, you can have all the water that you want."

Dom had my back, and I was certain that, by now, he knew I had his. "I'm parched like crazy. You must be, too."

"That's an understatement."

He moved in next to me. Plunged his face into the water, submerging his head for five, ten, fifteen seconds... at twenty he flung it out, sending a fan of icy water into the frigid air, "Wooooooha!" He vigorously rubbed at his head and face that had taken on a stubbled, rugged hotness. It made me feel less like the warrior I'd been all of twenty minutes before, and more like a girl. Just a girl. But I wasn't just a girl. How did he do this to me? I blinked hard to bring my brain back from Mars. He put his hand in the small of my back, making my return from outer-space that much harder. "You all hydrated and ready?"

"You know it. I take it you have a new transportation plan?"

"Do I ever. We'll be off our feet within an hour." He said with confidence.

In just under an hour we had trudged through Shenandoah National Park. The rocky and frosty sapphire terrain of the Blue Ridge Mountains was draped in a soft gray-blue sky. It was the middle of the day but the sun wasn't shining. It was muted, as was our mood, in anticipation of a long, frigid winter.

Dom and I were lugging ourselves along as we descended the chilly foothills. Evening began to roll in. I could smell a campfire but couldn't see it, or even another soul. We were starving, cold, sore. My face stung, fingers raw and numb.

And then, just as Dom and I hit our last peak, the sight of a sprawling pasture below us boosted our moods. We rushed down the hill and stood side-by-side, resting our elbows on a white post and rail fence. We watched some horses nibbling on stubbles of yellowed fescue grass poking through the hoarfrost. The one closest to us lifted his head, ears pointed curiously in our direction. "That big guy there, he's a bay." Dom said.

The fairytale-like scene of beauty and eloquence profoundly moved me. "And I thought horses were extinct."

"That's what they tell you in Los Angeles, eh?"

"Not exactly, but we definitely don't have horses."

"Well, you're not in LA anymore, Dorothy. Ready?"

"Ready for what?"

"To hitch our ride." Without missing a beat, Dom hopped the fence and turned back to offer his hand. Without a thought I hurdled the fence by myself. We were on their side of the fence now. Dom and I stared down the horse that seemed the most intrigued by our presence.

"How about we call him Buck?"

"Works for me. I hope Buck doesn't bite."

Dom chuckled as if I were kidding. I was only kind of kidding. "Are you sure about this? I don't know—"

"Man, you really *are* a city girl. Time to get you a good dose of horse country."

"I think maybe we should find a flighter I can get us into."

"Way too risky. This way we can cut through the backwoods to Anika's farm near Charlottesville." Dom slipped into a slow, confident walk towards Buck. He went right up to him and extended the back of his hand to the horse's nose. This richly dark brown beauty had big black eyes and a warm, strong spirit. I folded. Dom was right. He would be a great addition to our roller-coaster mission.

46

BUCK NEIGHED AND snorted along through the night with Dom and me mounted on his back. I sat in front with Dom's arms loosely wrapped around my waist. I don't know what I had been so worried about; horseback riding was amazing. We didn't even have a saddle, but because Dom had spent a lot of time on farms when he was growing up, bareback riding just seemed to come naturally to him. And he made sure that I was comfortable with it, too.

We were wiped out, delirious really, when we finally made the decision to stop and sleep. By that time Dom estimated that we were about three hours by horseback from Anika's farm. Dom had the kind of nature skills that didn't exist in LA, and it was a good thing he did. He scaled a young hickory tree with a shaggy bark that made it tricky for him to get traction, but he was determined. He managed to snap a low hanging, long branch and climbed back down with it, which he stripped and bent to hitch Buck to a much skinnier tree. We posted up under the grandest hickory within a stone's throw of Buck and were out cold within minutes.

***

Morning dew woke me with a shiver across my shoulders, my neck hairs stood straight as a mohawk. My back was surprisingly warm, though, and I realized that I was nestled into a full-on spoon with Dom. Somehow we had found each other to cuddle up tight as we'd slept. I didn't want to move, but I knew we had to keep moving. My stomach gurgled and growled, but Dom's was even more insistent, sounding like a monster shouting, "Feed me, dammit!" It helped to know that, once we got to Anika's, we'd be able to eat. Buck was raring to go which he let be known with a dramatic snort. We laughed, but the joy fizzled fast as reality set in. The second I tried to stand I felt an insane pain in my inner thighs. Oh— the trials of a city girl after her first time bareback riding. I clenched my jaw to suck back the excruciating ache and climbed back atop Buck for more. And we were off.

A thunderstorm pushed in shortly after dawn. At first it was magical, intoxicating, even. Deep colossal booms and sheets of water pounded down from a sad, pearly sky. We opened our mouths wide to the downpour. I hadn't seen rain in at least ten months, and even then it had been nothing compared to this. But the novelty got old real quick. We were cold. Heavy clothes chafed against our skin. Jeans felt more like sandpaper than denim. My soaked hair stuck in clumps like chilled noodles to the back of my neck. And good ol' Buck, whose coat was heavily caked with kicked-back mud, needed a bath even worse than we did. The rain magnified his barnyard stench times a million. Buck's hooves stuck in the earth and he had to work overtime with each step to pull them from the suction of gooey mud. The more we wished for the rain to stop, the harder it pelted down. We clung to the image of sipping on some steamy soup under a blanket by a fire. It seemed like such a distant dream during those three hardcore hours.

Based on Dom's flexer calculations, we still had about two hours to go when we heard a far off hiss. It wasn't the drones, I was sure. No, this time my body burned with the premonition of poison. A teeth grinding, acid on flesh nastiness was coming our way, a swarm of some sort of insect. But how could they be out in a storm like this?

"What is that?"

Dom pulled back on Buck's neck and made a clicking sound that told him to stop. We looked behind us. A giant, contorting mass of airborne blackness headed straight in our direction, but even as I blinked the haze of rain from my eyelashes, I couldn't make out what it was.

Dom tensed up, "No, no, no!"

Buck sensed a threat and started frantically tossing his head. I knew this couldn't be good. The auditory toxicity closed in fast.

"Hold on, Doro! Heeya, heeya!" Dom dug his heels into Buck, who neighed in distress and flared his nostrils into the air. Buck darted through the mud with all his might. I held on tight around his neck, a column of solid muscle. I peered over my right shoulder to see exactly what was on our tail. Through the unrelenting, machine-gun spray of rain that blasted me in the face, it became apparent— they were mosquitos, thousands of them.

"Heeya, heeya!" Dom pushed Buck harder and harder, but it was too late, the bloodthirsty army ambushed our heads, swarming in formation like a helmet. Buck flipped out, Dom and I were thrown to the ground and he trampled out of there.

"Run! They're deadly!" Dom screamed.

I swatted as the pathogenic pests formed a thick barrier around my face, up my nose, in my eyes, my ears, landing on my face and hands. I was as disgusted as I was scared. There was nothing I could do– I choked on rain and bugs that flew into my throat. "Dom!" I tried to scream out to him but it was muffled. I felt tiny pricks all over me, poison surging into my muscles. A metallic taste formed in my mouth. I lost my balance and, as I heard "waowaowaowao" and saw streaks of black, I succumbed to the virulent attack and dropped like a rag doll.

47

"HELLO, SWEETHEART. YOU are safe."

My vision made a slow dissolve in with fisheye distortion. I felt like I'd been riding a rowboat in the ocean. "Ughhh..." I squinted my eyes to make out a petite woman in her seventies kneeling next to me. She had long hair the color of soap suds and wore an oversized, beige Egyptian shirt with a pair of supremely worn-in jeans. It nauseated me beyond belief to look around, but I had to figure out where I was. Oh god– the room spun. I dry heaved, nothing in me to vomit but foam. The woman held a bucket up to catch it and rubbed my shoulder, "You're okay, you're okay. It's almost passed."

I felt like death. How did this happen? Why couldn't I see properly and how did I end up on this floor? The last thing I remembered was riding a horse with Dom. I mustered up just enough energy to mutter, "Dom?"

"He's just getting tea in the other room with Josie."

We must have made it to Anika's ranch.

"I'm Anika." Yesss– my blessings were too great to count.

Anika was good people, I knew it immediately. Normally it would take me some time to come to such a verdict, but this inherent goodness just emanated from her pores like raw garlic. She held a washcloth to my forehead. "Thank you," I mouthed, with barely any sound.

"Don't speak, Doro. Save your energy."

I rolled from the fetal position onto my back, which felt stiff as a board. I let out an agony-drenched sigh. My vision cleared to see beyond what was directly in front of me. This was the exact scene I had daydreamed about on our ride through the storm. Underneath an exposed beam ceiling, a fire crackled between two picture windows that framed a sweet little secluded farm. I was wedged into a comfy, worn brown corduroy beanbag.

"Doro, you're awake!" The sound of Dom's voice made me feel safe even though I was thoroughly incapacitated. He pulled another beanbag up next to me, sat down in it and reached toward me with a cup of tea. "Drink this."

I weakly lifted my arm. It was heavy and limp as a pile of wet laundry. I moaned in discomfort.

"I got it." Dom put the red ceramic mug to my lips and tilted it as he warned, "It's hot."

I blew into it and sipped the most glorious peppermint rooibos that ever was. It streamed down the back of my throat, warming me up and washing out the sour taste in my mouth. The fog behind my eyes started to burn off.

"You were poisoned, sweetheart." Anika said lightly. "I've

given you an antidote that should move through your system and have you back on your feet shortly."

"We made it, Doro." Dom's face lit up with the assurance that we were still on our path, just overcoming some heavy set-backs. "This is Anika, and Josie."

Anika got up and took a seat on the sofa next to her partner, Josie. I hadn't even seen Josie come in. I tried to smile to show my gratitude. It seemed to send a wave of good grace down my spine. I managed to take the tea from Dom. "I don't understand."

"Remember the mosquitos?"

Did I ever. I scrunched my lip and quivered in disgust with a little nod.

"S.O.I.L. They're fighting dirty."

"How? I thought I'd made us untraceable."

"I'm almost positive we were hunted down by a swarm programmed to find our blood. Seneca has our blood samples and the mosquitos were only attacking us but not the horse. It's a trick ripped right from the pages of the swarm warfare field manual."

Biological warfare. On me. Once again, I wasn't surprised, but I was upset to be the brunt of such a disgusting attack.

"What sickness?"

"Your saliva tested positive for synthetic Novuleria." Anika didn't try to pad the truth for even a second. I hadn't heard of Novuleria before, but it didn't sound good.

"It's a man-made disease with a specific purpose. Disorient

and kill." I was repulsed, but man, so fortunate that it hadn't killed me. I've never been the vengeful type, but someone definitely just had claimed exclusive billing on my hit list.

"Gregory Zaffron. He's a demon."

"Truth."

I could almost feel the cleansing process working its way through my bloodstream, and replenishing cells with the fire to burn down the malevolent Gregory.

"You, Doro Campbell, just conquered a battle of biological warfare."

Thanks to Anika, I had. But things still didn't make complete sense. I mean, Dom was fine and I was a bloody mess. "How did you slide by?"

"Dumb luck. My blood deterrents to mosquitos were established when I was a little kid and my parents took us to Africa for six months. If I hadn't been immune we would have been left in the woods for the raptors to feast on."

"On that note, let's eat." Josie chimed in. Josie was a unique-looking woman with mesmerizing features. Her sparkling lime eyes and caramel complexion glistened by the flames. I'm sure she looked younger than she actually was, which, if I had to guess, was about sixty. She had the same buzz cut as Dom, something we all joked about. She wore a white linen house dress, tan handmade moccasins and gold stud earrings. She told us about her interesting melting pot of genetic heritage: Native American, Irish, Korean, Russian, French, South African and

East Indian. And those were just the ones she was aware of. Her vast culinary repertoire reflected just that. While we'd been talking we could smell something tremendous being "whipped up," as she put it, for dinner. I picked up notes of turmeric and cinnamon waltzing with the cozy scent of crackling wood. We didn't have fireplaces in LA since they'd been outlawed before I was even born, but good home cooking was something I'd had almost every night. My mom is a spice master and that was just another thing about her that I missed in my Senecan life. To have this heartwarming treat of a dinner after the unmerciful treachery we'd just experienced was almost more than I could stand. I decided to offload all the negativity and anger I'd accumulated, and soak up new energy from this beautiful home where we were being surrounded with nothing but love.

Dom helped me to the dining table on the other side of the room, made from a fallen tree on their land. It had been hand-carved and sanded, and I ran the tips of my fingers along its smooth but imperfect surface. Anika and Josie brought us curried sweet potato and black bean chili, slow cooked southern greens with roasted citrus beets, corn bread, honey butter and sweetened minty rose water. Everything Josie made came from the land they lived on. The glorious smell made me sit up straight and I almost felt like myself again.

"This is officially the hungriest I've ever been."

"It's not surprising that you're hungry. Your body just purged everything it had in it," Anika said.

As we reveled in the meal, my body began to align with my mind. Anika and Josie listened, their friendly faces sympathetic as Dom explained everything we had been through, and where we were headed. Anika became visibly concerned with our beyond-precarious objective. "You had me right up until the point where you said you want me to perform a potentially fatal procedure on you. You two are so young, you have so much life ahead of you to take such a huge risk."

I left the lobbying to Dom because he knew them better. "You're right, we are young. But the only chance we have ever to become old is if we go through with this. Otherwise we'll just live in hiding up here and they'll eventually find us."

"I just don't know, Dommy." Anika was wavering. She wanted to help but feared the very real risk that what we wanted from her might end our lives.

"I understand it's asking a lot of you, but believe me, we've really thought this through. You're our only hope."

"And I understand that you think this is the way forward, but you two can't even begin to comprehend the magnitude of this."

"We can–"

"Dommy, it's not that simple. I promise you, it's not. I know it seems like it gives you superpowers, but you can't have a one track mind when it comes to this. A flexer implant is the ultimate of double-edged swords."

"We know. Don't we, Doro?"

"Absolutely. We are only in this for all the right reasons and none of the wrong ones."

"I promise, Anika. We'll be responsible." Dom pleaded.

Anika closed her eyes and lowered her chin to her chest. The fire's hypnotic crackle carried us through the next few moments. Dom got up and went to Anika. He crouched down to his knees and faced her. "If we don't go through with this, it will all be over. Doro and I won't have any chance at all. Please, Anika."

Anika took a deep breath. "Okay, but only after you two get a good night's sleep."

48

ANIKA LED US out through the back door of their little white house with navy blue shutters and a wrap-around porch. A swing sat just beyond a cute red barn. In the barnyard there were a few horses, goats, sheep, pigs, a regal old German Shepherd and a coop full of chickens. Their land must have encompassed at least forty acres.

We headed towards the chicken coop. There were three hens in there, plump as can be, and they were cluck, cluck, clucking away. "Oh be quiet, Pamela, these are our guests," Anika quipped at the biggest hen in the house. She moved aside some stacks of hay, took a broom and brushed away a section of the dusty remnants, revealing a hidden door made of plywood, flush to the ground. She lifted it up and signaled for us to follow her. "Please close it behind you. I would say we don't live on a farm, but, you know..." We smiled and I followed behind her, scaling down a creaky ladder. Dom pulled the door closed behind him.

Slivers of light shone through the slits in the hidden door and cut the cool darkness. I scrunched my nose and stifled a gag from the scent of moist chicken poop. When the waveguide ceiling lit up in a marshmallow white, illuminating everything in sight, my mind was too blown to register the foul odor. We were in a space of roughly a thousand square feet. Its white walls were coated in an inch of opaque swirling liquid inside which glowing sky blue graphs, charts and controls blinked into power. A hidden chamber of high-tech medicine was being hidden below a common chicken coop– incredible. In the center of the floor was a shiny silver plastic cylinder the size of a small flighter– a Biological Nanorobotic Fusion Chamber, otherwise known as a BioNan. Anika went to it and opened a small fist-size port in its side.

"I need the chip of whichever one of you is first."

Dom stepped forward.

"Are you sure?" I asked. This was my idea, so I didn't want him to have to go first in case anything went wrong.

Dom nodded resolutely.

"Requesting control," Anika addressed the BioNan.

A three foot wide, two foot tall, crystal control panel appeared in the air. She waved her hand over it, producing illuminated blue icons.

And just like that, a sweet little old lady morphed into a guru of technologically advanced medicine.

"Now, you're going to go down that hall to the bathroom. Shower real well and put on one of the robes you'll find in the closet."

Dom didn't hesitate. He had made up his mind and, once he did that, he never gave it a second thought. That was his style. I was scared for him, but the buzz of electronics was reassuring to me. Familiar. The flow of my blood and the electricity in these devices ran on the same wavelength.

Dom emerged wearing a robe. This was neither the time nor place to get all goo goo gaga, but, jeez, he looked good. And brave. Which made him painfully irresistible, if he wasn't already. Which he was. And that drove me crazy. The more I fell, the more I resisted. Like a rubber band, I was bound eventually to snap or sling forward. This was a massive game of tug-of-war, with my attraction to him pulling me from the inside, while the risky request we'd made of Anika pulling me from the outside. I was so scared for him, and yet I realized, if we didn't make it through this, we'd never have the chance to see what it could be like to be together— in Seneca or anywhere else.

"Okay, Dommy. You're going to swallow these sensors now and lie down." Anika handed him three tiny pills: yellow, aquamarine and violet. "They will dye your organs by the time you are situated inside the BioNan." Anika pointed him to the simple, stainless steel bench that extended from the wall of blue. Dom explained to me on our way here that Anika had been a professor at a nearby university which shut down her entire department when futurist medicine like the BioNan was outlawed. The university was set to destroy all of her equipment when a group of students pulled a heist just in the nick of time and brought it to Anika. It was probably this type of technology that had rebuilt G.W. after the crash.

"Just relax and let me take it from here." I appreciated that Anika was doing her best to send out the vibe of a fully confident expert.

Dom lay down on the bench.

A spinning whoosh sound powered up the BioNan. We all knew what could happen here, but nobody wanted to let their thoughts go there. The bench gradually disappeared into the BioNan, and sealed shut once Dom was inside. Anika moved to the front of her control panel and I moved behind her. I gulped and bit my thumb nail. My stomach turned.

Anika tapped at several of the blue icons on her control panel. A diagram of a body on a faint white grid scanned onto the wall. It was a rendering of Dom in yellow muscles, violet blood flow, and aquamarine organs. Anika moved her hands to form a sphere in the airspace in front of the control panel. An iridescent bubble appeared. She tapped twice on his aquamarine heart on the control panel, then pulled her hands back to the bubble, and a 3D heart appeared inside it. Right there, five feet in front of me, was Dom's precious beating heart. Different shades and textures showed the flow and pressure. Anika took her hands and revolved his heart on an axis, checking it over and entering numerical data from her observations back into the control panel. She then pushed the heart back to the diagram of his body with her palm. I was infinitely fascinated as she methodically pulled each organ out and did the same thing. I couldn't get over the fact that this aging hippie farmer was really a master of revolutionary medicine.

She then lowered her chin to her chest and brought her hands in a prayer formation up to her heart. For one minute, she breathed in and out in a controlled pattern, inhaling through her nose and exhaling deeply from the back of her throat. Then she brought her hands down to the control panel, lifted her head, relaxed her shoulders and slowly opened her eyes. She pulled a virtual robotic arm from the panel and, with her other hand, typed in code. A foot-long, double-pronged needle appeared in the robot's arm. Thank goodness I had overcome my fear of needles in Dom's lab, or I probably would have fainted watching this.

Anika pulled Dom's spinal column from his diagramed body and rotated it. Typed in more code. The BioNan emitted a vibration. I looked at her, hoping she'd reassure me that everything was going to be okay, but she didn't. Nothing existed other than what was in front of her. Dom's life... our future... was at stake. She tapped five buttons on the virtual robotic arm, and a series of clicks preceded a whirring sound inside the cylinder.

A screen that magnified an x-ray of Dom's spinal column appeared on the side of the BioNan. Anika moved down the control panel and zoomed in to magnify the area between two vertebrae that brightened up on the 3D image of his spine. She was exceptionally calm. I could easily recognize being in that sort of a zone. Everyone had his or her own version. Mine was energized. Hers was different. She seemed to purge all the crap that had no place in exactly what she was doing and bring herself down to a placid mindfulness. She pushed a command, and the whirr inside the BioNan crescendoed. I watched the virtual robotic arm move in and position the needle to inject into the lower third of the 3D image of Dom's spine. A muffled moan came from inside the cylinder. I turned, nervously, to look at Anika. Was he okay? Did it work? How long until we knew?

She ignored me completely, at one with that control panel. Next, she pulled up his eyes. More whirrs inside the machine. I watched the screen intently as a small robotic device held his eyelids open and electro-laminates were fitted to his eyes. A microscopic laser then embedded them onto the surface. This would allow us to see our computational activity inside our own eyes. Screens would no longer be necessary.

With that, the process was complete. Anika directed everything back into place. The sphere disappeared. The door on the BioNan opened. The bench started to come out. First I saw Dom's feet, then his legs... he wasn't moving. I rushed to his side. I couldn't stay back even if I wanted to.

"Give him a minute."

I nodded and waited impatiently as his body slowly emerged from the machine. I could see his chin, then lips, and finally his eyes. They were wide open and the glow above flooded his dilated pupils. He didn't blink. Anika came over to him, too.

"Dommy, you just take it easy now." As if pulled by puppet strings, his lips slowly parted. His electrifying eyes shifted to mine and crinkled into a smile. My heart fluttered. He was okay.

49

I LAY FLAT on the cold bench as it pulled me into the BioNan. Although this was an intimidating process, Dom's going first eased a lot of my fear and doubt. We seemed to do that for one another. He picked me up when I was down and vice versa. He had let go of the need to be in control and accepted this radical plan of mine as if it were as inevitable as the sunrise. I had started to let go of my mistrust of people and drift off into a world of possibility when it came to Dom. And here I was, inside a machine that would connect my brain to my flexer. More than half of the previous attempts at this had resulted in death. That was why the whole movement toward this high technology approach to medicine had shifted underground, and why Anika's lab had been dismantled.

The debate was legitimate. One side said that life was too precious and the outcomes too unpredictable to experiment with humans in this dangerous way. The other side believed that the potential for huge breakthroughs was too great not to attempt the creation of singularity between humans and technology. There were so many arguments. How would privacy be redefined? Would this allow us to live longer or shorten our lives? What would become of a world where information was wired straight into everyone's brain without the need to read and spend countless hours absorbing it? Ultimately, there were too many "what ifs?" The government jumped in to regulate these activities. Humans turning themselves into cyborgs was outlawed. But the people refused to be regulated. Which brought us to Dom and me– specifically me, laying flat in this BioNan.

As wide open as my eyes were, there was no light to let into them. I couldn't even see the inside of the vessel that contained me. I felt vulnerable. My shoulders and chest were exposed, my bare back was against the bench. The whirr kicked in. Here we go. I took a deep breath. A blue light flooded the chamber. My blue light. My mind raced. What if the lights went out permanently? I'd never been scared of death because I'd never had to be. But I realized I could die right then and there. I was scared. If I had to go now, I'd go knowing I had lived and I had loved. I never said goodbye, but there might be no such thing as goodbye. It might just be something we say but not something we ever do. In some incarnation of energy along the road to infinity, would we meet again? Whenever I tried to visualize what came next I always ended up with an image of speeding blasts of static. What would become of me when my heart stopped beating? My blood stopped flowing? My breath became harder, shorter. I tried to tame it, right then, just to see if I could tell what it would feel like. Death.

I felt a numbing pressure on my spine. It lasted ten seconds and then my lower back became warm. I dared not move. Strangely, at the same moment, my thinking shifted from death to life. What was it going to be like? What would I be capable of now? I was filled with a sense of hope and I imagined my re-emergence into the world. It couldn't come soon enough.

My head was locked into place by an unseen source of compression. I didn't resist. I felt something like cold metal lowering onto my eyelids and clamping them open. A liquid washed over my eyes, and then a film meshed onto my eyeballs. A searing heat formed a circle inside each eyeball. It didn't hurt, but my eyes felt dry, even with all the liquid that had just gushed into them. I wasn't thinking about anything now. The whirr slowed, then purred into idleness. All that was left was an empty echo inside the chamber. I identified my own breath. My heartbeat. My surging sense of wonder.

The bench pushed me out. In my rebirth, I entered a new world as a new girl. With my eyes wide open, the beat of my heart marched towards the future, my mind stretched far beyond the confines of my body.

It was go time.

50

WE DROVE AN hour from Anika's ranch to the banks of the James River. Anika and Josie had given us their old Toyota truck. It had been sitting dormant behind the barn for a half decade and they knew we'd put it to good use. Dom promised we'd be back to bring them to Seneca, but they respectfully declined. Anika and Josie loved their home and weren't convinced that Seneca was the answer to a better future for them. Still, they were supportive of our belief that it was for us.

Virginia was entrenched in its metamorphosis from fall to winter. Lush green had been ushered out by the most captivating shades of crimson, orange, and speckles of deep purple. The colors were heightened by their mirror image in the tranquil surface of the water, barely disturbed by wind lifting it into soft peaks. We pulled off the parkway that ran south from the ranch onto a one-lane gravel road snaking its way up to the water's edge. We got out of the truck and posted up to tackle the next phase of our mission.

The James River was such a peaceful place. No unbidden

noise from transportation systems, crowds, technology, or even our own conversation. The only sounds were the mild gusts of wind in the trees and the river's light current. Much of the wildlife that called this land of towering woods their home recently had dispersed to deeper, hidden places for the winter. We thought we were alone until we saw an agile doe and her majestic buck tiptoeing along the wood's edge. Dom and I sat still and watched them make their way.

"Can't we just stay right here forever?" Dom asked quietly.

It was an idealistic thought, an impossible dream, but I wanted to live in it, too. Run away from all the bad and just let our love flourish here in the tranquil Virginia wilderness. We could live off the land until the end of our time, whenever that may be. "I'm in."

This was our own personal, sickeningly sweet romance novel. Why did it have to end? This is what life should be, this and nothing but this. Then, in crept reality. I knew that the air we breathed wasn't as pure as it seemed. The quality of the land we'd be living off of wasn't quite so unblemished. It never had been. And it was partly up to Dom and me to change that.

We had agreed not to toy with the flexer implants- period- until we were far enough away from Anika's ranch because we didn't want to put her and Josie at any more risk than we already had. Now we knew there was enough distance between them and us. The deer were endearing, and having Dom at my side gave me a permanent buzz. But nothing could get me going like what

I was about to do. Even though I hadn't done it yet, I knew. I'd waited my whole life for this. I was born for this. The itch was too intense to wait another second. "I have to do it."

"I know."

I closed my eyes and let my thought process paddle into the technology that was inside me. My flexer chip took power from the energy sources that run through my body and received its commands from the neocortex part of my brain that processes conscious thought. After my conscious thought occurred, an instantaneous response from my flexer arrived in my brain.

I sent the command for my eyes to power up the FlexOculi Implant. This technology normally required outside power, but that was no longer the case. Because in regular life a FlexOculi would connect to a flexer on the outside of a body, but Anika had defied common practice and connected it to my spinal flexer implant. She was hands down the coolest old lady alive.

Although it was physically only on the surface of my eyeballs, the FlexOculi appeared to project a twenty inch monitor one foot in front of my face. Communication was established. Absolutely brilliant.

I could not believe it had taken me almost seventeen years to get one of these but, then again, I could believe it because there is no way my parents would have allowed it until I was eighteen. Part of the gelatinous coating on my eyes conducted wireless signals. Most people used these things for gaming. Well, *life* was my game.

I wanted to log in to my Veil– and, bam, at the tail end of the very thought, there I was. Inside my Veil. And my Veil was inside me. I sensed it. Every single bit of data.

Nothing– and I mean *nothing* could rock my world like this. It was beautiful. The future had become my present. An absolute gift. How fortunate I was to be alive and experiencing this. My body charged with euphoria, like a geyser bursting from the earth. I couldn't begin to comprehend the limitless potential within my own little temple of flesh and blood. As I sat on a river's edge in the middle of the wilderness, I realized that I could do anything, no matter where I was.

A tear formed in my eye, clouding the vision of my FlexOculi monitor and Dom just beyond it. He was toying with his own newly found internal form and function. When I blinked, a tear streamed down my flushed cheek. Everything was clear again. I pushed my focus beyond the FlexOculi to Dom. Without him, this wouldn't be. None of it. So many things had aligned for this to be my reality. I was overwhelmed. I had reached the peak of Olympus, but my heart lugged a deep, heavy load of sadness. I couldn't share my accomplishments with my parents. I so badly wanted to see them happy and proud of me. I didn't know when I'd get to see my mom again, but I just had to. I'd left without telling her I loved and appreciated her. I hoped she knew. My emotions took over, jumping spastically all over the place. My mental state was on an unpredictable teeter-totter. I swallowed the pain, pushing it deeper inside, and dredged the happiness up again. If only my dad could see me now. I held in a joy-filled cry. Instead, I reached out and pulled Dom's face in to mine. I had to plant all this emotional chaos somewhere that would ground me. Somewhere I could trust. Dom's tender lips.

As intense as our connection was, and as far away as I felt it take me, I knew that, in his kiss, I could be brought back down to solid ground again.

"Was that for saving your life after that mosquito attack, or have you just fallen for my irresistible charisma?"

"The mosquito bite." I said with a grin. He had to have known it was for everything.

I let out a deep breath the same way you do after a great big cry. I felt the same way, too, minus the sobbing it usually takes to get there.

"Now it's time to get down to business."

"Please. Just let me know what I can do."

"You just sit there and look pretty," I smirked.

Dom lay down, grinning as if he was ready to watch me in a peep show. I didn't blame him. This was some serious tech porn.

"I'm pulling the roster of all the Seneca Senators. I'll access the nanobot mainframe through my Veil where I stored the path, and then it's showtime." I harnessed my Veil to my FlexOculi that had momentarily gone into sleep mode, and I cross-referenced the Seneca Senators with the data bank of entangled Seneca citizens. Two hundred and twelve Senators were right there. And then, as I scrolled down the names, one in particular hit me like a ton of bricks. *Ellen Malone*. I'd had no clue that Ellen was on the Seneca Senate, nor did I have any idea what other positions she held in Seneca. After being momentarily stunned, I realized that my life had changed so radically following Ellen's arrival at my Culver City apartment, that nothing could shock me now.

I couldn't let anything hinder the path I was on. I knew I'd figure it all out later, but now my priority was to deliver the truth to the Seneca Senate. The nanobots were in their blood too, and, if they knew it, they would do something about it. How could they not? All I had to do now was procure the thought and issue the command, and all two hundred and twelve of them would instantaneously receive the message.

The notion of embedding and then controlling information in the minds of the most powerful individuals on the planet was mind-boggling. Even Dom had ditched the chill vibe he'd recently acquired for the early Dom-like serious stance from when I'd first met him. We both knew that what we were doing would change the course of life in Seneca, with impact far beyond. Hard to believe that a nagging feeling he'd had after his Necrolla Carne shot had taken us this far. We were headed into unexplored territory.

I thought of Anika, how she brought a sense of composure to her belief in a universal strength to push her vision through.

It was time.

Three, two, one...

And it was sent. Across a vast ocean of space and a tiny pebble of time, through the vessel of my conscious thought, two hundred and twelve Seneca Senators were receiving this message:

"My name is Dorothy Campbell. I am a Senecan. The information you are receiving is being transmitted to your brain via nanobots that were injected into your blood under the guise of the Necrolla Carne vaccine. The Seneca Observation and Intelligence League has hacked into the brains of every citizen of Seneca this way and is gathering information on each and every one of them, including you. If you don't believe it, you will be receiving the information they have about you right after this message. The data they are collecting is retrieved and stored inside a S.O.I.L. computer mainframe at Claytor Lake in Virginia. Fellow Senecan, Dominic Ambrosia, and I are currently at a location in the Aboves. Moments from now we will release to you our location, and then will comply with your requirement that we return to Seneca immediately."

The flexer chip data for each Seneca Senator was also stored in the mainframe. I transmitted the portal I had in my Veil directly to their flexers for each of them to access the mainframe on their own.

I turned to Dom. "I'm going to unblock our position now."

Any traces of fear inside him had vanished. This was all he had wanted all along — to have the truth about the nasty Necrolla Carne vaccine uncovered. He was a guy who valued truth above all else, and now his forced silence would be over. Now it was just a matter of making the most of our wait. I retracted my FlexOculi.

Just Dom, me and the James River. Dom took his boots off and put his feet in the water. This time his compulsive concern for his shoelaces and the placement of his boots were gone. He looked up at me with renewed hope in his eyes. This was one hundred percent, authentic Dominic Ambrosia. No fear, no control, no paranoia, nothing but pure Dom. How come, every time we were in this kind of live-or-die type situation he'd give me that look and I'd fall so freaking hard for him all over again?

"The water is freeeeeeezing!" he hollered in delight, as his legs submerged to just below his knees. I sat down next to him and squealed as I slowly dipped my toes. After a few seconds they went numb and I inched the rest of my feet in. The cold was nearly unbearable, but it hurt so good to feel so alive. Side by side, our feet dangled in the water. Dom looked over at me, scooted closer. Did I say I was falling hard for him? Scratch that. I was crashing!

"You have no idea how happy I am that you came to New York for me."

"Well, I wasn't just going to let it slide."

Nobody ever gave me the intense looks he did. I had to let my defenses down and just go with it. I felt safe and secure behind my walls but, as they began to crumble and fall, I felt safer in the freedom of not having them there... and of letting Dom in.

"I love you, Doro."

Oh. My. God.

Dom *loved* me. I couldn't gather myself to say it back, even though I felt the same way, times a trillion. My mouth hung open like a bumbling fool. I couldn't speak. This was so unlike me.

And then, before I had the chance to say a word, funnels of blue light blasted down onto each of us. Without any audible warning, we were ambushed, encased inside two separate spheres of light. I looked toward the sky to find the source– a silenced stealth flighter. I shouted to Dom, and saw that he was shouting to me, too, but we couldn't hear each other. Then the spheres coated over in a blinding light that even penetrated my closed eyelids. I covered my face with my forearm. I tried to initialize flexer communication with him, but there must have been a signal shield in the sphere in which I was encased.

The flighter lifted us quickly. The air became so shallow my breath couldn't grasp it. I choked on the freezing air. The blinding light flashed with blackness, evolving into a slow, dizzying bright blue and black strobe. My eyes struggled to see until stars took over the strobe and I passed out.

51

IN SIX DAYS of solitary confinement, I didn't see a single soul. Each day, a part of me suffocated just a little bit more. Sufficiently proportioned, health conscious meals were delivered to my living cube via a tube, similar to the meal hall system, only here the ceiling was just ten feet tall. Even though I'd had no physical activity in these past few days, I felt famished, pretty much all the time. I demolished every last crumb that entered my cube. I had an idea that the flexer chip burned calories from energy absorption, because it sure felt that way.

A single shaft of laser light ran across the center of the ceiling, varying in intensity in what I assumed was the same rhythm as the sun. In the dead of night, when the faintest light shined titanium blue like the moon, I lay on a white canvas cot a foot above the ground, with the friendly glow of my FlexOculi monitor to keep me company.

I wondered if Reba knew what had happened to me. Did they just use him for his gift and that was that, or was he privy to the top-secret information detailing my expulsion to the Aboves?

Had he sat in on Dom's exit interview, too, without having mentioned it to me? I bet he had. But I couldn't hold anything against him. I couldn't expect him to break his own honor code to the Seneca Society, no matter how close we had become. I wished I could connect with him, but for now it wasn't safe. Just because my future was in limbo, didn't mean I had any right to put his security at risk.

I concentrated on adjusting to using my flexer implant. S.O.I.L. was unaware that Dom and I had them, so we were still capable of communicating with one another. After two days full of sending messages back and forth, we had become old pros. We chatted the entire time we were both awake, and, when he slept and I couldn't, I used the time to sync my mind with the various Seneca doctrines and legal texts I accessed through the Seneca Public Library Veil.

Every Senecan had access to these texts via their flexer but, not unlike the Aboves, people generally didn't bother with the effort involved with being that informed. And I'd been no different than the rest– until now.

With my flexer implant, I was able to download information directly to my brain. Information surged into me. Mind expansion now occurred at lightning speed. Unfortunately, I found I had to go back fast and dump useless information in droves because the overabundance of information loading in to me was giving me migraines and obstructing the speech center in my frontal lobe. Good thing I had no one to talk to but myself. It was too much, too fast.

Without warning, the wall to my tiny cube opened up and I was overwhelmed with relief to see the first human being in days, even though it was a S.O.I.L. guard. It was time.

Cuffed and escorted by the men in blue, Dom and I emerged from our cubes of confinement into the hallway at the same moment. We both wore the same sullen expressions, but, the instant we saw each other, that changed. Neither of us had known that we'd been just inches away from each other this whole time. Although we shared a flexer connection, being disconnected physically had left a hole inside me. No advancement in human and machine merger could take away that innate need to be with the ones you love. I so badly wanted to take his hand... and never let go.

It was unnervingly quiet as we walked along the endless golden hall. Consumed as I was by doubt, worry and anticipation, it made every minute feel like ten. I felt prepared, but I still was deeply anxious about the process ahead. We had our bag of tricks, but there was no way we could be certain of theirs. We walked and walked and walked. S.O.I.L. guards, aligned like a bunch of gargoyles, were stationed every fifty yards, their bland faces unreadable.

Dom and I were still barefoot, our boots having been abandoned on the riverside, a million dreams ago. I didn't mind. The cold floor against my hot feet dealt me a great sense of physical relief.

Finally, we stopped. The two men in blue turned us to face the wall. A doorway opened up just as they did in S.E.R.C., only what was beyond this point was far different than anything we ever saw in session.

We were ushered under the golden archway and inside an absolutely awe-inspiring underground temple. It's towering ceiling was so high, I couldn't see just how far up it went. Luminous, almost heavenly light showered down on us from colossal, ornate salt crystal chandeliers. This light was alive and natural, yet like the carefully placed lamps used by professional photographers, it filled every crevice of our faces, leaving no shadows in its wake.

We were taken to two side-by-side podiums, in a line of twelve total. Dom and I seemed like two tiny black ants, swallowed up in this bright vastness. This wasn't a room. It wasn't even an auditorium. It was a natural salt mine the size of a medieval cathedral. Everything within it was carved out of salt or was a technological piece embedded into the salt. Even the floor was a solid and smooth fossil. The temperature had been carefully adjusted to about sixty-five degrees. Just right.

Elevated before us, carved meticulously along the crescent-shaped wall of pure salt, were two hundred and twelve thirty-foot figures of prestigious men and women. Just as Mount Rushmore depicted four of the United States presidents in granite, these intricate carvings did the same for the original two hundred and twelve members of the Seneca Senate. I would have liked to figure out who each one was but I had too much else to take in. In front of the colossal monuments lay a two-tiered cathedrae in which the actual senate members sat with opaque, flat-screen panels in front of them.

This was no longer an abstract body of power, learned about in session but never seen. Comprised of individuals from city and state governments, corporations, religious bodies, prominent world organizations of the Aboves; lawyers, doctors, artists, scientists, inventors, leading researchers and more, this was literally the finest and most varied sampling of the planet's brilliant brainpower. This was the one and only Seneca Senate, and it was staring right at us. They looked prestigious in Seneca blue robes like the ones you'd see on Supreme Court Justices.

As I scanned the faces of the members of the Seneca Senate, The President of The United States, The King of England, The Secretary General of the United Nations, The Dalai Lama, the creator of flexer technology, media tycoon, Julian Hollenbeck. Well over a hundred that I did not recognize, but could imagine were significant for their genius, accomplishments and global influence.

And here I was, Doro Campbell, along with my *boyfriend*, Dominic Ambrosia. We, two unruly teens, faced the most powerful assembly in the history of humankind. I was truly humbled. They watched us so intently, I felt naked. My plan suddenly seemed more like a child's science fair experiment than the genius strategy I had hyped it up to be. What was I thinking?

It didn't matter. I was committed now. And what other choice did I have, anyway?

I glanced over at Dom. He looked like he was about to pass out.

It wouldn't help if I didn't take in as much as possible about who I was up against, so I explored each face carefully. As I had learned during my stint in solitary confinement, that each member, nominated by another member, maintained his or her position in the Seneca Senate until that the member was expunged by a motion and vote by the group. Motions could come from the Senate, or any member of society that provided a petition signed by at least one third of their residential district. When a senator was voted out, the next three seats down each would nominate a new member. The rest of the senate would then vote, and one of those three nominees would fill the seat. Every four years, the Seneca Society chose a member of the Senate to become the Chairman.

Front and center, with one year left in his sovereignty, was Chairman of the Seneca Senate, Congressman Frank Wallingsford, and directly to his right, sat Ellen Malone. *Ellen Malone*. I couldn't understand why she'd never told me she was on the Seneca Senate and I didn't even want to begin to think of why she'd been there when Dom was whisked away from Brittany Gilroy's party. Or why Congressman Wallingsford let Dom be the scapegoat for his own son's fatal error. And even though my blood swelled like lava in a volcano, I kept my cool.

Nobody was going to play Doro Campbell for the fool. Not today. Hopefully, not ever.

Every citizen that came before the Seneca Senate was first read their rights and presented The High Doctrine of Seneca Society. A carefully crafted document, that was like The United States Constitution, in that it outlined the laws of Seneca, its judicial structure, and most importantly, the visionary motto that expounded Seneca's purpose–

"To create and sustain a world society in which the people exist and thrive in a singular culture of peace, equality, harmony and inviolable freedom."

Because I had spent my down time in solitude studying these texts in the Seneca Public Library Data Veil, I was primed to address the Senate. While I wasn't thrilled with some of the methods used to secure Senecan society, and the sincerity of a few of the players in it, a lot of what I had read inspired me. I'd developed a faith in this system, despite my previous doubts. Seneca's foundation documents persuaded me that if ever there was potential for social progress in my lifetime, Seneca was the path to it. I wasn't about to let a few bad seeds and contradictory ideals convince me otherwise. For my whole life I'd seen the poor struggle, the global economy in perpetual turmoil, while the sick just kept getting sicker. The planet was a helpless victim to millennia of human consumption. But here, in Seneca, the consciousness shift had found its footing and there was serious momentum for change. In Seneca, I experienced first hand living in a place where there was no such thing as being poor, the sick were healed and the economy was driven by forward thinking. The Earth had never seen as great a chance to heal as it did now. I had to grab this torch and run, and do everything in my power to help bring the heart of Seneca to the entire world. I couldn't just roll over and watch all of this progress get washed away by the corrupt agendas of a few.

Speaking of powerful people with questionable motives, just then Gregory entered the hall. Procedure was that all those involved in Seneca Senate sessions were escorted in, even high-ranking S.O.I.L. agents. His walk, which I'd thought was so great when I had first met him, was bitingly annoying now. He strode over to the podium directly next to mine and sneered under his breath, "Funny how things come full circle."

"Actually, it's a *semi*-circle." My disdain for him had multiplied like a viral epidemic since the last time I'd seen him.

I'm sure he wasn't too keen on me either, since I'd pulled the curtain back on his heinous covert operation. Meanwhile, to my other side, Dom looked exceedingly pale and unnerved. He had been profoundly victimized by Gregory and now the guy was just a few feet away from him. Well, Gregory was on the hot seat now and we were in the exact position we needed to be. I tried to grab Dom's attention with a quick barrage of flexes, hoping to replace his apparent agony with reassurances, but he was in no mood to receive them.

Proceedings were soon called to order by a man in a blue suit with the gold Seneca emblem on his lapel. "Senators and citizens of Seneca, your Chairman of the Seneca Senate, Number One, Senator Frank Wallingsford."

Here, in Seneca, Congressman Wallingsford was *Senator* Wallingsford. He had maintained his "Congressman" title in the Aboves. Kind of a sneaky maneuver, yes, but I found myself not rejecting it and, instead, seeing it as one of the compromises along the path to fulfilling the vision of Seneca's founders. Regardless, after what he allowed to happen to Dom, I was looking at him in a whole different light.

As Wallingsford stood, the panel in front of him lit up sky blue to signify he held the floor. "Senators, Seneca Advisory Committee, S.O.I.L. agents and officers, respondents, it is with great honor that I stand before you today and ratify this proceeding." He paused. All of the senators' panels lit up white, then faded back to opaque in an act of respect and acknowledgment.

"Today we have been called to emergency session on an issue of compromised security and internal deception. Parties present include the Seneca Observation and Intelligence League, with Chief S.O.I.L. Agent in the S.E.R.C. division, Gregory Zaffron, responding, and two expelled S.E.R.C. scholars, Mr. Dominic Ambrosia and Ms. Dorothy Campbell. We have received intelligence that demonstrates a breech in the freedom of all Seneca citizens. Agent Zaffron contests that both Ambrosia and Campbell have dangerously misinterpreted security procedures and that they pose a serious threat to the Seneca Society at large. He has requested a motion to be made at this hearing that we, the Seneca Senate, determine a solution to abolish this threat. We have been provided the intelligence from which Agent Zaffron and S.O.I.L. are drawing their conclusions. Now, before we convene and finalize a resolution, we will hear statements from all respondents."

Everyone kept quiet as Senator Wallingsford continued, "First respondent, Agent Gregory Zaffron. As a sworn representative of The Seneca Observation and Intelligence League, and with this motion brought against Ambrosia and Campbell, we, the Seneca Senate, hereby call you to the floor."

Gregory's podium panel lit up light blue. He pulled at his tie to loosen it a bit but still came across as remarkably poised for such a pompous jerk. I just crossed my fingers that his distinguished audience could see through his BS.

"Ladies and gentlemen of the Senate..." He paused between each sentence for dramatic effect. "Today, I am here with a heavy heart. I am presenting information the likes of which I'd hoped never to bring before you. The information we watch for, but never want to see. As you have reviewed in the intelligence we provided pre-proceedings, and can refer to today in the intelligence portfolios at each of your podiums, you can see that these two expelled S.E.R.C. scholars, Dorothy Campbell and Dominic Ambrosia, pose a great threat to the future of our society."

My last bubble of comfort punctured as I felt the judging eyes of the Senate membership directed at Dom and me. Gregory was in the process of bashing us thoroughly, and we just had to stand there and take it. The part that bothered me most was that we couldn't exactly deny what he was saying...

"Ladies and gentlemen of the Senate, this expelled S.E.R.C. scholar, Dominic Ambrosia, has identified, investigated and circumvented a highly confidential S.O.I.L. security operation known as Crystal. As you are all aware, one of the main initiatives under Crystal is to combat the Necrolla Carne virus. Many facets of that operation are contained strictly within the purview of S.O.I.L. Ambrosia was a recruit to S.E.R.C. under molecular nano-biotechnology. Our goal was to groom him as a trailblazer in Seneca's biomedical applications division. Instead, by harvesting blood samples and encouraging another S.E.R.C. scholar to participate in his rogue investigation, Ambrosia has triggered a disastrous stream of events. Ambrosia was warned by S.O.I.L. officials several times to cease this perilous path of inquiry. His disregard for such requests was not only an abuse of his privilege in S.E.R.C. and as a citizen of Seneca, but it has created a looming threat to the entire society."

Wallingsford's panel illuminated blue, which brought Gregory's back down. "Mr. Ambrosia, do you oppose any of these accusations?"

Dom leaned forward into his podium. He looked like he had seen a ghost. His voice was low and devoid of its usual spirit.

"No, sir, Mr. Senator."

"Very well, please proceed, Agent Zaffron."

Gregory didn't miss a beat. "Ambrosia then corrupted the bright young mind of fellow S.E.R.C. scholar, Dorothy Campbell, whom many of us believed in as one of the great young minds in quantum computing, to follow him down this path of self-destruction and to sabotage Seneca security. Campbell picked up where Ambrosia's abilities ended and applied her computer expertise to breaking into our system. Campbell made the conscious decision, a *choice*, to betray Seneca and alter the Crystal operation. She singlehandedly broke an encryption within The Necrolla Carne..." Gregory's voice resounded through every corner of this salt mine. "A security measure of the highest order, both in terms of technology and confidentiality."

Once again, Senator Wallingsford reclaimed the floor. "And, Ms. Campbell, do you oppose any of these accusations against you?"

Everything Gregory said was true. It just sounded so malicious when it came out that way. I wanted to object, but I couldn't. I needed to explain myself before it was too late. Before they identified me as the villain he had painted. "No, sir, Mr. Senator, but I just want to say—"

"If you don't object, then Agent Zaffron shall continue and conclude his statement, and then you will be provided the opportunity to justify your actions and respond."

I sank back. Thank god the ground was cold. Dominic looked over at me. A million unspoken words traveled between us in under two seconds. We had to rally our spirits and trump Gregory's manipulative logic with unity and truth. It was the only way.

Gregory was well equipped for the next phase of his attack on us. He held a wide stance, and grasped each side of the podium with confidence. Filling up as much space as he physically could and more, he owned it. He closed his eyes, tilted his head down as if he were extracting power from hell and took a deep breath from his nose. Everyone in the room avidly awaited his next statement. This guy was nothing if not a supreme actor. He raised his gaze and let loose an oratorical poison that even I didn't know he was capable of. I could just feel it seeping into the minds of the people who controlled our fate. "The ramifications are dire. Once the technological capacity to crack and manipulate S.O.I.L. encryption falls outside of our control, we can be assured the security of our society will be forever compromised. Quite simply, this one rebellious little girl gave herself unprecedented access to the minds of the entire population of Seneca. There is no telling what she will do with that capability. To us it's life and death. To her and her friends, this is just a video game, not real life."

"Please!" I couldn't control my outrage one second more. I was flabbergasted. *Little girl?*

Senator Wallingsford's panel lit up. "Ms. Campbell, you will have your opportunity to address the Senate. Until then, please refrain from interrupting."

Instead of speaking, I pushed the single button in front of me that I'd seen the others use to light up their panels and communicate agreement. With that illumination, my accordance was acknowledged. I was making political moves now. And this move was going to require me to sit and listen to Gregory's disgusting lies for just a little bit longer.

Through his projected fury, Gregory smirked, subtly enough for just me to see. "We warned her. She didn't listen. We took action. She revolted..." He turned aggressively towards me. "You can't expect that we would continue down this path, do you? To allow this subversive movement you have ignited to spread like wildfire and destroy everything these great men and women before us have given their lives to build?"

He was addressing me, with the most acidic, condescending rhetoric. I looked up to Senator Wallingsford, pleading for his green light to reply.

"Agent Zaffron, we appreciate your dedicated work to Seneca and I must agree that the safety and progress of our citizens is our priority. Is your address to the Senate complete?"

"Affirmative, sir. Senator Wallingsford, honorable members of the Senate, my utmost gratitude for your attention, and this opportunity to serve the great Seneca Society."

"Very well."

Putrid. Everything about him. His aggressive repertoire

blinded him to the possibility of intellectual competition from a sixteen-year-old. I had to be strategic, to consider how to use his arrogance. Even though it felt impossible to prove ourselves in the face of such a forceful agenda, I had to hold on tight to my belief that truth would prevail.

"We now call Dominic Ambrosia for a response and statement regarding the S.O.I.L. accusations against him which have brought us here today."

Dom peered down at his podium. I sensed that he was gathering the steam he needed from outside his own body, because whatever he'd had inside had been stripped to below the reserves. He suddenly lifted his head. He didn't look at me, didn't look at Gregory.

"Honorable Senators. I am sorry for causing such a disruption..." He took a long, agonized breath. *Come on, come on, bring out that gutsy guy I jumped cliffs with at Difficult Run!* I focused the thoughts in my own head and tried to forward them over to his. Just as quick as he caught my thought, he shot one right back, *Don't worry, I got this.* and continued on with his statement.

"When I got that vaccination that was supposed to control what they call Necrolla Carne, I felt deep down something wasn't right. No matter what, I just couldn't shake that feeling. Nobody around me had experienced any symptoms, nobody around me had even *heard* of anybody who'd experienced any symptoms, and there weren't any patients being discussed or interviewed on the B3 news— just a lot of talk about how dangerous it was. After my shot, instead of sensing that my body was being bolstered and protected, like the doctor said the vaccine would do, I felt a little bit slowed up. As if something was delaying my movements or decisions. It was just nanoseconds, but I couldn't ignore it. I had to figure out what had been done to me, especially because if it affected me, it affected every citizen of Seneca. Ultimately, I did. I looked into my own blood and saw something in there that could only have been put there by that Necrolla Carne vaccine... I could see that it was something computerized, but that's where I was stumped, for a long time. And then Dorothy Campbell came along, and I shared all of this with her, even after S.O.I.L. agents warned me to steer clear of further probing. But I had to find the facts. I had to. And now we can all see a perfect example of how the supposed facts that are presented to us are completely and intentionally misleading. That stuff in that folder S.O.I.L.'s given you, I'd be real critical of it."

After a long beat in which Dom allowed that to sink in to the consciousness of the room, he started speaking, softer. From his heart. "Yeah, in retrospect, I realize that maybe it wasn't the best way to go about things, but I still don't know what would have been. I had to find the truth. I had no other choice. And, honestly, I don't know what to do to rectify this, but what I will say is this: If the last thing I do here is reveal that the Necrolla Carne vaccine is responsible for human brain invasion, vital sign determination, biometric analysis and registration of brain pattern indicators, then at least I've been an honest man. Because that's what I believe. But the most important thing that I can testify to right now is that, no matter what you decide, you need to know I dragged Doro into this. She doesn't deserve the weight of this on her shoulders. It was all me."

No! Dom trying to take the fall for both of us was so *not* what I wanted. He was throwing himself in front of the bus for me. I loved him for it. And I hated him for it.

"Everything she did that got her in trouble was because of me. If you decide to punish me, please spare Doro. She is the ideal Senecan– strong, intelligent, fair. You were right to believe in her to begin with. Don't let me destroy that, too."

My eyes swept across the Senate. They shifted in their seats and whispered to one another. Ellen Malone looked down at me, and, while I wanted to look away as fast as I could, something pinned my eyes to hers. I tried to decipher what was going on in her mind from the look on her face, but she was inscrutable. I couldn't tell if she was disappointed, proud, worried for me, or what. I knew she couldn't protect me now. She was only one single individual here and this was no 'getting out of lockdown to go get chilaquiles' type of situation.

Senator Wallingsford broke in to lasso everyone's attention with his best, measured, politician's voice, "Thank you, Mr. Ambrosia."

Dom nodded and his podium went white.

"The floor is now open to expelled S.E.R.C. scholar, Dorothy

Campbell, for response and statement regarding the S.O.I.L. accusations against her that have brought us here today."

I was intimidated by the faces turned toward me and the fact that my fate was in their hands. But I was also driven— by the truth, by Dom's spirit, by the hope of this place. I knew we could help fix the problems if they'd just listen to us. Dom didn't want the weight of it to be on my shoulders, but it was, and he couldn't help that. I decided to take the blunt approach.

"Ladies and gentlemen of the Senate, thanks for letting me have this opportunity to tell you what really happened. I may be young, but I'm no idiot. Yes, I expected action to be taken against me. It was my goal, and I'm prepared for it."

A rumble moved through the Senate. Former Navy Seal, top ranking S.O.I.L. agent, Gregory Zaffron, was about to be challenged by a sixteen-year-old girl, in a room full of the entire judicial body of this accelerated form of government. It was *my* turn to get rhetorical. I turned to Gregory.

"Did *you* honestly think I'd continue to just let things be once I knew about the deceptions being played out in Seneca?" I shifted my focus away from Gregory's glare to address the Senate.

"We were chased, hunted, unjustly characterized as runaways on the national news, brutally attacked and left for dead in the middle of the forest, but that didn't stop us." I saw so many looks of astonishment that right then and there I could see the Seneca Senate, at least most of its members, had been unaware of Gregory's actions. "B3 News was fed blatant lies about the supposed Necrolla Carne Disease that in turn filled the minds of innocent Seneca citizens everywhere with fear about its destructive power. But we found out the truth. As a dutiful citizen of Seneca I take very seriously my social contract to The High Doctrine of Seneca Society, which is that: *We shall pursue and honor the truth above all else. For ourselves, for our fellow Senecans, for the ultimate, incontrovertible liberty of the Seneca Society.*

"Isn't it our obligation to chase the truth and come forward with what we've found? And, if not me, then who? *Who* is going to identify the problem, speak the truth and stand up for what's right? Dom and I knew we had to chase the truth. It was our obligation to this society."

I felt the wind against my back. "Corrupting people's blood with nanobots is the ultimate intrusion. Blocking memories and changing the course of people's lives without their knowledge or consent is cold-hearted manipulation. It's tyranny. It's enslavement. It's the farthest thing from what Seneca is all about, but it is exactly what S.O.I.L. is doing. Yes, I broke the quantum encryption and determined that all of us are being tracked and analyzed. Every thought in our minds and every movement we make is collected data, and *you* have no right to mine my brain for data without my consent. Nobody should have the right to do that to anyone else."

One by one, panels in front of the members of the Senate were lighting up, demonstrating their approval. I felt empowered by the lights. The sun shone on my face, beaming down through the salt-crystal windows in the dome above us. I noticed that Gregory's body language had changed infinitesimally, as he shrank back slightly, his shoulders slouching forward just a bit. The Senators couldn't see it but I could, and it gave me a burst of adrenalin. He hadn't expected them to respond to me like this because he thought he was invincible. That his misuse of power would continue unchallenged.

Just then I received an incoming flex, and it wasn't from Dom. *You're playing with fire, Doro. I have your back, but won't be able to protect you from what is to come.* It was Ellen. Oh my god. She had the implant, too. Slowly, Ellen Malone's layers were peeling back like a fresh onion. One by one, each tier disturbed me more than the last. I had no idea what was at her core and this wasn't the time to engage in a flex-off with her to find out. She flexed me again; *You'd better learn to use your new implant before some other people around here learn that you have it.* I scanned the faces before me. Many eyed me just like Ellen did, but I couldn't let uncertainty cripple my drive. And I couldn't trust that Ellen knew what was best, or that she would do what was right for me or Dom. This was my fight and I had to go by my gut instincts.

"Gregory wants to label me as an insurgent, and that's fine, because the truth is, if I didn't rebel against the wrongdoings of S.O.I.L., the foundation Seneca was built on could implode, and destroy everything you have worked to create." I took a deep breath and aimed my final blow at Gregory's campaign of deceit.

"Seneca is everything I ever wanted the world to be. Safe, fair, peaceful, dedicated to education in areas that actually matter. I see a future here where everyone has the opportunity to thrive and be the best they can be. But the tyrannies of an operation like the one around the fake Necrolla Carne virus, lying to people and intrusively penetrating their brains, are the fastest ways to quash all that hope. And someone like Gregory Zaffron, who perpetrates all these horrendous crimes, should in no way be a representative of the Seneca Society. The Seneca I believe in does not stand for oppression and hypocrisy. If this is put to an end before it is too late, Seneca really *will* be fertile ground for a whole new existence. The one people have always dreamed of. Freedom was never really possible here until these truths were exposed, right here, right now."

All of the Senators' screens lit up and I basked in the brightness.

"I hope that you will all see that Dominic and I didn't do any of this for our own selfish motives, or to play games or take control of anything. We just wanted to shed a light on the truth and expose a flaw that I think can ruin the future of the place I want to call home... Thank you all for listening."

Much to my surprise, and Gregory's despair, the room exploded in white light. Every panel on the Senate was illuminated. I felt amazing. My whole body buzzed from the surge of positive energy in the room. Ellen was deadpan,

315

maintaining a vacant stare. I knew she was pissed off that I had blown off her flex, but I was no longer worried about what Ellen thought. I looked at Dom. There was a glimmer of hopeful anticipation in his piercing eyes. In the end, the truth will always set you free.

As Wallingsford's screen stayed illuminated, a hush settled over the room. "We will now hear concluding statements from each one of you, in the same order, please. Agent Zaffron, you may proceed."

Gregory was fueled by the desire to win, to conquer two pesky teenagers, to remain in control. He showed no fear, and was filled with a malevolence that made my stomach turn. "Senators, we can all appreciate Ms. Campbell's sweet sentiment, but don't be fooled by a wolf in sheep's clothing in our midst. This sweetness is only skin deep. I ask you to let the hard facts that S.O.I.L. has collected and presented to you determine the outcome in the best interest of our society. Rebellion and assault on S.O.I.L. intel can only be a threat, not an ally to our society. Having witnessed the persistence of these two individuals as they infiltrated our security methods, I began to understand their capacity to disrupt. I stand by the current S.O.I.L. procedures, as they have been put in place in the best interest of all of us here today. We are dedicated to protecting what you are building– by any means necessary. Sometimes great success comes at a great cost. This is a perfect example of one of those times." He was resolute and cold-hearted. "On behalf of S.O.I.L, I, Agent

Gregory Zaffron, motion that, should Campbell and Ambrosia be found guilty of breech of our laws as outlined in the High Doctrine of Seneca Society, they shall be placed in solitary confinement until they are legal adults, at which point they shall be terminated."

A rolling thunder of private chatter emanated from the crescent-shaped audience elevated before us. Dom looked as if he hadn't just seen a ghost; he *was* a ghost. I don't think he'd ever expected it to come down to a moment like this. I, on the other hand, might not have been in my element running down a bridge and jumping off a ledge into oncoming traffic, but I was ready to rock in this war of words. We couldn't allow ourselves to feel helpless against a system that was there for us. I stared at Wallingsford, chomping at the bit for my opportunity to speak.

"Dominic Ambrosia. Do you have any closing statements?"

Dom looked at me, then back up to the Senate. "I just hope everyone sees the truth in what Doro is saying. There is nothing more to it. Seneca is my home now. I don't want to do anything to compromise that. I am only here to help."

Gregory muttered under his breath, "How cute."

I tightened my jaw, but was unable to contain myself a second longer.

"Funny," I spat. My glare ripped into Gregory. "To me it seems *you* are the one in breech of the laws of Seneca as outlined in the High Doctrine, so I think you should be the one who is terminated."

Gregory exhaled a puff of disgust and shook his head in feigned disbelief.

"And the fact is that it won't stop with Dominic and me. You will have to come back to the Senate and ask that more and more people be terminated. Because the reality is, people will eventually catch on to what you're up to. If the skills needed to ask the right questions and break into the system exist in Dom and me, it's there in others just as smart as us. There are bright people sitting even now in the most basic session available in S.E.R.C. They'll piece it together, too.

"The last thing I want to say, Agent Zaffron, is that if anything happens to Dom or me, the quantum entanglement you have established with every Seneca citizen, whether they're in Seneca or somewhere else in the world, will be broken and destroyed. But first they will get a very explicit message regarding what you have done. I've already coded it that way."

"You're bluffing."

"Then call me."

Gregory was speechless. It was the first time I'd ever seen him visibly shaken. There was a resolved silence in the row of thrones. My own silence was proud. It was all out of my hands now. I marveled at how uniquely different silences could be.

Senator Wallingsford stood. "Agent Zaffron, Dominic Ambrosia, Dorothy Campbell– please accept our appreciation for your statements in this session. The Senate will now convene and vote on a solution."

A mirrored blue dome appeared over the panel of Seneca Senate members. Dom, Gregory, the guards and I just had to wait. I grinned like a schoolgirl because I knew it would irritate Gregory. Gregory drilled his nasty eyes right back at me, but I could sense him cracking. Dom didn't even look up from his podium, he was so in the zone. None of us spoke. No matter how high the tension we were all trying to maintain poker faces.

After twenty-eight minutes standing in strained silence, the mirrored blue dome dissolved into the cool salty air.

Senator Wallingsford motioned Ellen Malone to the floor. "Senator Number Two will now give the determination and conclusion of the Senate."

Ellen Malone's panel lit up. I still didn't want to look at her, but I couldn't help it.

"Senators, Seneca Advisory Committee, S.O.I.L. agents and officers, respondents, thank you for affording me the honor to address you today."

The panels all lit up and, as they faded back to opaque, Ellen spoke with a command I'd never heard from her before. "I personally know these two scholars, and can attest that they are not a detriment to our society, but rather an asset. That is why it is with such pleasure that, on behalf of the Seneca Senate, I hereby dismiss the accusations brought forth today by the Seneca Observation and Intelligence League against Dominic Ambrosia and Dorothy Campbell."

The screens all went white. So did Gregory's face. And color

319

returned to Dom's. At the same time stupendous relief flowed through me, I had the thought that Ellen was a chameleon. Whose side was she on, anyway?

"In fact, the direction of fault is in choices made by our own S.O.I.L. Indeed, we are a society made up of human beings and, thus, error is unavoidable, especially in this stage of our collective infancy. Correction is in our blood, though, and our internal mistakes must be promptly and responsibly remedied. Moreover, we find it morally reprehensible that such intrusions were taken against not only the citizens of Seneca, but especially the league of Senators that have led you, Gregory Zaffron, and your colleagues, and have trusted you to be an instrument of their decisions. This is an issue we will address at a later time. Until the facts of this case are thoroughly investigated, you are placed on indefinite suspension from your S.O.I.L duties."

I thought about kicking up my feet like Gregory had in his absurdly machismo fashion that day in my room in S.E.R.C., but instead I let Ellen's words do the gloating for me. Gregory was beginning to look apoplectic.

Ignoring him, Ellen continued, "Although these S.E.R.C. scholars went against the system, what they're fighting for couldn't be more righteous. They represent the epitome of what we stand for in this society– *peace, equality, harmony and inviolable freedom.* Hence, we find it in the best interest for the future of the Seneca Society to reinstate Dominic Ambrosia and Dorothy Campbell as S.E.R.C. scholars. In addition, we would like to establish them as leaders of a new S.O.I.L. project where we will collaborate with them in discovering ways in which to break the invasive quantum entanglements. Simultaneously, we expect an effort on the part of S.O.I.L., with a newly selected Chief S.O.I.L. Agent in the S.E.R.C. division, to work towards a better, more just future of Seneca intelligence operations."

Senator Wallingsford's panel lit up. As Ellen Malone took her seat, he spoke calmly, and it echoed throughout the ancient salt mine turned judicial chamber. "Mr. Ambrosia, Ms. Campbell, do you accept this determination in your favor?"

Dom was elated. He nodded to me as if to say, "The floor is all yours."

I knew what I wanted. It wasn't too much to ask. "We will agree to it if you allow my mom and my dog to come live with me in Seneca, and Dominic's parents and brother, too, to live with him."

Senator Wallingsford moved forward to speak, but Ellen Malone's somber face caught my eye. No matter what had been done to me, I wasn't going to stoop to Gregory's level. I had to be my best me— so there was one more thing to ask for.

"And I further request that Ellen Malone's son, Connor, be allowed to come live with her."

Ellen became uneasy. She leaned into Senator Wallingsford, but he brushed her off, because he already knew what he was going to say.

"Considering the great positive change you have just brought our society, that certainly is not too much to ask. It would be a pleasure to have your loved ones join us. Welcome back to Seneca."

The man in the blue suit who had called the session to order promptly adjourned it and the blue dome rose over the Senate and lowered it below the surface of the salt mine.

Dom bounced down from behind his podium to throw his arms around me in an enormous bear hug. "You are seriously incredible, Dorothy Campbell. Do you know that?"

"See, I told you I wasn't spying on you that day we first met. I really did just think you were handsome. But now I think you're kinda smart, too."

Gregory began to storm out with his escort, but then abruptly turned toward Dom and me. "You think you're such geniuses. You're going to wish you'd never put your noses into any of it. This isn't over."

But it was– for now, at least. I smiled. Nothing could wreck this glorious moment, not even Gregory Zaffron.

52

IT FELT SO amazing to be back in S.E.R.C. A place that was once nothing short of bizarre to me in every way, shape and form, felt like home now. Familiar. And, armed with the knowledge that soon my mom and Killer would be here, too, I was at peace for the first time in a very long while.

It was Tuesday. My first day in session after everything that had happened. All I could do was look forward to lunch in the meal hall. I hadn't seen Reba since we were thrust together in that horrid memory wipeout, brainwashing attempt. I didn't want my first contact with him to be via my flexer implant. I owed him a huge "thank you" for having my back in there, and I had to give it to him in person.

I strolled into meal hall with pep in my step, ready to order a quesadilla and reconnect with my good friend. As soon as I spotted him at our regular table, my face lit up. I rushed over.

Reba was quietly eating alone. I snuck up behind him and stood there as I tried to think of something witty to say, but before I could–

"I knew there was a reason I just had to order this quesadilla."

"Reba!"

He spun around with a sprawling smile across his face. "Campbella!" he shouted as he sprang up from his seat and hugged me. We bounced up and down, laughing like goofy little kids.

"Que pasa chica?! I thought I was never going to see you again. I mean I *knew* I would but thought I wouldn't... if that makes sense?" His words were going a mile a minute, all blending together. Man, how much had I missed this guy?

"Somehow, coming from you, it makes perfect sense." We looked at each other in equal parts disbelief and glee, but that untouched quesadilla sitting there on the table had my name all over it.

"It's all you." Reba pulled my seat out like a courtly gentleman. We dove back into our mealtime ritual like it had never been broken. As I reconnected with my buddy and the best Monterey Jack cheese known to man, I told him all about how I'd seen my mom again, and how Dom and I had been handed a most just resolution by the Senecan Senate. I spared our conversation the details of my new assignment by the Senate, because they'd made sure to impress upon us that it would be a top-secret operation. But Reba seemed to know at least a little something of what went down.

53

TWO DAYS AFTER our arrival back in Seneca, Dom and I began our declassification project under the wings of S.O.I.L. They didn't want to waste any time, but they also didn't want to distract us from what we'd originally been brought to do here. We started to meet every Monday, Wednesday and Friday after sessions ended for the day. An empty acoustic carrier would take us on a ten minute trip from S.E.R.C. to the Claytor Lake computer center. We always arrived just three minutes after three and stayed through dinner. Crazy to think that only a few weeks before, we had been on the run from S.O.I.L., and now we were spearheading our own S.O.I.L. operation.

One of the great ironies was that Gregory was obliged to serve our project. Once a week he flew down to Claytor Lake to assist us and make sure we had everything we needed. He definitely bit his tongue a lot and did what he had to do, but I could tell it was torture for him. I wasn't into causing people discomfort, but there was a sweet satisfaction in seeing Gregory so alienated.

Dom and I were given the privilege of naming the project. We decided to call it The Brooklyn Project both as homage to the New York City borough's "strength in unity" motto, and to the place where our own triumphant journey began.

Our leader, Magnus, was a S.O.I.L. agent, fluent in both Operation Crystal and Necrolla Carne. He was an Albino Korean, with extremely light blue eyes, the color of purified water reflecting the LA sky and spiky blond hair. Impeccable blue S.O.I.L. attire covered his lean, five nine frame. We knew nothing about Magnus other than his first name, though, come to think of it, it could have been his last name. Oh, and that he was allergic to walnuts. He would track down people's snacks like a bloodhound, to make sure there weren't walnuts anywhere near him. It was like his kryptonite. Magnus disclosed everything about Necrolla Carne to us. Well, *everything* as far as we knew. Meanwhile, each of the fifteen hundred people that worked in the Claytor Lake computer district only knew the tidbit of information they needed to get their jobs done for the project.

Dom and I set up in a domed room that overlooked the vast floor of data analysts and tech staff that worked at computer hubs. We were on the other side of the blue mirror now. I sat in front of a panel that displayed the mainframe data which I had remotely accessed and used to break my own entanglement. The entangled brain of every citizen of Seneca resided there. I know I said nothing could surprise me, but this glimpse into the utter enormity of Crystal proved me wrong.

Our DNA categorized us all. To put it simply, we were

grouped alongside those who were most similar to us genetically. Although we didn't know it, the specifics of each of our DNA was the fundamental data that had been collected and tested prior to our offers to join Seneca. Elaborate DNA profiling was used to ensure that the entire population abided by the society's regulations. It was how Seneca's citizens were protected from disease, both physical and mental, and also how optimal procreation scenarios were projected. Basically, aside from being recruited on the basis of knowledge and skill, it came down to the science of who we were.

On Monday we had gone through one huge lot of DNA profiles and removed the quantum entanglement that had been placed between the Seneca mainframe and their bloods. Nobody felt a thing. They wouldn't even realize that something had happened. It was the most rewarding experience of my life to pull the trigger and break each entanglement.

On Wednesday we paced our way through the second group of DNA profiles. One by one, Dom pulled up data ports on each Senecan, and then passed them off to me to apply the quantum entanglement break code. We'd store the confirmation record and move on to the next one. Our routine became second nature.

We were able to joke with each other and talk about other things in the midst of our work, nearly forgetting that it was a super confidential, technologically grand application. We grew closer and closer by the day, attached at the hip around the clock. If we weren't together, we were FigureFlexing. Yep, Dom and I had become one of those sickeningly cute couples.

Something felt peculiar to me that Wednesday afternoon, though. I wasn't sure what it was, but there was something in the air. It was kind of like that game where you'd feel a tap on the shoulder, but when you'd turn around to look, there'd be nothing there. I did notice, though, that Dom was staring at me all the time. The only time he'd look away was to double-check his work. I'd gone from trying my darnedest to get this guy's attention back in September, to December, when he wouldn't quit looking at me.

"You know, it's not nice to stare."

"Whoever said I was nice?"

I poked him in the side. He hated that. Like I hated it when he would hold my legs down and tickle my feet. Really, I hated anything that had to do with feet. As our poke-and-tickle routine was going on, we didn't notice Magnus standing there with his arms crossed in a supreme look of displeasure. We both quickly straightened up, and got back to our computers.

"Glad you guys are having so much fun. This isn't a serious operation or anything."

"My apologies, Magnus, I just can't resist this girl. Can you blame me?" Dom was back. My confident, sarcastic, "blue combat boots," who wasn't intimidated by the authoritative set. He was so much more attractive this way. I couldn't wait until the end of today when we could hop on our private acoustic carrier ride for ten minutes alone together before going back to our separate residences.

Magnus couldn't be bothered. He rolled his eyes, "Just get through the second batch of profiles and we'll call it a day." And he left the room.

We shared a grin and got back down to business. It was quiet for all of fifteen minutes, just clicks and taps as the entanglements were dismantled, one by one.

"Oh yeah, now *that* is one good looking genetic profile."

I looked over. Dom was biting his bottom lip, looked at me deviously out of the corner of his eye.

"What are you doing over there?"

"Oh, just checking out some hot chick's DNA."

I scanned outside the window to see if Magnus was around. "You're gonna get us in trouble!"

"Worth it. Oooh lala."

"Stop!" But I was curious. What was he doing?

"You sure you want me to stop? I think you'll want to see this."

"What!?"

"You, lovely. *You...*"

I double-checked to make sure Magnus wasn't watching, rolled my desk chair over to Dom's. He nodded up to the monitor that contained a DNA profile. It was mine.

"You're into that sorta thing, aren't you? Bar graphs, charts?"

"You know me so well." I checked out the data on me. My name, residential sector location and my DNA profile. It was all right there.

"Sexy profile."

I nudged him, "Thanks... I guess."

"While we're here, we should cross our DNA profiles to make sure we're not related or anything," he joked. "What if we have an ancestor in common, like twenty generations ago? Don't you want to know?"

"Gross. No. I don't even want the thought in my head!"

And then Dom clicked down one profile below mine on the screen, "Whoa... take a look at that."

"What?"

He didn't answer. He just moved in closer to the monitor, his face glowing blue. From the look on Dom's face, I gathered something pretty astonishing was on that screen.

"What? Tell me!"

"This anonymous DNA profile... is a fifty percent match to you."

"Huh?" I was completely bewildered, "That's impossible. Unless they already have my mom's data in here." There were only two people who could match me at exactly fifty percent. My heart rate started to climb.

"Nope. Not your mom. The person with this DNA is in South America. Puerto Lopez, Colombia. And unless your mom is really a man..."

"Dom, seriously, stop playing. This isn't funny."

"Doro, I'm not playing."

"This is impossible. That could only be..." My eyes widened, stomach dropped. My heart plunged into my throat.

"My dad."

Acknowledgements

My hubby, Aaron. Our steamy late night science talks, your unwavering support of my dreams, and enthusiasm for Seneca helped me write something I am deeply proud of. I literally could not have done it without you. I am so grateful. I love you. p.s. By "late night," I mean 9pm.

My mom. You've gone above and beyond in so many ways. I love you and can't thank you enough for helping with our girls, bringing positivity into our home and reading my pages over and over again. But especially for always nurturing my unfiltered curiosity.

My agent, Chris Tomasino. You believed in Seneca to no end and invested so much time and knowledge into shaping this book into what it is. Thank you for everything.

Seneca Rebel's cover designer, Miss Anonymous. It's a special thing that my art and yours will live together forever in harmony. Thank you for your vision and having fun with this.

Michael Shields, Chris Thompson & Across the Margin, you've jumped into this like a cannonball into the pool and have rocked it since day one.

No Mimes Media, Behnam Karbassi & Steve Peters. This whole beyond-the-page Senecan experience wouldn't be without your energy and bright ideas.

Mark Gamsey, Sara Rassi & Chris Prosser for your bringing your stunning photography into the Seneca mix.

A special thanks to my peeps who have championed me since well before Seneca— M. Lee, Charlotte, Magnus. All my friends who read Seneca Rebel when it was fresh on the page to offer opinions, guidance and support— Brittany Beale, Katana Collins, Claudette Sutherland, Anika, Jeanne & Staci Hart. My sisters Zeena & Serena, for each contributing in your own ways.

And my world class, one-of-a-kind, constant group text— Katie, Chrissy & Christina, for keeping it real and brightening my days.

My sweet pit bull Athena passed away shortly before this book went to print. For nine-and-a-half years she was right by my side when I was writing. I am extremely fortunate to have had such a loving, loyal companion in my life. I will miss her forever.

I have had the privilege of learning from some seriously outstanding teachers over the years— from Hunter Mill Country Day School to Oakton Elementary to Luther Jackson Middle School to Oakton High School and Virginia Tech. Many individuals who dedicated themselves to educating have had a profound effect on me, and hopefully that is echoed in these pages.

Every single person that reads this book, I am honored you have given your time to such an important part of me. Until next time, stay curious.

Rayya Deeb is a screenwriter and Virginia Tech Hokie, born in London, England and raised in Northern Virginia. Seneca Rebel is her debut novel. She lives in Los Angeles with her husband and two daughters. Visit her at www.rayyadeeb.com

Made in the USA
San Bernardino, CA
25 October 2016